EMENDATUS

Ages of Claya - Book 2

Whitney H. Murphy

ISBN: 0-9976951-2-9
ISBN-13: 978-0-9976951-2-0

'Emendatus'

Corrected.

When life's portrait doesn't match the frame

we've so carefully crafted.

When the world doesn't fit

the ideals we've so prudently carved to hold it.

When the songs we hoped to sing seem strangely,

stubbornly

out of tune

and the winds take a path we hadn't planned,

hadn't dreamed—

when perfection's cut short

and we rise on weary feet,

lifting our broken visions

to amend it.

Whitney H. Murphy

Part One

1

She's found at the shore when morning comes— when the clouds overhead have furrowed themselves together, breaking only narrowly along the horizon to reveal the setting twin moons beyond. The sky lies like a wrinkled blanket above the earth, stretching from the edge of the land over the wide face of the sea, gray and weary. The sign of a nearing storm. But the rain has yet to come.

She's found like a leaf on the pale sand, lying with her little arms spread and the sea sprinkled like tears over her sleeping face. Asleep—despite the restless sea that stirs and leaps nearby, threatening to swallow up the child and pull her away into its depths. She couldn't be more than three years old. A child of the *arai*, the human race. Lost, or abandoned. And she lies clothed in faded silk that bears the subtle sheen of threads woven in the lands of the far west—beyond the ocean that only the strongest of ships dare to cross.

The tide is rising when they find her at the western shore—dark waters drawn by the face of the greater moon as its twin eclipses silently over it. But the people of the woods don't fear the surge or the ominous sheen of weakened moonlight along the waves. They come softly, not minding the cool lap of the sea at their ankles. They gather around with wide eyes and gentle gasps slipping through their pointed teeth.

A human child!

They whisper among themselves, staring up and down the wide, sandy shore, searching for any sign of a ship. But only splintered remains join the child on the sand. Fractured, sodden shards of tortured wood.

A sudden wind comes billowing from the north, etching grooves and wrinkles into the face of the sand all around. And now a subtle rumbling can be heard, echoing from the darkening clouds that hang low on the horizon. The voice of a troubled sky. There's little time.

The girl hangs limply in their arms as they lift her from the sand. Her amber curls fall aside like a curtain from her pale face. And now the rain has come. It begins to mist over the shore, spotting the sand and stones in its path.

Quickly now!

The people of the woods step nimbly, bearing the child away from the tossing waters of the sea, away from the wind and rain that begin to dance all around them—vanishing into the shadows and safety of the trees.

2

There's a subtle trembling in Mother's hands when she takes the bowl of fresh water he holds up for her.

"Thank you, sweet child," she whispers to him. She leaves a little kiss between the windblown clumps of dark hair on his forehead before turning to the woman who lies beneath a thick blanket on the floor, breathing deeply. It's Ifana—the kind lady who's lived for years with her husband in the cabin next door.

"Come now, I'll help you clean him," Mother whispers as she kneels to soak her apron in the water.

Beside her, Ifana nods—silent tears drawing lines down her flushed face. The newborn infant in her arms lies motionless as they dab away the fluids from his tiny body. A darkened, almost purple body. He doesn't cry, doesn't move. Mother said there's something wrong—something that can happen to children who come too soon. But she hasn't explained. None of the adults have. But they all seem to know something. They speak with hushed voices, bowing their heads and wiping the shimmers from their eyes as they gather around their neighbor and her newborn son. At seven years old, Tolaiyë can't define it. But he can feel the heaviness in the room. He can *see* it, pressing down on the shoulders of everyone who enters. It seems to hit them like a sudden wave at the door, stealing away any happy thought that might've been carried in on their faces.

Now they help Ifana wrap her baby in a blanket. And the tears begin to cascade anew from her weary eyes. Mother looks down, cupping her hand over her lips the way she always does when something terrible's happened. Something that can't be fixed.

"She's coming! From the woods!" The man's voice shocks everyone from their silence. The father of the baby. He comes running into the room with wild eyes, pointing out through the door he's left wide open behind him. "There's a chance," he tells his wife, voice wavering. He drops down beside her, pulls her close. "There's a chance. We have to let her try."

The visitor from the woods makes no sound at all when she comes. Standing beside the door, young Tolaiyë nearly leaps from his place when he turns to see the slim figure that stands suddenly beside him. A thin creature whose narrow shoulders stand only a little higher off the ground than his own. She stands clothed in a simple tunic—has arms, legs, hands, and feet, as any ordinary human being would have. But she isn't human. She's smaller and covered in dark, short fur. Tolaiyë's every thought is swallowed up in her massive, shining eyes—eyes that gleam with an oddly violet hue—and the broad ears that hang flat against the sides of her head. The visitor matches everything he's heard about the people of the woods. But seeing one of them in person is somehow stranger than he's always imagined. Almost frightening.

Silence falls thickly over the scene. Every gaze in the crowded cabin turns to watch the furred figure that stands in the doorway. Young Tolaiyë holds his breath behind his teeth. But the visitor from the woods pays no mind to the staring faces that surround her. She moves with slow, soundless steps across the room and lowers to her knees beside the weeping mother, placing a slender hand on the newborn child's gray head. Then her wide ears twitch subtly backward, and her eyes turn up to capture Ifana in their bottomless gaze.

"I must hold him," she whispers.

For a moment, Ifana simply stares back. And when she raises her son at last in shaking arms, there's a new glimmer in her face that Tolaiyë can't understand. Like the weary flicker of a lantern in the night. He looks instinctively to Mother—then to the faces of the adults who stand all around, hoping to find the answer. But they're all statues. Speechless, motionless. Watching the visitor with unblinking eyes. They watch with tight jaws as the newcomer takes the tiny child with one smooth scoop of her arm and lays her hand over his little chest.

What *is* this creature? Tolaiyë can hardly bear the stillness in the room. It seems to last for an eternity, threatening to swallow the entire cottage and everyone in it.

Until it's broken by a sharp, sudden sound. It's a sound he's heard many times before, in the village. The sound of a newborn baby's piercing cry. The heaviness that drowned the room only moments before is abruptly overthrown—pushed aside by a sudden chorus of gasps and exclamations.

"Healed!"

"Alive!"

"He moves!"

"He cries!"

"Gods be praised; the child lives!"

A once still and silent newborn has begun to wail and stretch out his tiny limbs—and the voices of all those who look on seem to come to life along with him. All marveling, all wondering at the miraculous event before them. Tolaiyë alone watches the broad-eared, fur-clothed stranger at the center of the room. She returns the squirming infant to his parents' quaking arms, giving only a silent nod in answer to their tearful, breathless thanks. And she rises to her feet, turning back to the door that was left open at her entrance. She's nearly over the threshold when she pauses in her place and turns to stare back at Tolaiyë with a violet gaze as profound as the night sky. A wild gaze. Seemingly motionless—like the gaze of some untamable, unknowable creature. Then she turns away, slinking out the door and vanishing into the shadows of the woods. And little Tolaiyë remains frozen, with his heart threatening to burst from his ears.

* * *

"That baby was ill, wasn't he?" he asks Mother as she helps him spread a freshly washed blanket over his bed that evening. It puffs the faint scent of summer wind into the room as she tosses out the corners and shakes out the wrinkles.

"He was dying, child. None of us expected that poor little soul would live to this hour," she tells him. She glances at him over her shoulder, showing him a gentle smile. "But our friend Lídei saved him today. Now I suspect he'll live a long life. Our little village hasn't seen anything so marvelous since the morning the moons aligned five years ago."

Outside, the last beams of daylight fight to peer through the trees. Glancing out between the half-open shutters, Tolaiyë can spot Father's tall silhouette in the garden—sauntering, bending down here and there as he gathers the rakes and little shovels left lying between the rows. Preparing for the coming rain.

"Mother, where do the people of the woods go when it rains?" The sight of the violet-eyed visitor sticks like a stain in his mind. Those wide, bottomless eyes . . .

"I'm sure they have shelters of their own."

"Where do they come from?" He slumps to his knees near the foot of the bed, resting his chin on the edge as he lets a thoughtful frown fall over his face.

Mother crosses the room to close and latch the shutters. "They've dwelt in these lands for many generations," she says. "The clans of the voránjevin were here long before our people came down from the old kingdom."

"From Sketza."

"Yes—from the lands of Sketza, far away to the north."

The old kingdom. Tales of the far north have been told in the village for as long as Tolaiyë can remember. The land tucked away into the northern horizon, where the earth is bold and stony. A land where the ancient trees rise to towering, marvelous heights overhead, fingering the sky. A place Mother and Father chose to leave behind. They came with many others, journeying from the north with young dreams carried fondly in their pockets and the gleam of the southern skies framed crisply in their eyes. Father says they came searching for things they couldn't find in Sketza—that many of their kinsmen came in search of new lives, away from the troubles of the old kingdom. He always puts the same stern expression on his face when he speaks of those days, shaking his head and letting out his breath in one long sigh. As if the story's far too long to ever be told in one sitting. He's never explained much more, and Tolaiyë's never asked. Father's family was among the first to settle in these lands, just north of Emér, the inland sea. In those days, Father was just a boy. And the people of the woods were the only neighbors he knew. Now Sketzan families can be found in a handful of settlements scattered throughout the forests and hills of North Emér.

Kneeling on the earthen floor, Tolaiyë's knees begin to tingle with numbness. He shuffles his weight. "Have we taken this land from them, the people of the woods—the voranjev . . . ?" He struggles to remember the word.

Halfway across the room, Mother's kneeling to poke a fresh log that lies heavily in the fireplace, and the light of the flames casts a warm red-orange glow across her face. "No, my son. They never remain in one place for too long," she says to the flames. "Their people can be found nearly anywhere. Our friend Lídei and her clan often roam the woods near our home. But there are times when we don't see them for many months." She rises now, a basket of sun-dried wrap tunics and loose trousers under one arm. "Come now, we're nearly finished. There's likely to be a few more that need mending," she tells him, bringing the laundry to the edge of his little bed.

Tolaiyë shuffles reluctantly to his feet and snatches a stiff pair of trousers from the basket. Father's working clothes—still chilled from the evening wind they were just pulled from. Despite being well worn, they have yet to earn any tears.

"The voránjevin people know far more of these lands than we do," Mother explains as she folds a shawl with several quick flicks of her wrists, looking it carefully over. "They've spent many years exploring all around the inland sea and beyond."

"Beyond?"

"Yes, child—the western shores, the barren south, and far away to the east, where the forests end and the hills turn to golden, blowing sands. There they found Rand to Molsó, which we call the Sand Sea."

"A sea of sand? Can we go to see it?" Tolaiyë's fingers grip suddenly tighter around the half-folded trousers in his hands.

Mother laughs. "Maybe someday. It'd be an adventure told of for generations if we did," she says—and there's a familiar melody in her voice. A soft thrill to the edges of her words. She smiles up at him again. This time, vibrantly. "There's a song about it, the Sand Sea," she whispers.

All the people of North Emér have their songs. But no one seems to sing so often or so whimsically as Mother.

She snatches another tunic from the basket, letting the notes slip calmly from her lips.

I've looked to the east
Beyond treetops
Where the plains melt like morning light
Beyond hill and horizon
Can you reach it—
The endless sea of golden sands?
A place of dreams
Where only Thought can walk?

3

The woods are alight with soft green and azure hues. As if every tree hides candles beneath its branches that set its leaves aglow like countless tiny lanterns—all frosted with the silvery shine of the night stars above.

It's a place she's come to in dreams before, many times. Always at the very deepest hour of the night, when even the wind along the treetops seems to fall idly to sleep. An empty place that seems to watch her, wait for her. The dream comes every night now, and every night it remains unchanged.

But tonight is somehow different. The air seems to leap like static at her skin, and all around the trees seem to lean in with eager eyes, watching closely. She wanders for ages through the leaves, stepping carefully between the trees, searching the shadows. The woods aren't empty this night. There's something waiting, not far ahead. Somehow, she can feel it. It calls her, pulling her strangely forward.

"Éliva."

The voice is nearly too soft to hear when it calls her name. A whisper. Who has spoken it? She presses forward, bending to glance between the dark bodies of the trees.

"Éliva."

The voice comes floating again to her ears—now so near that she finds herself spinning sharply around to face the one who calls her. But no one stands waiting when she turns. Only a little grove of young trees greets her, flooded with white, ethereal light. The source of the light seems to float in the air near the center of the grove—a tall rod hovering vertically between the leaves. It sits motionless in the air, suspended only a short height above the ground. An ornately engraved and painted staff with a shining orb hanging weightlessly in the curving crescent shape at its top. Like the staff of an ancient king. Light pours like soundless white flames from its edges, now rising in intensity and engulfing all that surrounds it. Such consuming whiteness, swelling, *blinding*—

The dream leaves her with a sudden flare of silvery light, and she sits up so sharply and suddenly that she nearly rams her forehead into the branch hanging low over her bed. Another dream! Just as they've come to her for months. But this time . . .

She breathes. The sun's early rays have only just begun to light the woods all around, but the trees have already let out their sweet blossoms, casting their delicate perfume into the breeze. Morning. The air's already warm. She swats the frizzed hair from her face, too impatient to give it the thorough brushing it needs. There's no time now.

Lídei sits only several paces away, her dark color nearly blending into the shadow of the broad tree at her back. Éliva's spotted before she can rise to her feet.

"I see our sweet girl has slept in," Lídei remarks softly without looking up from her weaving, a calm smile spread across her face. For the voránjevin of the Shardehn clan, early mornings are usually spent hunting and preparing fresh meats, or tending the little gardens. But Lídei can nearly always be found weaving—sitting quietly someplace where the young daylight peers in through the canopy and sets a little patch of grass aglow. Éliva's often accompanied her in the mornings, watching the voránjevin woman's thin fingers move with fluid motions between the threads. Earthen tones—browns, reds, and grays—all winding seamlessly together at her touch. Mother Lídei. She's always said that weaving in the morning light helps the peace stay rooted in her heart. Of all the voránjevin people who make up the Shardehn clan, none has been so like a mother to young Éliva as Lídei the weaver.

"It wasn't on purpose, I promise." Éliva lets herself sink to the grass beside the little stack of unwoven threads, tucking her knees to her chest. "That dream came to me again."

"Mm? The dark forest again?"

"Yes, but this time . . ." The dream flashes softly across her thoughts as she struggles to describe it, and her words slip away. It was such an oddly familiar voice that came to her.

Beside her, Lídei pauses in her weaving, a single dark thread lying over her palm. Her giant violet eyes turn to catch Éliva in their gentle gaze. "What else have you seen in this dream?" she asks.

"I'm not sure what it was. It was like a tall walking staff. But it seemed somehow . . . somehow"—the word seems to hover shyly at the edge of her breath for an instant before slipping out at last—"alive."

"A living thing?"

"Yes, and it called my name," Éliva nearly whispers.

For a time, Lídei says nothing in reply. She gathers her weaving and lays it all together carefully on the ground at her knees, breathing deeply before looking back to Éliva. "I've never told you. But it was a dream that led me to find you ten years ago," she says. "I dreamed again and again of the seashore, of the cold waves crashing in. I hadn't visited the shore in years. Yet the dream persisted for weeks." She reaches over to tuck a stray wave of Éliva's long hair aside. "And when I followed the dream at last to the western shore, there you were. Right where I had always stood in my dream each night."

"A dream?" Éliva murmurs.

She was only three years old the day she met Mother Lídei, and the recollection of it has become so blurred and surreal in her young mind. The memory of waking to the sight of unknown faces—furred faces—with such large, painted eyes. Waking to the sound of voices that whispered unfamiliar words, gasping and murmuring all around.

It's no secret that Éliva's not like the other members of the clan. At only thirteen years old, she stands a good head taller than nearly all the brothers and sisters of the Shardehn. And while their bodies are clothed in thick fur, Éliva's skin is pale and almost hairless. Her eyes are nowhere as wide and vibrantly colored as those she's always seen around her. And while the faces she sees each day are all framed by broad, flat ears that hang down to the jaw, her own face has always been surrounded by a seemingly untamable mass of amber-brown waves of hair that cascade from her head.

They say that from the time the clans began many generations ago, Lídei is the only voránjevin mother who's ever dared to take in a child of the arai. A human child.

Lídei turns back to her weaving. "More often than not, dreams are only random, meaningless visions," she says, "but there are times when they become something real to us."

Éliva blinks, letting the thought unfold carefully at the center of her mind. *Something real.* Until recently, no dream of hers would ever fit that description. But the recurring vision of the dark forest is unlike all that have come before it. It's tangible, the way imminent summer rain is tangible. It's inexplicably whimsical—yet vivid as any waking day. Every night she finds herself wandering there between the cool shadows of the trees—searching but not finding. Looking for something or someone she can't name. Something *real.* Now she's found something at last. A voice and a carved staff bathed in blinding white light. But the new discovery only churns the questions in her heart. And creates more.

Mother Lídei was once led by a dream. Perhaps Éliva can learn to be led as well. But who calls from the dark wood?

The thought stays with her all morning long—drifting and weaving silent circles around every motion she makes, every word she speaks. It floods her mind as she helps the others prepare the meats from the morning hunt; dazzles her focus as she follows Lídei around the camp and surrounding woods, tending the gardens and gathering dirty blankets for washing.

Who calls?

The longer it echoes in her ears, the memory of the voice in the dark forest seems to knit an ever-stranger path into her heart. It distracts her well into the evening, until the sun is sinking behind the western trees and casting light in sharp, orange-yellow streaks along the forest floor. She walks idly back from the hills south of camp, hardly noticing the dying light as it flits between the leaves.

That voice . . . has she heard it before?

The idea triggers soft thrumming in her chest. But it's thrown abruptly from her mind when she raises her eyes to find a tall figure standing in her path, only a few paces ahead. A man. Not a voránjevin *heln*, but a human man.

"Oh—" A startled gasp leaps from her throat as she stops in her place.

The man stands clothed in dark gray and blue tones, in silk more intricately embroidered than Éliva's ever known was possible. And his gaze is unyielding. "Éliva Trafos Ilánehl." His voice falls strangely echoless in the afternoon air. And that name . . .

"I . . ." She tucks a clump of her rebellious hair away from her face and behind one ear, unsure how to respond.

The man brings a hand to his hip, a subtle smile drawing across his short-bearded face. "I suppose you may've long forgotten that name. Or perhaps you lost it in the sea the day you came to this land," he muses.

"Do you know me?" Éliva stares back, fingering the thick hem of her shawl.

Never be too quick to trust a stranger. Lídei's oft-repeated advice comes floating softly to mind.

The man's stare is motionless. Almost unnerving. "I've known you for many ages," he whispers. "Since long before you were born near the Black Shores of the far west. Long before your family boarded a ship that would never reach its destination, before the gods left you helpless on these shores nearly ten years ago."

Éliva's breath catches stiffly in her throat. The Shardehn have always supposed that she came from beyond the sea. But all these years, the greatest evidence has survived only in her own scattered, fleeting memories. Images and voices that have long since faded. And she's never hoped to revive them.

Who *is* this man? There's something unnamable in the odd glimmer of his golden-brown eyes. Something about the lack of contrast in the shadows on his face, or the way the light that falls down in spots from the canopy above seems to miss him altogether. Something just beyond words.

"You knew my family?" she asks the man, somewhat surprised to hear how level her own voice remains.

"I'm simply someone who knows what you are," he tells her.

Éliva's response chokes back in her throat. "What I . . ."

The stranger shakes his head. "You're not one of them, Éliva. No, no. Not another creature of the woods, like those who've watched over you all these years."

"They've told me that there are many clans and nations of people like me," Éliva tells him. "The arai, the race of Man. But I've never wished to leave the Shardehn."

The man laughs. A smooth, almost musical sound. "Yes, all of Claya is filled with the clans of the arai. But even *they* aren't like you," he says, and the laughter in his eyes turns suddenly stern. "You're something much greater."

There's an uneasy edge to the hissing tones in his voice. An off-note that sends subtle tension crawling along Éliva's limbs, urging her to move—to dash away into the night and back to the safety of the Shardehn. She glances around. When did the sun fall so far below the horizon? On all sides, the woods seem suddenly dimmer. But the strange man who stands in the middle is darker yet. He seems to know her. Maybe he truly does know all about her and where she came from. But an odd sensation follows after him, like the darkness of the coming night.

"Who are you?" she whispers, shuffling carefully sideways.

The man's smile returns—scarcely visible in the failing light. And despite the fact that he stands several paces away, his reply seems to breathe directly into her ear.

"Your brother."

The words flush like cold water through Éliva's thoughts, and she opens her mouth to question—

But the man has vanished—gone without so much as a quivering leaf in his wake.

4

Every nation finds names for its children. Many honor their sons with the names of their ancient forefathers, or adorn their daughters with the titles of queens from ages long past. But the people of Sketza have ways of their own. They've long lived apart from the lands beyond the western sea, away from the trends and traditions that dwell there. And it's long been a custom among them to name their children not with single titles, but with songs.

"In stone no hands can find the blood of sorrow."

Stone. Mother's always said that in poems, the word refers to Claya itself. The earth. She and Father say that the name they gave him means *joy*—that in all the earth, no sorrow can be found. And so from the beginning they've called him *Tolaiÿe*, "of joy." There are few who know his song in full, and those who do rarely speak it. But over the years, Tolaiÿe's preferred it so. A song seldom spoken has a way of becoming sacred. Like a simple yet delicate gem that's kept in a carved box. Only to be revealed at life's most significant moments.

* * *

"Our lord Talek, the son of Rand, is growing weary of the stubbornness of these western families. How long will you deny the king your loyalty?" The man and his companion are rough edged, with stained blades at their sides and the remnants of forest living all over their rugged figures. Greased hair hanging in clumps, trousers worn almost black at the knees. They wear the plain red-and-gray tunics of the king's men. Soldiers of Rand, come from the east.

Father stands with one arm resting loosely over the handle of his rake. "You need not ask," he tells them. "These people have no king. Not since the time they left the borders of our homeland and not today." Several other men from the village have gathered beside him, all watching the two strangers.

"These people?" the soldier spits at the dirt. "We'll see what they become if left to their pleasures— lawless, scattered over all the land like the *parafa* you adore so much." He gives his companion a stiff clap to the shoulder, motioning toward the eastern woods and their inhabitants. But his gaze passes over young Tolaiyë as they turn to leave—and pauses there. "No matter. The world will soon be free of your curse . . . when the king's army arrives at your doorstep," he sneers, glancing the boy over before turning away.

Nearby, several of the village men let out curses of their own, stepping forward with their fists and their shovels held firmly. But Father puts out his arm, calling them softly back as the soldiers vanish down the hill. When he turns to look over his shoulder at his twelve-year-old son, there's no sign of anger in his eyes. Only something else. Is it . . . sadness?

"Don't mind them, son," he says.

The curse. It's stained the village of Ethein for twelve years now. The reasoning behind it is simple. Of all the families who came to settle these lands, none had any record of a child being born with black eyes. Until Tolaiyë came. Mother says his eyes were black from corner to corner the day he entered the world. No hint of color, no whiteness at the edges, no shine. It was three weeks before the blackness faded, giving way to the greenish-brown hue that Tolaiyë's eyes bear today—the warm coloring that's always led the villagers to exclaim how remarkably he takes after his father's face.

Curse.

Mother and Father never used the word—but it was only their close friendships with the other families of Ethein that kept them from becoming outcasts. And when word of the black eyes reached the people of surrounding settlements, the village of Ethein became a place seldom visited. It became a place mentioned only in whispers, in rumors. Most especially among the people of Rand.

Rand.

A common word for "ocean." It was the title given to a man who led countless Sketzans to settle in lands that lie several days' travel to the east. Many believed him to be the true king of Sketza. They said he was destined to create a new kingdom in North Emér for his people—that he would rule over lands as vast as the sea, from the western coast to the borders of the far eastern sands. But his time ended long before the lands of North Emér could be entirely explored. Now his son reigns in his stead. And Talek, the son of Rand, seems to keep an ever closer eye on the families of the western lands, who claim no allegiance to him. His soldiers have come often to Ethein and the other settlements northwest of the Emér Sea, demanding goods, announcing decrees. But today they came with threats.

"They're men of words alone—no sense wasting our strength against them," Father assures his neighbors as he turns back to the gardens. Maybe he's right.

* * *

That evening, the trees on the hills are restless. They seem to toss themselves wildly against the darkening sky, whirling and waving their long branches as the wind moves over them. As if they hope to warn the people of some impending danger. Tolaiyë pauses to watch them in the back garden, where he kneels pruning the vines. Listening. Now the wind rises again in a sudden gust, and all around the trees seem to lift their voices to greet it. Somehow, they're speaking. But their words are hushed, scarcely audible above the rushing of the wind. And they speak strange words, old words. Whispering.

"Is something amiss?" Mother's voice comes drifting to his ears, and Tolaiyë's surprised to find that he's risen unconsciously to his feet. He turns to see her watching calmly from several garden rows back.

"Did you hear them?" he calls back to her.

"Hear what, child?"

The wind suddenly loses its vigor and falls back to a soft sway all around as Tolaiyë pauses, searching for words.

"The trees," he says, "their voices."

Mother only stares silently back at him, a mild expression painting her face. Hesitation. Then she tugs the glove from her left hand and reaches up to wipe the moisture from her brow. "What did they say?" she asks.

Tolaiÿë glances to the trees again before answering. They've ended their dance, but a sleepless stirring ripples on in their dark leaves. When he turns back to Mother, the setting sun has begun to light half her figure with sharp shadows and warm colors.

"They spoke of eternity."

5

The sash has blown itself into a loose knot. It flaps and twists like a dark flag near the tree's crown, visible only in random gaps between the swaying branches. Éliva takes a moment to confirm her footing on the bough below before reaching out one hand to snatch the sash's blowing end and pull it gently free. She lays it hastily over her shoulder, fastening a quick knot at her opposite side to keep it in place, then runs a hand over the length of it, searching for snags. The fabric is dense, worn soft over years of use. And somehow undamaged. Relief gusts like the passing afternoon breeze over her heart. A handful of the clan's oldest sashes had been rinsed and hung to dry in the morning. It was an unusually strong gust of wind that lifted them free from the low branches and scattered them all throughout the trees just southwest of the camp. The kind of wind that comes like a sudden omen before a storm. But the rain has yet to arrive today. And it's fortunate. Éliva's spent several hours searching and gathering the sashes—many of which had been tossed high into the trees. Black skies and thick rain would have made them nearly impossible to spot.

The sashes are treasured possessions among all voránjevin people, often handed down from one generation to the next. Lídei says the voránjevin people have worn sashes over their left shoulders since the beginning, long before they came to these lands from across the western sea. Every sash carries the colors or emblem of one of the clans. When worn as a wrap, the thick folds of the sashes are perfect for carrying an endless array of things, from supplies for the hunt to an infant needing comforting. The uses are as endless as the tales that surround the origin of the sashes—stories told nearly every night beside the campfires of the Shardehn.

Éliva takes her time returning to the forest floor, trusting only the firmest branches for footholds. This may not be the greatest of the ancient trees in these woods, but it's certainly tall enough to offer an intimidating view from its upper limbs. And Éliva prefers not to think about how merciless the earth below would instantly become, should her foot slip.

The day's still hot when she returns to the camp of the Shardehn at last, carrying a spark of excitement in the lightness of her steps. Lídei will be thrilled to see that the last of the scattered sashes has been recovered.

But she isn't alone when Éliva finds her. A gray-furred heln kneels beside Mother Lídei with the stone-carved posture of a hunter. He turns at the sound of Éliva's coming, and she finds herself momentarily struck by the vibrant amber-yellow hue of his eyes. He gazes back for a fleeting moment longer, unblinking, and the air in the grove becomes suddenly sharpened.

She's seen the gray heln once before—when the Shardehn first came to camp near the western shore of

Emér, several years ago—and he frightened her then, without so much as looking at her. Without saying anything at all. Now his gaze seems to leave a hot scar in her mind. He turns away after a moment longer, murmuring something softly to Lídei before slipping off into the trees. Gone.

Éliva breathes again, moving to Lídei's side. "Was it something I did?" she asks softly.

A bitter smile comes to Lídei's calm face. She sighs, still watching the trees where the heln disappeared. "Sweet girl, don't let him worry you. My son often appears angry to those who don't know him. He has a stern gaze," she says, turning to look at Éliva. "I'm sure he just noticed the dark shimmer in your eyes."

The dark shimmer. The shadow. The black flickering. It's something Éliva's tried to catch in the mirror countless times but never succeeded. A fleeting dark shadow that conceals the white and emerald colors of her eyes for just a moment—only when someone else first glances at her—before flickering away. Lídei says the arai can't see it, but the voránjevin can. Says it must be the sign of someone born for a special purpose.

But what purpose?

Éliva pulls the sash from her shoulder, kneeling to fold it carefully in her lap. "Why doesn't he stay with the Shardehn? Is he serving as a messenger between the clans?" she asks.

"Faleth left the Shardehn long ago to dwell with the Iftav—the clan of his father," Lídei tells her. A brief sparkle of gladness lights her expression as she catches sight of the old sash that lies folded between them, then fades as she moves away in her thoughts. "His father, my Drinehn, always carried such love in his heart. When the arai came from the north, he was among the first to befriend them, to learn their speech. He and I went often to visit them. Even after our son was born." She shifts her weight as she talks, reaching to grasp a few thin waves of Éliva's hair and intertwine them gently through her dark fingers. "It was an arai woman who taught me how to braid."

Drinehn. Éliva's often heard his name mentioned among the Shardehn. It's a name they mention only with soft voices and bowed heads. A name held reverently beside those of the greatest keepers of the clans.

"Did he fall ill?" she whispers.

Lídei shakes her head as she finishes the first braid and reaches for a new set of strands to work with. "My Drinehn gave his life many years ago, to save a family of the arai. My son was your age, just thirteen years old, and he's worn a stern face ever since the day his father left us. Over ten years ago now." There's something old in the sound of Lídei's words. Worn, broken-in—like the way a pair of sandals becomes soft with time, or the way the words of ancient songs tend to melt through the ages until they blend into the music itself.

And there's something else—a subtle stirring that pulls at Éliva's heart. "Drinehn . . . he isn't far, is he?" she says.

Lídei pauses midway through the second braid, looking up with a subtle new gleam at the edges of her eyes. "No. He's never far from me," she whispers. "I'll join him where he is, someday." A faint sheen of wetness glistens over her eyes as her fingers move again, capturing the words and weaving them into the braid she creates. Locked.

* * *

The night is still when it comes. Silent enough to hear the delicate rustling of birds' feathers and the faint calls of creatures hidden away in the great depths of the woods. Not a single leaf stirs. It's a night too silent for sleep. Éliva sits beside her blanket with her back to a tree, watching as the moons shift in and out of sight behind thinning clouds and the darkened canopy above. Wondering. The night is calm but sleepless. All around, the forest is not unlike the dark grove in the dreams that've come so many times to her mind. The place where a voice has called her. Beckoned her . . .

"Can you feel it?"

The words are scarcely louder than a murmur, but they pierce the stillness of the air with a sharpness that nearly startles Éliva to her feet. The man who spoke them stands only several paces away, almost entirely disguised in the shadows of the trees. A human man she's met once before. The stranger in silk from the southern woods. The arai who knew her name.

How long has he stood there? Somehow, he's crept past the evening watchers, farther into the camp than any uninvited guest should be able to venture. Éliva breathes. Who . . . ?

"This is the camp of the Shardehn. How have you come here?" she whispers, fighting to dispel the soft shiver that climbs her spine.

The man only smiles—an oddly sharp-angled grin. "The earth is waking," he tells her. "The wind speaks of it. The trees speak of it. Even now your time is near." He holds his hands out from his sides as he speaks, palms skyward.

The entire Shardehn clan lies sleeping all around. More voránjevin than any single man could hope to fight off. There's no reason to fear him. But this man is somehow different. His voice sends a kind of coldness into the air—the sort of bitter cold that seeps smoothly into the bones, into the heart. How had Éliva not noticed before?

Now the man's figure seems to fade, waning into the blackness that surrounds him. *Vanishing.* Éliva strains to make out his shape in the shadows, reaching soundlessly toward the edge of her blanket and fingering the little dagger that lies sheathed there.

"Are you a spirit?" Her question scarcely rises above the loud thrumming of her heart.

But the arai doesn't answer. And when Éliva blinks to look again, there are only trees and shadows where he stood. Spirit or man, the intruder is gone.

6

The trading post has changed little since he last visited, nearly six months ago. The goods are most certainly all new—pelts, blankets, grains, and dried meats—but they lie stacked in the same order as always, neatly arranged in their places for visitors to peruse. A thick-figured man appears from behind a tower of quilts, squinting closely at the metal brackets pinched between his fingers. A wooden crate large enough to carry a boar rests at his feet, its broken clasp already partly mended. Now the man looks up, and a sudden grin breaks across his broad face.

"My good man Kehljen! A few moons have passed since you last came to my post," he calls out, tipping a bearded chin at his guest. "How fares my friend from Ethein?"

"Well as ever, Galdehn," Kehljen calls in return. The pack he carries has begun to feel like a pile of rocks. He loosens the ties and lowers it carefully to the grass.

"And your boy, Tolaiyë? Hasn't come with you this time, I see," the tradesman remarks as he rummages at the back of his shop, searching for an empty sack or crate.

"Not this time—though he would've loved to. But they were lacking a set of able hands in the gardens," Kehljen tells him. Tolaiyë's always loved to visit the trading posts, dreaming up each trip to be some thrilling adventure into the deep woods.

"Well, I imagine his aid is well appreciated. Strong boy, that son of yours. That'll do," Galdehn says, setting the crate with the half-mended clasp on the ground between them. "What needs has the village today?"

"*Káneva* oil, if you have it. Otherwise, your best root extract," Kehljen tells him. The vegetables from his pack fill the crate just beyond the chipped and ragged brim. He shakes the empty pack over the grass, stepping back as the dirt and crumbs cascade out beside his feet.

"*Káneva!*" Galdehn pulls a slate from his table, eyeing the new goods and scribbling down a few jagged numbers as he speaks. "Just traded a load of hard grain for several barrels of it, not three days ago. Has there been some accident in Ethein?"

"Nothing terrible. Just a few men with rope-scalded palms in need of a little relief. Our supply's run low."

Galdehn gives a slow nod of approval. "Glad to hear there's no tragedy among your good people. Not like the eastern regions these days. The stories that pass by my table as of late aren't anything any *káneva* or hearty extract can fix, of that I'm certain," he says.

"The people of Rand?" Kehljen raises an eyebrow as he tips his canteen to his mouth.

"Aye, my brother. If you've any mind to keep your families alive, don't let them be wandering anywhere too far in the southeastern woods. Strange things are about."

Somewhere in the grove behind the shop walls, the sound of laughing children echoes. A half-muffled melody. The tradesman's family at play.

Kehljen finds a seat for himself among a few stacks of rugs. "Have the people of Rand turned against each other?" he asks.

Galdehn shakes his head as he lifts the newly filled crate to a place near the back wall. "Men are vanishing," he says. "Men and women alike. Even several soldiers of Rand now. Vanishing into the southeastern woods—just south of Kehnin and west of Votyón."

"Vanishing? That's only a few days' journey from here. Are they not familiar with those parts?"

"Familiar as any of us would expect to be. Some say it's the families of the western settlements messing about, attacking in secret. But you and I both know that couldn't be so." He tips his head to one side in disapproval, thick whiskers ruffling with the frown at his lips.

"No, our people have never sought battle," Kehljen agrees.

"None truly know, but I've a feeling the people of the wild have had a hand in this." Galdehn waves a finger loosely toward the south. "They've never had good relations with the men of Rand, not like those in these parts have with Ethein."

Kehljen fails to catch a surprised chuckle before it slips out from his throat. The tradesman must be making a joke. "The voránjevin clans? Surely not, wouldn't you say? I'd never expect such a thing of them. They've been nothing short of gracious with us since the day we first settled these lands," he says.

But Galdehn shakes his head, eyebrows furrowing together. "I know it, brother—know it as well as you. But the wild folk come in many tribes. Many colors and many minds. And some of them may not be so fond of us as we think," he murmurs somewhat softly, as if the trees nearby were listening in. "You might ask them next time one of their folk visits Ethein. Who knows what they'll tell you." Now he turns to weigh a full jar of oil, adding just a few ladles more before securing the seal.

Kehljen watches silently on, wondering. The kindness of the people of the woods has always inspired him. The suggestion that they could have any part in harming human lives seems out of the question. *Ridiculous* even. But Galdehn's never been one to speak lightly. And there's an anxious edge to his usually jolly smile that sews something cold in Kehljen's heart. Something difficult to name.

Galdehn sets the sealed jar carefully in Kehljen's pack, securing it snugly in place. "These are becoming strange times, my brother," he says. "Let's walk them carefully, eyes open." He offers a hand, which Kehljen takes in a grateful shake. Strange times indeed.

7

She's nearly asleep when the voice calls. Floating somewhere in the gap between waking and dreaming, unsure of anything. But the voice comes like a wave of the sea to her clouded mind—slipping into her veins and pulling her awake, urging her to rise.

"Éliva."

She opens her eyes, blinking until the scene comes into focus. It's an almost moonless night, but the woods are aglow, flooded with edgeless green-and-blue patches of light. No different than the dreams that have crowded her mind each night. But tonight she isn't dreaming. Not this time.

The world is silent as she rises to her feet. As if time and all those living in its grasp have somehow frozen in their places. At every side the camp of the Shardehn sleeps on, entirely unaware of the white light that now streams through the woods nearby, streaking through leaves and across motionless, sleeping faces.

"Éliva."

The voice calls again, and the pale light swells and sways mildly between the trees. She turns toward it, wondering at the calmness of her own steps. Maybe her heart should be racing. Maybe she should be afraid, should turn back and hide until the safety of morning returns. But there's a deep and abiding peace that rises from the earth and tumbles like fallen leaves over her shoulders. A serenity that seems to melt away any wariness in her bones, any tension in her breath. This is the night the dreams have prepared her for. A night she's waited for. Somehow, she knows it.

"Éliva."

The voice whispers into the center of her heart, echoing from just behind the curve of the next tree. And when she steps onward, the grove beyond is a gleaming pool of white light. The one who calls her floats weightlessly in the air at the center of the clearing—a creature she's gazed at before in dreams. But tonight it's more than a vision. The bearer of the voice is a tall, limbless being, like the staff of a magnificent queen. But *living*. Its intricately engraved surface, the single shining eye hanging in the crescent shape at its top—every detail exactly as it was in the dreams. And the light of its presence floods the woods all around, beaming near the brightness of the morning sun. She pauses several paces away, momentarily lost in the splendor of the sight.

The being speaks. "Child of gods, the time has come." It uses old speech. A language from ages long past. "The duty to which you are called, the calling of those in the heavens, lies before you. To protect the free will of the children, to stand as messenger before them, and to present the fate of Claya at the footstool of the goddess. That it and all its realms may become whole and eternal."

The words sound like an old song to Éliva's memory. Words of a covenant, a promise. Something promised long ago—a *lifetime* ago. It churns and ripples at the edge of her recollections, fighting for clarity.

The creature's single eye shifts silently in its place. "Do you accept this call?" The question sounds, and all the night seems to gather near to listen in. As if all nights have awaited the coming of this one, this moment—watching tirelessly through the ages.

The answer swells up from somewhere ancient in Éliva's mind, recalled from a lifetime long past, rising to her lips despite the questions that flutter through her mind. Despite the apparent lack of explanations. The answer is right. She can feel it.

"I accept."

A new flurry of light flickers along the creature's slender sides in response to her reply, sending the shadows into a wild dance at the feet of the trees. "Reach out your hand," it whispers.

For an instant, Éliva can only remain in her place, eyes unblinking. Breathing. When she raises her hand at last, fingers loose and palm turned to the night stars, all the days of her life seem to fall suddenly away. They melt into the night at her back, leaving only this moment. Only here, only now.

The silver light that emits from the being at the center of the grove rises to a more brilliant shining now, radiant as the sun. It bursts outward in a blaze of blinding whiteness, engulfing the girl who stands breathless at its edge and surging through every strand of her being, igniting like morning rays in her bones. Like the winds of a thousand summers rushing together—powerful, pure, and warm. And when the light subsides, falling again to a soft, silvery glow, the world has changed. *Éliva's* changed. She opens her eyes to find a gentle glow emitting from her own hands, her arms, her feet. Where a plain tunic once hung, shimmering robes now clothe her thin figure, draping over the grass like the gown of an empress.

Breathe, sigh.

She tests the feel of her lungs, blinking slowly, marveling. Somehow, she's become something new—or stepped into a life that seems new, yet feels undeniably familiar. Feels *right*.

"Rise, *sasarian* daughter. This Farian is your servant. It will uphold you in all things." The one who called her to the grove softly announces itself as it drifts nearer in the night air.

Farian. Its name finds a comfortable place in her memory. Like the name of an old friend, or a sister once forgotten. And the undeniably familiar word it called her . . .

Her thoughts are pushed aside by the sudden chorus of sound that seems to erupt in all directions. The sound of beating hearts—thousands, *millions.* Hearts beating in the woods nearby, in distant northern territories, in the lands far beyond the western sea, and everywhere in between. Hearts that sing, hearts that weep. Human hearts living in every stage of life, full of every dream and every longing ever imagined. They thrum on together in one impossibly massive choir, each singing its own song and echoing endlessly against the greatest rhythm of all—the great drum of the heart of Claya itself, buried deep in the earth.

She gasps. "Farian, what are these heartbeats? Why do I hear them?"

The Farian turns in the air, making a slow rotation. "It is part of the call of the *sasarianë*, to watch over the children of Claya. To you it is given to hear all their joys and sorrows. This servant will teach you. You will learn in time," it tells her.

All joys, all sorrows. Éliva closes her eyes, listening. So many living souls! When did the world become so filled, so alive—such an unending symphony? And the more she listens, one melody seems to ring out above the rest, somehow chiming more loudly, more clearly, than any other. A young heart, not far away to the northeast. The heart of an arai, a boy of the western families in North Emér, who stands beside a well, drawing up a satchel of water . . . Who?

Someone comes, stepping softly through the trees toward the clearing now. A presence Éliva could never mistake. She opens her eyes.

"Lídei."

The voránjevin woman pauses with gaping eyes at the border of the trees, glancing slowly between Éliva and the glowing Farian that remains floating in the air nearby. "Sweet Éliva, I should have seen it. Should have known," she murmurs.

Éliva smiles. "I'm beginning to remember now, Lídei! There's something I promised to do. A role I promised to honor ages ago. It's still coming back to me." She gathers her robes, stepping nearer.

Lídei takes her hand. "There was always something powerful in you," she whispers. "The power that brought you to our shores. Now I see it. You're one of them—one of the race the clans have watched for and spoken of for generations. One of the sasarianë."

Sasarianë—it *is* the word the Shardehn sometimes spoke of throughout the years. Until now, it never seemed significant. Now it's what she's become. But what does it really mean?

"Come, servant of the gods. There is much you must learn," the Farian's voice chimes mildly at Éliva's ears.

She glances over her shoulder at her guardian's motionless figure, then turns back to Lídei's waiting gaze. "I'll come back. I'll visit the Shardehn," she promises.

Lídei nods, the light of Éliva's reflection forming white and silver stars in her wide violet eyes. "Go, child," she breathes, giving Éliva's hand one last grip before letting go. A grasp that sends soft flutters of energy flowing between their palms.

Éliva rises to her feet, and the wind rises to meet her. It swells and folds like silk on all sides, lifting her free of the earth. And the grove falls quickly out of sight altogether.

8

Young Tolaiyë's never minded when Father asks him to fetch the evening water. The gardens of Ethein are so still, so serene, when night falls. Painted—like the scenes Mother sometimes creates with the colored dyes she buys from Galdehn's post. The light of the twin moons has a way of pulling different natures out of ordinary trees and hills. As if the earth itself falls into a trance each night, lulled to silence by the slow turn of the white moons across the sky.

The night breeze has paused in its place as he comes to the well, and the water brought up in the first scoop of the ladle still carries the warmth of the afternoon sun. Clear and stony flavored. Its rippling face catches the pale color of the greater moon as he tips the ladle into the water cart—and it catches something else. A white glow, purer than the moons, far brighter than the stars. The southwestern horizon's entirely alight when he turns to see it, lit by a column of light that rises like a great pillar from the trees, surging into the night sky and away through the thinning clouds.

Tolaiyë stands motionless at the sight of it, watching as light falls like frost over the curves of the land until the moment carries him away entirely. And for a fleeting instant, he's no longer staring at the horizon, but into the gaze of a glorious being. An angel cloaked in silvery radiance, whose countenance shines with the light of the morning. A goddess with eyes like the dawn.

When the vision falls away from his eyes, Tolaiyë finds himself lowered to his knees, leaning limply against the stone mouth of the well, breathless. And only the moons and flitting stars light the southwestern horizon, fighting for brilliance against the blackened night sky.

Part Two

1

Father never seems to talk long when a weighty issue's on his mind. His sentences become simple, fleeting—cut short by the mild tilt of his chin and the tightness of his breath. Only the most essential words are spoken. Nothing more.

"Don't hesitate to leave Ethein if you have to. The Shardehn can help me find you when I return," he murmurs as he tugs his shawl into place. "The men of Rand can be ruthless."

Mother reaches to tighten the straps that hold the water and supplies to his back, a mild crease forming down the center of her forehead. "We'll be just fine. Be swift, love," she whispers to him.

He takes her hand. "Shouldn't take more than four days to reach their capital settlement," he assures her, then turns to his son, eyes stern. "Protect your mother."

There's a kind of power in Father's presence as he gives his command. It's something Tolaiÿe's noticed from the time he was young, though he's never managed to define it. Mother carries it too. It's the strength that's always kept the three of them bound inseparably together despite whatever circumstances may arise—a power that only seems to follow men and women who wouldn't hesitate to give their lives for someone dear to them.

Tolaiyë nods.

Eleven years. For eleven long years since the last soldiers of Rand appeared at Ethein with their threats, the people of the western settlements have managed to remain free of a king's rule. For eleven years the people of Rand have pestered—first with written decrees, then with messengers. And later, with armed bands of soldiers. Insisting, threatening. The rule of Talek will not be stunted, they say. A brave new lord reigns in North Emér, they cry. And he will claim the borders of his kingdom for the good of his people. How dare the settlers of the western forests deny his sovereignty!

Now the king's armies threaten to enforce the king's rule, marching westward with their soldiers, no longer planning to negotiate.

At twenty-three years old, Tolaiyë finds himself wondering how the peaceful families of the western villages could ever muster the strength to overcome an attack from the east. Father's one of the few of his generation who's learned to fight with a traditional *sénsin* rod—a dense rod roughly the length of a man's leg, carved from the dangerously acidic wood of the *chikáton* trees that grow along the edge of the plains. The powerful burn of *chikáton* wood makes learning to fight with a sénsin rod a more delicate matter than most villagers have time to master. One mistake and the burning wood can melt through clothes, skin—even bone—with little difficulty. Father's almost always practiced with the sénsin rod sheathed in a snug metal sleeve to avoid any risk, although he never seems to need it. Tolaiyë's never seen steadier hands or surer footing.

"It rarely pays to be brash," Father's always said.

He was right. But these days, the people of the western settlements have little time for training. The vast majority of them have only enough combat experience to chase the occasional unwanted wildlife from their gardens. By contrast, they say the king's army always has at least one sénsin-trained fighter for every ten blade- or spear-wielding soldiers.

For most settlers west of Ethein, fighting isn't a promising solution. But perhaps they'll find another answer.

After weeks of counseling together, and after what seemed like endless debating among the villages, a plan for a peace treaty was created. Father and six other men of the western families were selected to deliver the treaty. With luck, they'll find an audience with the son of Rand himself. It's one last attempt to avoid the impending storm—a dark tempest that seems to rise over the horizon despite all efforts against it.

The other men have arrived now, trudging over the hill with their loose hats and worn coats, walking sticks in hand. Father lays a strong hand on Tolaiyë's shoulder, then turns to leave a kiss at Mother's lips before turning stiffly eastward. In the five years since Tolaiyë left Ethein to live near Ontrágo to the northwest, Father's never once set foot in the lands east of Galdehn's post. Watching the men slowly vanish down the east hill and into the speckled shadows of the morning forest, Tolaiyë fights to dispel the impulse that rises up and presses against his chest, urging him to follow after them. They'll be back. Hopefully.

2

The sea wears a gray-and-silver-laced cloak as the morning light lies along it, churning sleeplessly over itself. The sea's been her place of solace since the night the Farian came to her, over eleven years ago. A space where the endless voices of the world seem somehow less overwhelming, despite ringing more clearly than ever.

Swell, rise. Sink, recede.

The waves magnify and soften the sounds of the earth with every rise and fall. An endless rhythm. This is her realm. Standing in the air above the swaying waters, Éliva watches the slow curve of the horizon.

"Farian, these many years you've taught me to commune with the earth. Now its voice is always singing, a sounding bell to my heart." She closes her eyes, listening. "I hear all that live in Claya. And there are so many . . . so many lives. But what can I give them? How can I fulfill my purpose?"

She listens for a moment longer, waiting, then opens her eyes to find the Farian floating soundlessly beside her. It turns in a slow circle.

"This servant will show you."

* * *

The Shardehn people often spoke of the lands of Ataran, far over the western sea—telling stories of adventure and grandeur that had always entranced Éliva's young heart. And now, after more than eleven years, she's visited the many cities of the western continent herself. She's ridden the wind to distant shores and hilltops, walked unseen through ornamented plazas, gazed at ancient towers and the bustling roads that lie in curving, winding paths between them. She's wandered through countless forests, valleys, and mountains. But today the Farian guides her elsewhere, to lands that stretch north and south along the eastern shores of Ataran, where only a few lonely heartbeats can be heard along the outer edges. Empty, wild lands. And at the heart of it, ruins lie like crumbling bones among the grass and vines.

The sky is a marvelous, blustery, blue and ivory scene when she descends amid the ruins. Great billowing mountains of white plumes glide calmly by overhead and cast their shadows over the sunken remains of bricks and carved stones that lie all around. The earth's healing in this place. She can feel it. There's old sorrow floating like dust along the ground, hanging between every tree and broken block of pavement.

"Many lives must have been lost here, long ago," she whispers. "The earth has wept for this land. I can hear the echo of its weeping even now." She turns to the Farian. "What is this place?"

Her guardian shifts its single eye as it drifts into the air before her. "This truly is the grave of many," it tells her as it continues floating northward, as if it's caught in some unseen current in the air. "Come."

Éliva follows, stepping softly through the tall grasses that fight to overcome the remains of walls and foundations. The earth is reclaiming what was always its own.

In time the greenery gives way to a long stretch of taller ruins—tilted, solitary walls and severed archways; cracked and shifted stairways that no longer lead to anywhere in particular. The Farian floats on, guiding Éliva to a place where the shattered framework of what must have been a towering domed rooftop encircles a vast circular floor. Three of the four weathered stone columns that occupy the space no longer carry any burden, but remain reaching nobly for the sky, as if hoping to prevent the collapse of the clouds that drift high overhead. Éliva pauses between them, gazing up at the intricately carved crowns.

"This was once a great city, wasn't it?" she murmurs.

"One of the greatest. The city of Tekéhldeth." The Farian comes to a stop near the center of the wide floor. "She who came before you once walked these lands. She came as a servant of the gods, as you are now."

"And you served as her guide, as you now do for me?"

As she turns to meet her guardian's one-eyed gaze, a cloud passes momentarily by, darkening the pale colors of the sun-bleached stones of the ruins.

"Yes. The darkness of this place had grown too great. She came to oppose it, in hopes of saving the lives of those who yet lived in its grasp," the Farian replies, its smooth sides catching the sunlight that begins to slide back into the scene. "She gave her entire self in order to give them another chance to live and act for themselves. And in so doing, she was not able to remain in this sphere."

Her entire self. Éliva steps in a slow circle, wondering how the faintly colored tiles at her feet must have looked the day her predecessor walked across them.

"She gave her own life?" she asks.

The Farian's eye makes a subtle turn. "And saved the remnant of this land. They became a new race. A people who would live on to one day raise up the one called to take her place," it tells her.

For a moment, Éliva's thoughts are paused in their place. It was the Shardehn clan who found her lying helpless on the shore, who let her live among them throughout her childhood. A voránjevin clan. A people whose ancestors once journeyed from beyond the wide ocean to find Glesia, the eastern continent. The forests surrounding its inland sea have been their home for generations. But they've never forgotten the land of their beginning—never ceased to commemorate the fact that they once belonged to the realms of Ataran, far over the western sea. Spoken word and a handful of written records have extended the memory of their families through the ages. Now, as Éliva stands at the heart of what was once their greatest city, years of fireside tales and legends told by starlight float softly back over her mind. She heard them all in her youth. The Shardehn, the Iftav, the Taufeth—all ten clans often spoke of their western heritage, a proud legacy as ancient as the forests themselves. But now the Farian uses a phrase to describe them that Éliva's never heard—not in all the timeless stories and songs of the clans. *A new race.*

"They became ... a new race? Farian, what changed when they left this place?"

"They were born anew from the ashes of what they once were. No longer of the arai, but a new race."

Reborn, changed. The concept is wild, *astounding*. And yet even now, as she hears the distant flutter of voránjevin hearts beyond the sea, Éliva wonders how she hadn't seen it sooner. After all these ages, humanity still echoes in the inner soundings of their heartbeats. Like a subtle chime in a chorus of thrumming strings and drums. She only needed to listen more closely. How had she not noticed before? The arai and the voránjevin—two races that are suddenly interwoven in her mind. Two children of the same birth.

But this memory, the knowledge of their true origin, must have been long lost among the clans. And who among them would accept it now?

The Farian drifts soundlessly to her side. "You are called to the same role as your predecessor," it murmurs. "As she served to protect the freewill of the children of Claya, so will you."

Éliva breathes, ignoring the wind that gusts through the columns and sweeps the curls from her shoulders. "But how can I serve in the place of one who did so much? One so great? What can I possibly do?" she wonders aloud.

"There was a promise made before the days of Claya. Do you not recall?" the Farian answers.

"I do."

"It was one promise, which called both her and you to this role. You are bound to the same right, the same ability, the same power. The heavens have given you many gifts, and trust you to use them as you will for the good of this world."

It's true. Éliva can feel it in the light that courses through her being, the light that's dwelt within her since the night it arrived and blazed the mortality from her bones. The Farian's often said that the sasarianë are raised up when the world needs them most. Should the darkness that destroyed this ancient place return, young Éliva would somehow have the same power to extinguish it as the sasarian woman of old. But the thought sends a cold tightening through her lungs. Could it return?

"Farian, the darkness that dwelt here . . . how did it come to be?" she asks, and the wind seems to hear the question, swirling and gasping through the surrounding crumbling bricks with suddenly renewed vigor.

Her guide makes a slight turn in the air. "There can be darkness in the hearts of all the children of Claya," it tells her, "and it is given to all children to do with it as they will. This choice even the sasarianë must make. There are some who make darkness their power."

Éliva's breath catches momentarily at her lips. The darkness that once consumed this land and turned it into a sinking grave—the force that drove away all survivors and has warded off all civilization ever since—was created by a sasarian? Someone like herself? And it was another like her who rose to stop it. It's a strange and harrowing thought that the light she was given could be turned to blackness, used against the very purpose of its bestowal. But it's happened before. This ruined land stands as a witness.

Could it happen again?

3

Some say that traveling by moonlight is a risk rarely worth taking. An idle step in dark woods lures the demons out from hiding, they say. Terrible luck, dark omens, encounters more frightening than can be told—all have supposedly come to unsuspecting travelers in the night. Kehljen's never been one to follow after wild tales. But of all the nights he's spent traveling, none have brought him so near to believing the old superstitions from the north as this night. This night, the air carries an odd reverberation—off tune, like the twangs of a stringed instrument long uncared for. As if some unanticipated event might wait behind each new tree or stone in their path. But the men of the peace treaty press on. They've opted to walk until weariness forces them to rest—then pause for no more than is absolutely necessary. Time is short.

They've endured two days of traversing hill and forest, weaving along the borders of streams and ponds, occasionally clearing new paths through stubborn thickets. Two days, and the men have exhausted all conversation. They trudge eastward through the dark trees in silence. Only the solid thumping of their steps accompanies them as they move warily along, led by the stars and the light of a single torch. At this pace, they hope to reach the meeting hall of King Talek by the afternoon of the third day. But the night seems endless.

They've carried the torch in turns, with the bearer always walking in the lead. And tonight's second shift has fallen to Kehljen. Aside from the constant distraction of holding the flame aloft, leading with the torch is a simple job. One he hasn't minded taking over for the older men on occasion, when their weary arms need a rest.

But he hasn't carried it long this night when a loud gasp from several paces back shakes him from his thoughts.

"We all right?" he murmurs over his shoulder, turning to squint at the men who follow him in the dim light. They've each paused in their steps, glancing at each other with drowsy, puzzled looks.

"Thought he was behind you."

"What's that? He stumbled?"

"Vandel, was that you?" a man named Daln asks the darkness behind him, bending to peer under a long sweep of branches that hangs nearby.

Kehljen holds the torch out at arm's length in hopes of better lighting the scene. "Plenty of places to lose your footing 'round these parts. We'd best be care—"

But his words fall abruptly away as he catches sight of Daln vanishing suddenly into the leaves with nothing more than a stifled exclamation.

"What in the . . ." The man beside Kehljen stomps gruffly into the shadows after his kinsman, striking aside the leaves in his path as he goes. "Daln, you clumsy—ay!" He hasn't placed his fourth step before he drops abruptly to the ground himself, jerked by one leg into the dark foliage and out of sight. And this time, there's no question. He didn't trip—he was *pulled*.

Panic rises in a cloud of confusion among the four travelers who remain standing. All at once they scramble to pull their daggers from hidden scabbards, fumbling with flustered, weary hands and stubborn layers of clothing.

"*Kateo!* Curses! There's someone here, men!"

"Arm yourselves!"

But the moment rises too quickly to meet them. Another man is jerked away into the shadows before his blade can be raised. The next is taken while distracted by the sight of his kinsman's lifeless body falling partially back into view at his feet.

"On the right!" Kehljen shouts as he spots movement in the leaves, jerking a short hunting blade from his satchel.

But the last man can scarcely turn his head before he's fallen to the earth. Dead. All six of them, dead. Kehljen turns again and again in his place, watching all directions, clutching his dagger in one vein-creased fist with the torch in the other. Breath comes in stiff bursts through his lungs as he fights to ease the wild thrumming of his heart.

Be loose, be calm. Be loose, be calm.

He's backing slowly eastward when a dark figure appears beside the nearest fallen body, hunched over. A small figure with eyes that shine like the lesser moon when they catch the fickle light of his torch. It's a gaze he's seen before, often in the woods near Ethein. A voránjevin gaze.

But how could it be? The people of the woods have never . . .

Now the figure rises to its feet and comes stalking toward him through the leaves. Kehljen backs away, wondering if his startled mind can recall how to speak their language, wondering how many others may be prowling nearby. The Shardehn have always been peaceful. But these woods are far from the borders of Ethein—perhaps far into the hunting grounds of some other clan. But why this? Why, why would they . . .

The attacker has come close enough for Kehljen to spot the dark waistcloth that clothes him— something often worn by the males of the voránjevin clans. A hunter's garb. He's near enough to leap at Kehljen's blade-bearing arm. But now the stranger stops, looking over his slender shoulder at the second figure that's appeared beside him. A taller voránjevin who's gripped the hunter's arm. The newcomer shakes his head, glancing at Kehljen with startlingly orange eyes before murmuring a single word. It's a word Kehljen can recognize, one his mind races to recall the meaning of as the two figures vanish away into the night, leaving him alive, puzzled, and entirely alone among the dead.

That word!

He learned it before, ages ago—used it when he practiced speaking to friendly visitors from the woods. Something they had called him when they saw little Tolaiyë climb into his arms. He's kneeling to cover the eyes of the body nearest him when the meaning of the word comes at last to his mind.

Talo. Father.

4

"Slowly now, take a drink." She holds a water satchel to the waking girl's mouth, helping her sit up on wobbly knees. They're always terribly thirsty when they first wake. Thirsty enough to catch the scent of water from half a day's journey away and crawl desperately after it, if they must.

"*Dei k'efahen,*" the girl breathes. "I can't see . . . too . . . too blurred." She tips her head forward to let out a deep, wet cough. Her newly formed wings rest loosely folded at her sides, dark feathers gleaming with the moisture of her long sleep.

"Your vision will clear very shortly, remember? And it may very likely be sharper than before. No need to fear," Lídei assures her, laying a palm to the young one's heart to monitor the warm surge of energy there. The girl's strength flows like static waters beneath her hand, coursing through every muscle and tendon, every vein. And a healthy heart thrives at the center of it all. Lídei nods in approval. "Now give us a good stretch," she urges. "Those new wings have been cramped for many days, as I'm sure you can feel."

The girl moves slowly at first, tipping carefully to bring one foot forward, then the other. Now she breathes the morning air deep into her feathered chest, unfolding her wings to their full length. They're massive—spanning across the little grove and reaching their tips into the surrounding leaves. A wild grin erupts over her young face. It's an expression that Lídei's always loved to see on the faces of those who wake for the first time as a *virit*.

Virit, "the big eagle." It was the first form the ancestors learned to transform into, ages ago. A smaller body with short legs and immense, powerful wings in place of arms. Feathers form a short tail and cover all but the face—which remains unchanged. Some voránjevin find that the natural colors of their fur are magnified after a change, leading to a brilliant array of hues in their newly grown feathers. And all who change into a virit stand several heads shorter than their original height. But it's expected. After all, to ride the wind beside the eagles, one must be as small and light as an eagle.

The process of changing one's body to a new form usually takes more than a month, and can be challenging in more ways than one. But the skill's been perfected over generations—and it's become an irreplaceable asset to the clans. It was the ability to change into the virit form that enabled the ancestors to fly over the great Atayu Sea and come to these lands. Now, each clan relies on virit messengers to provide prompt communication between camps and scouts. And the virit isn't the only secondary shape a voránjevin can take. A finned form built for water has long enabled clans along the coast to wrangle in entire schools of fish at once.

Some say there's no limit to the shapes a voránjevin body can adopt. But from the time the first ancestors arrived on these shores, no new forms have been achieved. The clans have thrived for so long with the options available to them, Lídei's never expected anything more. With the sky and the waters in their grasp, what more could be needed?

It's a long-standing tradition within each clan to watch over those who have fallen into the deep sleep that accompanies the *ek'let'eh*, "the changing process." Someone must watch over their glossy cocoons as they sleep, always ready to bring them food and water when they wake, and bathe the sweat and blood and fluids from their new, drowsy bodies. It's a role Lídei's played for years. But despite seeing hundreds of her people wake in new bodies over the years—sometimes as eagles, sometimes with fins, sometimes with their original form again—the miraculous event of the *ek'let'eh* never ceases to spark wonder and fascination in her heart.

"I can see! Thank the gods!" The new virit sighs in relief as she brings her wings back to her sides.

"Very good," Lídei tells her. "You'll want to make your way to the stream when you're ready—blood and things can quickly dry on those lovely feathers. The morning hunters should be returning with fresh kills very soon."

The young one nods, smiling excitedly to herself as she turns toward the stream that paves a cool path through the trees to the northwest. It's a decent walk. One she can use to test out her wobbly new legs.

Lídei's turned to rinse a bit of wetness from the tips of her fingers when a familiar gray figure comes stepping out from between the eastern trees. She smiles.

"You certainly have your father's firm gaze," she calls out to him, "with the addition of a stubborn frown."

As he comes walking toward her, a mild smirk finds its way into the corner of her son's mouth—for only a moment.

She brings a gentle palm to his cheek, looking him over. "Has Onei come with you?"

"She's gathering news from the south," he tells her, glancing subtly in several directions before looking back to her. "You still dwell so near to the arai village."

Lídei nods. "The hunt is bountiful here. And we've had no reason to go elsewhere," she says.

There's an uneasy edge to the orange gleam of Faleth's eyes. Something's upsetting him. His ears twitch softly backward. "Mother, the Shardehn should move on, leave this place," he tells her.

She takes a moment to watch him, tracing the tension in the rise and fall of his breaths. "What's happened?" she asks softly.

"The arai of the east are coming."

"The men of Rand?"

"The arai have never been united. Now they play at the edge of war." Faleth sighs, folding his arms and leaning back against a tree.

Lídei tips her head to look at him sideways. "How have you come to hear the plans of the eastern arai?" she questions. "Do the Iftav no longer dwell toward the east shore of Emér?"

"We're always moving."

Odd, Lídei ponders. The Iftav have remained along the northeastern shore of Emér for years, only rarely journeying farther northeast toward the lands of Rand. But if their messengers truly are so far northeast . . .

"Have your scouts heard any news of the arai from the western families who were sent to propose a peace treaty to their neighbors? They passed by this way, but we haven't received word for more than ten days." She shakes out a moisture-spotted rag as she talks—one she used only moments ago to dry the forehead of the waking virit girl.

Faleth looks up at her. "Heard of them? I came to tell you about it. My scouts found the bodies of western arai men in the woods not far from the first village of Rand. They failed their mission," he tells her flatly.

"Slain? By the people of Rand?" Lídei gasps, suddenly forgetting why she had just been reaching for a bowl of water.

Faleth looks off into the trees. "Killed. All six of them," he says.

"Six? But there were *seven* men who left from the borders of Ethein. Among them was the father of the boy we've watched all these years."

"I know the man's face." Faleth nods. "He wasn't among the dead. Though I doubt he reached the lands of Rand alone."

Lídei lets herself slump slowly down to sit in the grass. Kehljen . . . is he gone? Of all the families of Ethein, none has become dearer to Lídei than that of Kehljen and Kadeis. The thought of telling Kehljen's possible fate to the kind lady Kadeis sets a bitter weight in her heart. She closes her eyes, lets herself breathe and think through the possibilities. No need to assume the most terrible outcome. The man may still be alive. He *must* be.

Faleth's mild voice pulls her back. "Mother, your clan may've carried too much hope for the arai. They're a hopeless race, lovers of violence. The men of the east are coming. They'll destroy the village Ethein and bring war to all the families west of it," he murmurs. "Let them fight their battles. If they choose to slay their own, it's of no concern to our people."

Lídei shakes her head. Faleth's never been fond of the arai. "We've befriended the people of Ethein. We can't simply abandon them. At the very least we can warn them," she tells him. But Faleth's unconvinced. She can see it in the firmness of his jaw. Solid, unmoving. She returns to her feet. "Why do you worry, my son? The Shardehn won't be endangered. What does it hurt to aid our neighbors?" she asks, suddenly more aware of the tightness rising into the air all around. The tension that always follows her son like static when the arai are mentioned. This time, it seems sharper than usual.

Faleth lets another deep sigh escape his teeth. "I don't worry for the Shardehn. The men have never been a threat to us. They never will be," he tells her. He steps away from the tree, shrugging the stiffness from his shoulders. "I only wanted to warn you. I'll send my nearest messengers if anything worse arises." He gives her a deep bow before turning back toward the east.

Lídei watches him go, struggling to name the imbalance that edges silently into her bones. A sour sensation. "Faleth," she calls after him as he leaves, "the rumors of the eastern woods—what have you heard of them? They say that people of Rand have begun to vanish again in the woods there. The western families have only ever fought in defense of their settlements. It seems odd to me that they would devise such attacks. What do you know of it?"

The gray heln pauses in his steps and turns to look back at her with a stare so like that of his father's that it sends a pang of loss through his watching mother's heart. "Those arai are animals. It's likely the doing of their own soldiers," he answers.

But Lídei can see the lie in his teeth. Hiding, like a little dagger behind his back. "Don't lie to me, Faleth."

The gray heln shakes his head. "The arai are good enough at slaying their own kind, Mother. They need no help from us," he assures her. And he continues on his way, blending into the shadows of the trees.

5

Mother's had a new way of laying the dish rags to dry since Father left for the east. A tight-elbowed, stiff-shouldered way. She tosses each one over the rim of the washing tub with one swift motion, then tugs the corners straight with a firm jerk— her lips forming a straight line across her face all the while. Twelve days have passed since Father left. Twelve mornings that've found Mother sitting up beside the fire, watching the dawn through a door propped partly open. The men should've returned by now, or at least sent word. All of Ethein knows it, though no one dares to mention it. And the longer the days roll on, the more often Tolaiyë finds himself glancing impulsively toward the eastern hills.

When a figure appears at last along the eastern edge of the village, it isn't a man from Father's company. Or a man at all. The people of the woods are often mistaken for children from a distance. But as this one comes walking in the afternoon light, Tolaiyë catches sight of an unmistakable pair of violet eyes. The eyes of the first voránjevin he ever saw. A *filíl*, a woman of the woods. He pauses with his ax held in one hand, a half-split log on the grass at his feet.

"Good sister, what news from the Shardehn?" Mother calls to the visitor as she rinses the last dish from her bucket.

The little voránjevin woman comes slowly, the short fur along her head and broad ears shuddering mildly in the westward breeze. The thick sash worn over her shoulder bears a deep scarlet hue—a color that reminds Tolaiyë of the wildflowers that always grew beside the hunting cabins in the northern woods. A color like the dawn and red earth blended together.

Her voice is nearly a whisper when she reaches Mother's side. "You're likely the strongest woman I've known among the people of Sketza. Your strength will be needed now," she says. A faint accent slides into the edges of her words.

Mother kneels down to look into her friend's dark gaze. "Lídei, has something . . . gone wrong?"

They say the people of the woods have ears in every grove of trees. What have they heard? Tolaiyë leaves his ax propped against the house and steps softly to Mother's side. Lídei glances to him for an instant before turning back to Mother's expectant stare.

"Kadeis, my people have found the bodies of six men sent to make peace with the east. Slain, in the woods not far from the lands of Rand," she tells. "But take heart—the man Kehljen was not among the dead. He may yet live."

Father. Tolaiyë's lungs become suddenly rigid. A faint tremor passes over Mother's shoulders beside him as she brings her hands to her face, a wet shimmer leaping up in her pale eyes and piling at the edges of her lashes.

"Not my Kehljen," she breathes.

"He may be finding his own way back now. I'll keep our scouts in the area—but Kadeis, you must listen to me," Lídei breathes. "You can't wait here. The men of Rand are coming from the east. They bring war, and the village of Ethein is the first in their path."

The wind sends a gentle whip over the treetops, tugging wisps of dark hair from Mother's loose braid.

"You're right. We can't remain here," she tells the grass.

Lídei lays a slender brown hand on her shoulder, looking into her eyes. "No—and the Shardehn can't leave our friends for death to take either," she assures.

"You'll aid us?"

"If the people be willing." Lídei nods. "Tell them to leave what they can spare, and to gather at the southern border of the village as the sun hangs over the western trees tomorrow. There the Shardehn will meet you. We'll take you into the protection of the woods south of here. No men of Rand will find you."

* * *

When morning comes again it brings an odd, consuming silence along with it. A profound silence unlike any Tolaiyë's experienced before. As if the wind has stopped in place—paused to watch the rising dawn together. Mother lies motionless on the bench beside the soft-glowing embers of the fireplace, asleep. Tolaiyë sits up, and the usually subtle sound of his blanket creasing seems to clash and clamor against the unmoving air. He reaches to unlatch the shutters beside the bed.

And then he hears it.

It comes like a sigh in the morning light. A voice—soft, murmuring at the edge of his hearing. A voice that's somehow familiar, though it's impossible to name. It's come to him for days now, always at the stillest moments, always calling him by name. Calling him to the east. He's kept the voice to himself for days, wondering what it could possibly mean. Wondering if he's become delusionary. But the more the voice comes to him, the less Tolaiyë can ignore the growing pull in the deepest corner of his heart, dragging him. The east is calling.

"Does it look like rain?" Mother's waking voice finds him standing beside the half-open window. He turns to see her reaching to stoke the white coals on the fire.

"Not at all," he tells her.

She pulls her long hair into one thick bundle over her left shoulder. "Good," she says. "We don't have time for rain today."

The day passes like a rushed, fluid dream. From the moment the sun's rays find their path over the hills until the shadows grow long from the west, all the people of Ethein are gathering what they can from their gardens and homes. They stack supplies into shoulder bags and little wagons, stubbornly finding space for cherished heirlooms in their cramped pull carts. Some families left that morning to journey northwest to Hadón or beyond, seeking safe haven in the larger settlements. But the majority remained behind. Now, as the daylight pales and weakens along the horizon, the open grove at the southern edge of the village becomes steadily filled with hushed voices—a little crowd of villagers with their humble packs and carts, glancing anxiously toward the border of the trees and whispering together.

They say the true nature of the people of the woods has never been seen. Leaving nearly everything behind to follow them into the forests may be a terrible risk. After all, there are times when they seem more like wild animals than anything else, with their fur-covered bodies and massive, odd-colored eyes. Unknowable, unpredictable. But the Shardehn have shown a pattern of kindness from the beginning, despite their foreign nature. And they offer friendship—which is more than the soldiers of Rand have ever proposed. Accepting the aid of the Shardehn may be a great risk indeed. But one worth taking.

The grove has grown dim when the voránjevin guides appear. They come stepping out from the graying columns of the trees with the dusk flickering in their bottomless eyes, with only the soft rustling of leaves to announce their arrival. Seven of them—more voránjevin than any locals of Ethein have ever seen at once. Each with the same thin, childlike stature. The little crowd of refugees shuffles at the sight. All around, children tug at parents' shawls, pointing and questioning breathlessly. Men and women readjust shoulder packs and exchange cautious glances with their neighbors, silently analyzing the scene. Lídei walks at the lead of the guides, singling out Mother among the many faces that watch her.

"Are they all here?" she asks.

Mother glances to the families who stand eagerly waiting with all they can carry, then looks back to her friend. "All who will join us," she says.

"Then we'll delay no longer," Lídei affirms. She murmurs to those who follow her. They nod in acknowledgement before turning back to the darkness of the woods. "Your people can follow them—they'll lead along the most level paths. I'll walk at the rear with Kadeis of Ethein."

Mother smiles as she motions for the others to follow the guides into the maze of trees ahead. "They'll lead us," she assures them.

All at once the grove begins to echo with the sound of footsteps and rustling grasses as packs are lifted and little carts are tugged into motion.

"We may never be able to repay your people for this kindness." Mother kneels to thank her violet-eyed friend.

Lídei stares calmly back, a plain expression on her furred face that Tolaiyë's come to recognize as a voránjevin smile. "The Shardehn have never been a clan that stands idly when friends are in need. The survival of these families will be payment enough," Lídei answers.

And she says something more. But Tolaiyë doesn't hear it. Instead he turns unconsciously to the darkening east—turning to face the sound of a voice that rings again like spring rain over the trees. The voice that's called him in the stillest moments, beckoning him for days.

"Tolaiyë? Is something wrong?" Mother stands watching when he turns back, eyebrows raised in her pale forehead. Lídei looks on beside her.

Tolaiyë stares back at them both, searching for the right words. "Mother, the east. Someone calls me there. I . . . I think I might be able to find Father," he tells her.

"East? There are only armies and death to the east, my son. Your father is finding his way back even now—I'm certain of it. He still lives." Mother fails to hide a tremble at the edge of her voice that pulls terribly at Tolaiyë's heart.

"Is it a voice that calls you? A familiar voice?" Lídei asks with a whisper.

How does she know? Her stare seems to pierce into the inner corners of his mind. As if there were some truth hiding there in the darkened edges of his memory that she's always known. Something Tolaiyë once knew, but no longer remembers.

"It's a voice I've heard before. Though I can't say where," he tells her, and the words sound so ridiculous to his ears. He shakes his head. "But maybe I'm just losing my mind. Maybe I—"

The voránjevin woman steps closer, motioning for him to come down to her height. Tolaiyë lowers to his knees in the grass, unsure what to expect or how to act. Mother joins him. When Lídei speaks, her words are scarcely louder than the evening breeze that grazes over the grass.

"This is a voice you must follow. But as your mother warns, to follow it straight east from here would not be wise. There's another way," she says, and she points two slender fingers toward the south. "Go southeast, to the shores of Emér, and follow it as it curves. Not more than three days' journey along that path, you'll find one called Afai. A man who once dwelt among the people of Rand, and a friend of the Shardehn. He can guide you safely from there."

Mother's gaze darts between Lídei and her son. "This voice he hears . . . do you know what it means?" she asks.

But Lídei only stares silently at Tolaiyë, unblinking—long enough to set loose uneasy flutters in his chest. When she speaks again at last, looking back to Mother, the setting sun has just slipped behind the western trees entirely, leaving only shadowed hues in its wake.

"Your people can't see it, can they? The dark shadow that flickers over this boy's eyes," she says.

Dark shadow? The supposed curse of the black eyes is known to many, but those who believe it only ever speak of the blackness in Tolaiyë's eyes at birth. No rumor or superstition has ever mentioned anything more. Mother opens her mouth as if to reply, eyes full of sifting thoughts, but no words come. She shakes her head.

"There was once a human child who lived among the Shardehn," Lídei continues. "A girl whose eyes bore the same shadow. The voice called to her as well."

"And she followed it?" Tolaiyë asks.

Lídei gives a slow, single nod. "Many years ago. She was led to the answers she was searching for. Led to her purpose . . . although it's something I've yet to fully understand."

Answers. Purpose. The words seem to cling at the center of Tolaiyë's thoughts, persistently remaining despite his effort to think around them. *Purpose.* There was a purpose, wasn't there? A reason to come into this world—something that was planned all along. What has he forgotten? Or is it all a daydream—the idle thoughts of a sleepless mind?

Mother's hand appears on his wrist. There's a glimmer in her eyes that's difficult to place. Like the mingled hues that often paint rain clouds as they break and dissipate against a clearer sky.

"Tolaiyë, I've always sensed that you carried unique gifts. Even as a child you often told me of the voices of the trees and the songs you could hear the earth singing. If this voice that calls you is one you must follow, I won't stop you," she whispers. "But promise your mother that you'll keep yourself safe from the men of Rand."

"I'll be all right, Mother."

"He can send you word as he travels, through our scouts," Lídei assures. "There are some who understand the language of your people. But darkness comes quickly. The boy can rest with the Shardehn this night and make his way at dawn." She turns toward the darkening forest, motioning for them to follow.

Mother rises to her feet. Tolaiyë follows, sending one last glance toward the east as they step into the curtain of the woods.

Tomorrow.

6

The silver waves of the Emér Sea are restless when he stops to watch them from the northeastern shore. As if some invisible force quakes the seabed far below, shifting and churning it endlessly. He's come to the shores of the inland sea only once before. Long ago, when Mother and Father brought him to see it as a tiny boy. Watching it now, Tolaiyë marvels anew at the seemingly endless gray face that rolls out from the sands at his feet. After just under three days of walking, standing still is a simple treasure.

Word from Ethein came to the Shardehn the morning he left on his journey. It was three of Lídei's scouts that spotted the invaders. The soldiers of Rand came creeping across the borders of the abandoned village before the sun had fully risen, less than a day after the Shardehn took the local families into the protection of the forest. A parade of men at least two hundred strong, all wearing the gray and red colors of Rand, all bearing spears and blades and sénsin rods over their broad shoulders. A foul-smelling group, the scouts said. The men seemed amused to find the village empty.

They wasted no time making themselves comfortable in the empty houses, picking their way around what goods were left behind. It's not certain how they might have treated the families of Ethein, had they found them. But Tolaiyë doesn't care to imagine it.

"These are strange times among the people of Sketza. How is it that a young man of the western settlements walks alone to the north shore?"

The man's voice comes sailing like cold sea spray on the afternoon wind, startling Tolaiyë's thoughts. He turns to find a rusty-bearded man standing in the sand several paces to his left, dressed in an earth-colored ox-hide coat not unlike the one Father inherited from his family. The kind many men carried with them from the northern lands of Sketza years ago.

"I come south in order to avoid the lands of Rand. I'm told there's someone living along this shore who knows a safe passage to the east," Tolaiyë answers.

The bearded man reaches up to idly finger his short whiskers, gazing momentarily out to sea. He has the pale skin of someone with far-western heritage. A shade not often seen among the earthen-toned people of Sketza.

"Yes, I've had a feeling for some time now that someone was coming," he murmurs. "Who gave you word?"

"I come from Ethein. Our friends the Shardehn sent me this way."

The stranger's eyes grow suddenly wide as he steps nearer, moving his hands to his hips. "The Shardehn!" he remarks. "The kindest people you'll ever find in North Emér. Known them all my life."

A man who once dwelt among the people of Rand, and a friend of the Shardehn.

Lídei's words echo faintly across Tolaiyë's mind as he turns to face his company. "It was Lídei of the Shardehn who sent me this way," he explains.

The man pauses his steps in response, a broad smile on his face. He glances to the line of trees that guard the shore before turning back to Tolaiyë. "Then I suppose you know my name," he says, and he waves his hand. "Come, brother. The Emér is brewing. A storm approaches." He turns to the south and starts off along the sand.

Tolaiyë hefts his shoulder pack and follows warily after, wondering. Maybe this isn't the man Lídei described. It may be foolish to follow after him. But the stranger has an interesting warmth to his smile. And there's something about the way he saunters with his hands tucked away into his pockets that makes him seem as harmless as the ancient grandfathers who always watched the morning from their porches in Ethein. It's the subtle yet undeniable glow that so often follows those who carry a good heart.

The man's little cabin isn't far. Only a short walk toward the south and up a little hill to the east. It sits nestled among the trees that stand staring out to sea, simpler and more humbly built than any found in Ethein. Inside there's only room for a little fireside table, a narrow bed, and a loft. All evidence of the man's living is somehow stuffed into every open space—three chipped clay bowls stacked on a shelf above the fire, baskets filled with blankets and tunics and coats pushed somewhat neatly beneath the bed. Nearly every open space of wall is full of pegs and little hooks that hold a seemingly random assortment of everyday items. A pair of well-worn leather gloves, three belts, ladles, spoons, and a hatchet with a studded cover.

"I owe my life to Lídei and her people. I trust anyone she'd send my way," the man says, snatching a glove to check a little pot of water that hangs over the fire. He motions toward a seat beside the table. "My name's Afai. What can I call you, brother?"

"Tolaiyë, of Ethein." The chair is cushionless, made of simple wood. But Tolaiyë's back seems to melt into it.

"Ethein. I see. No wonder you've come to know the Shardehn. What cause do you have in the east? They say it's only an endless sea of sand beyond the plain. An empty desert. Traveling alone may not be wise." Afai opens a little cupboard and rummages through a few jars as he speaks.

"In all honesty, I'm not yet sure how far east I'll need to go. I'm searching for my Father," Tolaiyë explains. "He was among the men delivering a proposal of peace to King Talek. All of his company was found dead on their way. But we hope that my father survived."

Afai pauses to look over his shoulder, emerald eyes catching the light of the fire. "Killed by the people of Rand?" he asks.

"Or so we suppose."

"Where were their bodies found?" He pulls a jar from the shelf.

"Near the southwest boundaries of the lands of Rand. Not far from their westernmost settlement," Tolaiyë tells him.

Afai spoons a familiar-smelling herb into the steaming water. The same herb Mother often uses to calm her mind after a long day's work. "Southwest edge . . . the woods there hide a greater threat than the soldiers of Rand." He waves the spoon in the air, single eyebrow raised.

Tolaiyë frowns in thought. "What sort of threat?"

"I come from a settlement called Votyón, about two days' travel northeast of here. Not far from the area you've mentioned. From the time I was very young, my family and I enjoyed the friendship of the Shardehn people. Most especially Lídei and her companion, Drinehn." Afai pours the tea into two cups, moving aside as the steam billows up from their brims. "I was nine, helping my father and the other men build a shelter for storing grain. Someone didn't steady the roof beams well enough. And when one of them came down, I was under it. My father was the only one near enough to stop it from crushing me. These were massive beams, mind you. Far too heavy for any one man to lift alone." He sets the cups down on the table and settles into the second chair, looking up at Tolaiyë. "You know of the Shardehn. I'm sure you've seen something of the abilities carried by the people of the woods."

Tolaiyë nods, thinking back. "I've seen their touch heal the sick and the dying, from time to time," he says.

Afai takes a sip from his cup, breathing in the steam. "They can do much more. They call it *Hitérian*. The ability to move energy through their bodies at will. They can pull the strength out of your muscle as easily as they might take a stone from your open hand. It's how they hunt. And they can channel their own strength into others, if they choose," he says.

"You've seen them do this?"

Moving energy. It sounds like something from a legend. But then, who aside from Mother and Father would believe that he hears voices in the wind and the trees? There's plenty of mystery in this world, Tolaiyë tells himself. Who's to say what strange abilities the voránjevin may or may not have?

Tolaiyë tests the temperature of his tea. It tastes like home, with a slightly stronger hint of sweetness.

"Lídei and her companion were there that day," Afai tells him. "It was Drinehn that saved my father and me. He put his hands to my father's back and gave all his strength, saving the man's life at the expense of his own. My father was able to hold the beam just long enough to shuffle aside." Afai shakes his head, as if the event were still too much to believe.

"Was Drinehn caught under the beam himself?"

"He was too weak to move in time. It pinned him across the middle. The men nearby heard our cries and came running. But they weren't as familiar with the voránjevin people as we were. When they saw creatures from the woods, they panicked. Didn't understand. Lídei and her boy couldn't fight them off alone. They were forced to leave Drinehn's body behind." Afai takes a long sip from his drink. "My father tried to stop them. But they say it's a terribly bad omen for a structure to fall and injure anyone during construction. They burned the entire site to the ground that day. Drinehn's body included. The people of the woods have been considered little more than demons ever since to those in the eastward settlements who know of them. But they had it all wrong. My family will be forever indebted to Drinehn for his sacrifice. His son's only a little older than me. He's held his father's death against us ever since. Against me especially."

"Seems like there's still so much I don't know about their people. I never knew that Lídei had a son," Tolaiyë adds.

Afai nods. "His clan stalks the woods not far north of here. But their scouts can be found all throughout North Emér. The Iftav. Any Sketzan would be unfortunate to meet them. I came to live here in peace only after the Shardehn helped keep my location a secret from the Iftav."

Another voránjevin clan, aside from the Shardehn. Mother has sometimes spoken of the many tribes of the voránjevin people. But only the Shardehn have ever appeared in the lands surrounding Ethein. And they've only ever come in peace. It seems odd to hear of a tribe that would dislike the Sketzans—even pose a threat to them.

"You think the Iftav may have killed the men of the peace treaty?" Tolaiyë asks.

"It's certainly possible."

"But what motive would they have?"

Afai pokes out his lower lip, turning his palms upward. "You can guess as well as me," he says. "I only know that the Iftav are likely to hassle any man who crosses their path." He rises from the table, pouring one last swallow for himself before leaving the cup beside the wash bin. "You're welcome to remain here and rest as long as you need before you move on. That loft isn't half bad with a blanket or two."

"Thank you. I don't mean to burden you long," Tolaiyë assures him.

His bearded host waves a hand in the air. "It's no burden, brother. And besides, I'm beginning to feel that I won't be remaining here much longer myself."

* * *

The night is full of wind. It whips and thrashes against the cabin walls, searching in vain for its entrance again and again. The rhythm of it lulls Tolaiyë into dreams as fretful as the sea waves outside. Tossing, surging. Until she calls. This time, the voice belongs to a woman.

"Brother."

The wind has stopped entirely when he opens his eyes. He rises, leaning to glance over the edge of the loft. Afai lies motionless, hands tucked behind his head and a gentle rasping on his sleeping breath. And the cabin's lit. Not by the fading fire at the hearth, but by unearthly green and sapphire glows that hang throughout the scene—soft points of light that seem to drift like dust in the still air.

"Brother."

The voice calls again. Outside. Tolaiyë reaches for the ladder and steps carefully down, not bothering to find his coat. The cabin door lets out a low, drowsy creak as he lifts the latch and swings it open. A sound scarcely louder than his footfalls. Beyond it, the night's aglow like an evening festival. And the sea! He turns, and the silver and turquoise glimmering that rises from the still waters of Emér dazzles his eyes, beckoning him closer. He steps down the hillside, walking until the cool sand comes to meet his feet beside the shore.

"Brother."

The one who calls him stands suspended in the air above the waters. A goddess draped in long, gleaming robes. Amber curls cascade over her shoulders and frame the shining brilliance of her face. A face he's seen once before.

"Brother, we're waiting," she says. "Come to the east, beyond the Sand Sea."

7

The door's heavy bar latch makes a solid clap against its brace as it's thrown back, echoing off the cabin walls and jarring Tolaiyë from sleep. He sits up on a single elbow to peer over the loft's edge. The door remains partly open below, welcoming in the brisk morning air and a little flood of white sunshine.

Was it a dream?

He slips into his coat, leaving the clasps undone. Outside, the sea catches the first morning rays and dashes them into slivers and sparkles across its calm face. The sea's returned to normal. Afai kneels near the edge of the trees a few paces away. A reddish-brown-colored voránjevin stands talking with him. A petite female. She whispers to Afai and nods before turning to stare at Tolaiyë—her massive, tan eyes unblinking. Then she turns and vanishes into the trees before Tolaiyë can manage any kind of reaction.

"You speak their language?" he asks as Afai returns to his feet and comes sauntering toward him.

The bearded man shrugs loosely. "I learned as a boy. It's awfully useful around these parts." He pauses to bring a broad hand to Tolaiyë's back. "By the way, I'm coming with you to the east."

Tolaiyë blinks. "Has something happened?"

"The Iftav have caught wind of my hideout. I can't stay here," Afai tells him, beginning toward the cabin.

"I plan to go farther now—farther than the lands of Rand," Tolaiyë answers.

Afai stops in his place, looking back. "Beyond the lands of Rand?"

"To the Sand Sea—maybe farther."

For a moment the two of them stand in silence, the breeze lightly tossing the hair on their heads. Then Afai claps his hands together. "Well, in that case, we'll need a wagon!" he announces, and turns again to march up the hill.

Tolaiyë follows slowly behind as the man rummages through the cabin, tossing random blankets and crates until he finds a little sheathed blade.

"Traveling together in these lands is too likely to attract attention. You can go straight east from here, through the woods. I'll take another way." He ties the blade to his belt, then reaches for his pelt coat. "One and a half days' travel straight east will bring you to Rand's Mark, a stone marker that stands at the edge of the plain. I'll meet you there with everything we need when the sun's high tomorrow." He shows a broad smile as he steps out the door, heading south. He's gone a few paces before Tolaiyë calls after him.

"What if the Iftav find me on the way? Is there any defense against them?"

Afai glances back, shaking his head. "No need to worry, my brother. If they do find you, they won't hurt you. Not you," he calls back.

Not you? The answer makes no sense. Wasn't it just last night that "any Sketzan" would be unfortunate to meet the Iftav?

"You're free to take any food you can carry. I'll bring the rest! If you don't show up at the meeting place after three days, I'll send the Shardehn scouts to find you!" Afai shouts over his shoulder as he disappears over the next hill.

Standing alone beside the cabin, Tolaiyë lets his breath ease out. Not long ago, the world seemed to take only ordinary turns. But now Father's been missing for two weeks, and Ethein's been taken away. Now he finds himself setting off on a journey to the Sand Sea with a stranger he's barely met, guided by dreams and voices he can't explain. When did it all begin? He wonders, but the answer floats aimlessly out of reach. The path to the east will be long. Maybe far longer than he can fully imagine. But he can't help feeling that the answers lie somewhere along that road. Waiting.

8

It's only a matter of days before the frightened word of tradesmen and travelers alike spreads throughout the western settlements. An entire village! Empty! Void of life, they say. Left to be scavenged by the soldiers of Rand. And how dare the savages of Rand lay hands on the prosperity of Ethein! Land cultivated and beautified by years of devoted laboring—simply taken!

Some say the soldiers slew all the families of Ethein who didn't flee northwest to the larger villages. Others believe the people were made slaves and sent to the east. Terrible claims and suspicions rise and float across the land like dust in the wind, stirring fear and panic and anger into the settlers of the western forests. And in only a matter of days, the borders of Ethein are filled with men of the west, hidden in the evening light. Men come to avenge their neighbors.

They ambush the soldiers of Rand on a night when the clouds black out the twin moons. They come with daggers and hatchets, spades and garden hooks—any sharp edge and strong rod they can gather. Only the roughest of battles can be expected from the men of the east.

But this night, nothing happens as expected.

The soldiers have only a handful of watchmen wandering the dark lanes between the gardens and cottages. They seem strangely startled by the villagers who appear with clubs and pitchforks. And now those same villagers—farmers, gardeners—begin a victorious march through the empty settlement. Reclaim! Reconquer! One house at a time, they push their way through—chasing out any soldiers they find, scowling and hollering as they go. Some soldiers attempt to fight back before finding themselves surrounded. Others simply flee weaponless into the night, vanishing into the trees. Where has the ferocity of Rand's men gone? The scene makes no sense at all, but the villagers don't care to question it. They press forward with weapons held high and excited shouts at their throats.

Until the terror of the soldiers becomes their own.

It happens slowly, silently—undetected at first as men begin to be lost in the crowd. Present one moment, gone the next. But as the night deepens, they begin to disappear while following at one another's backs, or while in midconversation with a comrade who happened to glance momentarily away. In time they begin to circle back over paths they've only just crossed to find their friends and brothers collapsed to the ground. Fallen, where no soldier of Rand remains to attack them.

How could it be? The westerners begin to search frantically through the shadows, chasing after every sound, determined to capture the enemy that eludes them at every corner. Until groups of thirty standing men turn to twenty. And twenty turns to fifteen. And panic begins to creep like cold fog between their scrambling feet.

Then the once-victorious farmers find themselves retreating from Ethein as quickly as they marched into it when the night began. They run with the shadows at their heels, not daring to glance back— chased and scattered by an invisible death. Driven out by what can be nothing less than the curse of Ethein. The curse of the black eyes.

9

The sun has yet to fade entirely in the west, but already the boldest stars can be seen peering out through the cloudless face of the sky overhead. Glancing up through the canopy as he walks, Tolaiyë can't seem to recall the name of the white star that hangs directly overhead, always accompanied by a little sprinkling of silvery dust. It's a star sometimes spoken of in old rhymes and fireside tales. How could he forget?

Father's old friend Galdehn always said that walking through the woods with your eyes to the sky is a sure way to sprain an ankle. But it isn't a log or stone that brings Tolaiyë's feet to a stop. The sudden appearance of a blade at his throat and a fist gripping his shawl do just as well.

"This one must be awfully lost, sir." The man's breath is foul enough to kill, even from an arm's length away. He wears a tattered red and gray tunic full of stains. The colors of Rand. "Last I checked, the critters of them western villages don't come within seven days' walking of these lands." He tips his chin to give Tolaiyë a good look over.

A handful of others come stepping out from between the trees, eyeing him with their crooked grins and dirt-stained faces. Thieves. One comes nearer than the rest, folding his arms as he leans against the boulder at his back. He spits. "A Sketzan from the west? In these parts? Sure looks like it with that getup. Alive even!" he exclaims. His men burst into coarse laughter all around. "We ought to fix this, y'know. King Talek would frown on this indeed!" He shakes his head in pretended dismay. "I got myself a nice new hunting blade here. Maybe we oughta—"

The ringleader's words are cut suddenly short as a horrible gasp erupts from his teeth. His spine arches sharply backward before he clutches his chest and falls limply to the ground, lifeless. A slender figure stands on the boulder behind him, one hand still outstretched where the thief's back had leaned a moment before. A voránjevin. Gray furred, with a vivid sunset color to his eyes and a dark sash draped over one shoulder. His face is expressionless by most human standards. But after seeing so many voránjevin faces in recent days, Tolaiyë manages to identify the hint of a single emotion in the creature's gaze. Disgust.

The other thieves have no time to react—no time to make any sound at all. They drop like poisoned insects to the ground, knives and spears clamoring out of their hands and into the stones and bushes surrounding them. Then Tolaiyë finds himself standing in a circle of voránjevin faces. Their small stature makes them seem almost like a crowd of children gathering around. Children with giant eyes that shine up at him like a collection of colorful, polished stones.

"Thank you," he whispers.

The burning sensation in his legs comes as a surprise. It begins at his calves and spreads rapidly to his midthighs, melting away the strength there and forcing him to his knees. As if his body suddenly weighed down on his bones with ten times its usual mass.

. . . as easily as they might take a stone from your open hand.

He can feel the touch of little hands at his back, gently tugging at the strength in his lungs, threatening.

The gray voránjevin leaps down from his boulder and steps closer, murmuring a few words to the others along the way. He stops a single pace from Tolaiyë's face, orange-yellow eyes lit like candle flames in the evening light. "What brings you eastward?" He speaks Sketzan with surprisingly clear pronunciation.

"I search for my father, Kehljen. A man of Ethein and a friend of the Shardehn," Tolaiyë tells him.

The voránjevin glances to one of his fellows, then back to Tolaiyë. "What men have you met in these woods?" he questions.

Tolaiyë looks briefly to the bodies that litter the ground nearby. "Only dead men," he says.

"Someone hides from us near here. We'll find him," the gray creature explains, pointed teeth poking into view as he speaks. "These are dangerous times for your kind. It would be wise to leave North Emér far behind you."

Tolaiyë opens his mouth to speak, but his interrogator calls softly to those who follow him, and without warning the entire company slinks away into the leaves. They vanish soundlessly, leaving only a few quivering branches in their wake. And Tolaiyë remains kneeling alone in the midst of fallen thieves. Alive.

Heaven's Gate.

The name of the white star comes drifting at last to his mind. A little late.

10

A strong wind is whipping over the trees as Tolaiÿe comes to the edge of the plains the next afternoon. It grabs hold of the tall grasses and sends them tipping and bowing in rhythmic patterns over the land. Here the forest gives way to untamed hills as far as the horizon extends, an open vastness that startles the eyes and snatches one's breath, much like the shores of Emér. But the waves of this sea are unmoving. Not far to the southeast, a stone tower only a little taller than a man rises from the earth, watching over the sunbathed scene with perfect stillness. The meeting place.

A small wagon full of covered baskets rests beside the stone marker, its pulling ox lying unharnessed and peacefully lapping at the grass at its chin. Afai's reddish hair stands out in wild contrast against the greens and grays that sway all around him. He rises from a lazy slouch beside the wagon and steps to the stone tower, slapping a hand to its dark face. "You found it," he calls out. "Rand's Mark."

Tolaiyë raises a hand to shield his eyes from the sun's glare as he crosses the open space between them. "Rand built this?"

"This was the farthest south he and his explorers ever came. They built this tower before turning back and swore that their people would soon fill all the lands surrounding it. I suppose that prediction may yet be fulfilled, in generations to come." He gently coaxes the ox to its feet, attaching a harness across its thick shoulders. "This is Kyn—one of the cattle I've kept in the grove south of my cabin. She'll pull the supplies for us. Assuming we can find a bit of game now and then, we should have plenty of food for the journey."

It only takes a moment to secure the little wagon before they set off toward the east, with the wind gusting them along. Kyn follows obediently at their backs, occasionally nibbling at Tolaiyë's shawl from behind.

"How did you know the Iftav would let me live?" Rand's Mark is already a shrunken shadow on the horizon when he remembers to ask at last.

Afai's eyes grow wide. "They actually found you?" He curses. "They're getting quicker. It's good that we're headed east."

"I had a run-in with thieves, first. Seemed like men who once served in the army of Rand," Tolaiyë tells him.

"And the Iftav appeared as well?"

Tolaiyë nods. "Only moments after the men. They let me continue on my way, after killing all eight of the thieves," he recalls. "They asked about you."

Afai laughs. "You don't seem very shaken, considering what you went through!" He pulls a water satchel from his belt as he walks, and tips it to his mouth.

"For some reason I felt calm." Tolaiyë loosens his pack and tosses it into the wagon, wondering briefly why he hadn't done so at the start, before looking back to Afai to ask again. "How did you know they wouldn't hurt me?"

The bearded man doesn't answer immediately. He stares ahead over the rolling hills as he returns the cap to his satchel. "The voránjevin messenger told me," he says.

"The one you spoke to yesterday? What did she say?"

Afai glances over at him, biting the edge of his bottom lip. "She said you were born with a sign. A sign that means something to their people. They can still see it when they look at you," he explains. "Sound like anything familiar to you?"

Your people can't see it, can they? The dark shadow that flickers over this boy's eyes . . .

"Lídei mentioned it once. The people of Ethein say I was born with entirely black eyes. I was kept hidden until the blackness faded sometime after my birth. Some have called it a curse," Tolaiyë tells him.

"Is that so?" Afai snaps a thick reed from a bush as they pass it by, idly stripping away the outer layers as he walks. "Well, if it keeps the Iftav off your back, I wouldn't call it a curse. I bet that's why they may've left your father alive too."

Tolaiyë smiles. The man makes a good point.

* * *

That night, a sea of stars lights the hills. Silver blues, deep violets, and sparkling points of light all stirred together in a breathtaking spread across the sky. It's the kind of sky Tolaiyë never tires of watching. They camp near the cover of a broad tree that rises like a lone sentinel on the plain. Tolaiyë leans back to watch the light of Heaven's Gate from the wagon bed, ankles crossed. Afai sits in the grass against the wagon's wheel, mending a tear in the heel of his shoe by the light of a little flame.

"My father once traveled to the mountains that rise at the start of the Sand Sea," Afai says. "I can go with you at least that far. You intend to go much farther?"

"Maybe," Tolaiyë answers. "Though I won't know for certain until we arrive."

Below, Afai nods softly as he finishes binding the leather in his hands. Then he turns to look over the wagon's edge. "I won't force you to open any secrets, my brother. But this'll be a long journey. Likely longer than either of us has ever dared. I've got to ask: What's your true reason for seeking out the far east?"

His question comes so plainly, so bluntly, that Tolaiyë finds himself at a loss for words. "My true reason?"

Afai lets an odd smirk set creases in his bearded cheeks. "You and I both know it seems unlikely that your father would wander as far as the Sand Sea on his way to deliver a peace treaty." He almost laughs.

Tolaiyë takes a long breath and moves his hands behind his head. "I can tell you. But it'll sound strange," he says.

"No worry there. I've seen and heard plenty of strange things in my days."

As strange as this? Tolaiyë wonders, hesitating. But Afai didn't seem bothered by the idea of the curse. Maybe he isn't as easily frightened as other Sketzans.

"Since I was young I've been able to hear the earth whispering."

"The earth? Speaking?" Afai sits up a bit in his place.

"And the wind, the trees—all of them. They all have voices. When my father vanished, I heard the hills calling me eastward. Originally, I had planned to visit the settlements of the people of Rand in search of him," Tolaiyë continues. "But the armies of Rand were on their way. And when we had to leave Ethein, Lídei insisted that I come south to avoid the soldiers of Rand. To find you along the shore of Emér."

"I see," Afai murmurs. "But it still seems like your father would be there among the people of Rand, if anywhere. Right?"

"I thought the same," Tolaiyë agrees. "But when I reached the shore, I heard the earth urging me onward, to continue east. And now there's another voice calling me to the Sand Sea. Maybe beyond."

"*More* voices?"

"The new voice has come from someone I saw once before, in a dream. When I was just a boy."

Afai shifts his shoulders, looking back out over the night hills. "You're right. It does sound strange."

"My true aim is still to find my father. Maybe it doesn't make sense, but there's something in the far east that'll help me do that. I can feel it," Tolaiyë explains, relieved to have finally found the right words. "And it *is* strange. Hopelessly strange. I only hope my father is still alive and safe in the meantime."

"Well, there's no telling what we'll find out there. Our feet may very well be the first to step beyond the gate of the Sand Sea. I've got no other escape from the Iftav, it seems. And anyway, I can't let a young kid like you go venturing alone to the far east." Afai sighs, shakes out a thick blanket over the grass, and lounges back.

Tolaiyë closes his eyes, listening to the sleeping hills. It's a warm night. The first of many to come along a path that seems to weave endlessly on to the east.

11

Only four days have passed. Four days since the soldiers of Rand were chased like cowards from the abandoned lanes of Ethein, and since the men from the western families found themselves fleeing for their lives from the shadows there. Four days, and already a strange whispering has risen up like a dank scent in the evening winds, gusting in all directions. Rumors of vanishings, of shadows that creep. Tales that can't be explained.

They say the curse has risen in the lands of Ethein. A dark haunting that follows after any who step into its grasp, biting at their heels with every turn. Even the huntsmen don't dare to wander too near, but make wide paths for themselves to the north, for fear of the curse that stalks there. The curse of the black eyes.

Part Three

1

The captain's laugh is coarse and riotous. The sort of hearty sound that can be heard beyond the thickest walls and rooftops. Here in the army's camp, with nothing but the open forest on all sides, the sound seems to reverberate endlessly through the trees.

"The nearer we come to our target, my good captain, the more I suspect that you and your men should lead tonight's seizure of Ontrágo," Talek calls out as he comes walking to the man's morning campfire. "Your laughter alone may very well send the rebels fleeing in terror."

"No doubt, good king! Woodland critters are all quick to fleein' at the slightest noise! But I dare not steal the honor this night." The captain raises his broad-rimmed flask in salutation. The handful of soldiers gathered around his fire follow suit, tipping their heads in agreement. The captain's long been known as a man who laughs at any situation—even at times when death may be a real possibility. It's a trait that some might call strange, or even a hint of madness. But it was that very trait that led Talek to appoint the man as a captain. An army can always use the strength of men who never fear threats.

"If you insist." Talek gives a humble bow. "The men and I are setting out now. I expect we'll be in position by the afternoon."

The captain rises to his feet, bringing a fist to his wide chest. "Very well, good king! We'll find our place by the southeastern border and await your signal."

* * *

The day's even younger than anticipated when Talek reaches the planned vantage point with half his army that afternoon. The woods north of the western settlement of Ontrágo are steep and dense—the perfect place to hide an army. As one of the most crucial trading posts on the west side of North Emér, situated only several days northwest of the ghost land Ethein, this village makes a logical starting point for the occupation of the western settlements.

The stubborn rebels. It's been nearly two months since their so-called curse left his soldiers unwilling to set foot near Ethein. This time, no foolish superstitions can provide a simple escape. With Talek's men closing in from the north and the captain's battalion flooding the south, Ontrágo will be easily surrounded. Violence will be avoided if possible, but the westerners must learn to honor those who govern them. To respect their king's authority. All these years they've lived like children. Wayward children. But the new kingdom must be established in unity. And a little chastisement will ensure that all falls back into schedule. Or so the son of Rand supposes.

But the day's still young when the king's small army finds themselves facing the resistance of the

Ontrágo settlers alone. No aid arrives from the south when the king's signal is sent. Not as the afternoon wanes on, not as the evening settles in over the hills. And the village becomes unruly. Farmers, tradesmen, craftsmen—all are quick to push back against the soldiers' agenda to take control of Ontrágo. They prod their limits, testing the patience of the king's men. Night has yet to fall when stiff negotiations turn quickly to violence. Then Talek's small team of men is battling to quell the chaos long into the night, securing the borders of the settlement, detaining rioters, confiscating weapons. Morning's white rays are peering again over the eastern trees by the time the last rebel's restrained— and the soldiers of Rand, though standing, are nearly sleeping on their feet, cursing the captain and his men.

Traitors! Idle cowards! How could they abandon their assignment—such a simple role? And what a difference another fifty men could have made!

The soldiers are enraged. But Talek the king meets the morning with a terrible uneasiness in his chest. A sickening, tightening sensation that stirs deep in his heart, threatening his weary mind.

"I'll be leaving for the east within the hour. Be ready at the edge of the woods," he tells a handful of his men as he refills his canteen. "The remainder of the troops can maintain our hold here for now."

"Understood!"

In the many years the captain's served over the armies of Rand, never once has he walked against the king's orders. Never once has he shied away from battle, let alone an easy assignment to secure a village. There must be some uncommon reason why he never arrived with his army. And though he has no evidence to guide him, Talek finds himself dreading the answer.

2

The roaring wakes them first. A distant whir that grows from a hiss to a wild gusting. Rolling and tumbling over itself, surmounting all in its path until it comes like a churning mountain across the desert dunes. A raging storm. The anger of the Sand Sea.

Thirty-two days of walking brought them to the edge of the desert. Aside from an occasional shrub or scampering desert critter, the sands are void of life, and Tolaiyë and Afai are forced to rely entirely on the remaining supply of grains, dried meats, and fruits in their humble wagon. And the sun is merciless over the sands. A single morning beneath it was enough motivation for them to adjust their plans. Now, after another fifteen days, they've become entirely accustomed to spending the heat of the day asleep beneath their makeshift tents, then traversing the silver dunes by the light of the stars and twin moons each night, with their shawls and blankets tied like pelts over their backs.

But today, the Sand Sea doesn't care to let them sleep. And its roaring voice comes with only a moment's warning.

"The ties! Check the tie-downs!" Afai gasps as he wakes, scrambling onto his knees before he can finish his breath. "I'll get Kyn's head covered—the tie-downs!"

Tolaiyë fights against the tent walls that bat wildly on all sides and crawls out beside the wagon, reaching frantically to secure the ropes over the supplies while the sand whirls and whips all around. One knot's blown loose. He reaches desperately to snatch it—but the storm has already come. It arrives like a sudden wall before him, deafening. A force that tosses the wagon violently over and sends Tolaiyë tumbling helplessly backward for what feels like an eternity through the biting sand. He fights to keep his eyes closed and tucked behind his arms as he summersaults head over knees and shoulder to shoulder, tumbling until his feet manage to dig into the dunes, and the weight of the sand piling at his back brings the spinning to a stop. The wind is a thrashing beast at his back, his neck, his arms—a million stinging needles that pound ruthlessly over him.

Until it ends.

Not gradually, but suddenly. The roaring winds end so abruptly that Tolaiyë remains crouched at first, head cradled in his dust-coated arms. But the stinging gale has gone away, falling to little more than a whisper at his ears, beneath even the sound of his own breathing.

But . . . the storm . . .

He shakes the desert from his hands, making an effort to clear the grit from his eyes. When he opens them at last and peers out over his half-buried elbow, he spots the storm. It rages on, no more than four paces away. But Tolaiyë remains untouched. The winds curve like walls on all sides, encircling him in a column of stillness while the world beyond is cloaked away, obscured in the endless swell of the golden sands. Overhead, a clear and radiant sky can be glimpsed—as if Tolaiyë's somehow fallen into a massive glass cylinder at the heart of the storm. And he isn't alone. A gleaming rod has appeared in the space directly ahead, floating effortlessly in the still air. The tall scepter of a king or some mighty lord. A pure and piercing light emanates from its intricate surface, pouring most brightly from the silvery stone that hangs freely at its curved top. An eye. Somehow, the scepter is alive, watching Tolaiyë with a gaze that seems to burn through the very core of his heart. And the creature speaks—

Then the column of whirring sands that encircles the scene falls suddenly away. Its walls collapse, and all around the broken remnants of the storm fall lifelessly to the ground, showering down like golden, shimmering rain onto the dunes. Tolaiyë finds himself sitting alone and speechless in the midst of it, nearly sunken in the sands that now glimmer at the returning presence of the rising sun.

"*Ayteo ha,* great gods alive! How are you not dead and buried!?" Afai's hoarse voice comes calling from behind.

Tolaiyë looks over his shoulder to see him peering out from behind the overturned wagon, some thirty paces away. How indeed? Tolaiyë stares as his disheveled friend comes stumbling out into the open. When he finds his voice at last, only the words of the creature in the storm come to mind.

"South. We need to change our course, head to the southeast," he shouts back to Afai. "We'll find something we need there."

* * *

They've only walked for a few hours on the second evening of their new course when the dunes begin to change their shape. Jagged slabs of dark stone begin to jut out from the sands in random places, forming little channels and troughs that Kyn seems to enjoy weaving through. She tips and bobs her long head as she tugs along, like a calf at play. In time the sands give way to great sheets of layered stone. And after days of trudging the dunes, such solid footing is a heaven-sent dream.

Afai never questioned the idea to turn southeast. In the two months that Tolaiyë's traveled with him, the red-bearded man hasn't questioned *any* changes in their path. He always seems to shrug off the uncertainties of the journey with surprising ease—slipping his hands into his worn pockets, letting a calm smile fall over his face.

"This'll all be just fine," he always says. "I can feel it."

It's possible that the path leads to nowhere in particular, and that they'll find themselves starved and parched to death in the middle of the Sand Sea before any destination falls within their reach. But Afai's quiet confidence has begun to seep its way into the daily pattern of Tolaiyë's thoughts—alongside the recurring assurance of the voice that still calls in his dreams. The voice of the scepter. Somewhere beyond the sands, their destination lies waiting. And somehow, they'll find it.

The sun is still hanging sleepily along the horizon as great stone ledges appear along the path. The earth slopes gradually down as they continue along a southeastern angle, and they're forced to help Kyn ease the wagon over several knee-deep drops to the sandy stone footing below. Tolaiyë's midway through guiding the wagon's front wheels over a little edge when an odd scent comes drifting into his breath. A hearty, fresh sort of scent. Like the savory taste of wind that's just passed through a thriving summer prairie. He doesn't see the palm leaves at his back until they're tickling his neck.

"Trees!" he gasps.

Afai's just shuffled up onto the ridge above to handle the back of the wagon. He looks up with a start, eyes wide. "Sweet mercy!" he breathes. "We've been led right, my brother! Look there!"

Tolaiyë turns to peer through the palms that crowd his shoulders. Just beyond the next ledge, a little jungle of desert trees rises from among the stone and sand. And beyond them . . . could it possibly be?

The two men scramble to aid Kyn over the last ledge, then unhook her harness to let her roam free among the trees. The ox tips her wide nose high into the air, nostrils gaping wide. She wastes no time trotting off through the palms toward the sound that now rises above the wind. The sound of water. Tolaiyë follows after, unable to hide the smile on his face. In time the stony hill to the northeast reveals its southernmost side: a fractured cliff face with fresh water pouring in a handful of little falls from its depths. It creates a natural spring that pools over the stones below and forms a series of wide, shallow ponds among the trees.

"We've found ourselves an oasis!" Afai's almost laughing. He throws off his shoes as he leaps down to the water's edge. "And it's a good thing—we were dead men for certain! I'm liking these voices in your head more and more, my friend!"

Tolaiyë laughs. So much for quiet confidence.

The water is paradise. It pours with a sweet taste from the rocks, soothes their parched throats and dry lips. Afai's always carried a basic soap along with him for treating potential injuries. Now they combine it with bowls of fresh water to wash away weeks of sweat and dirt from their weary skin.

Kyn wades into a shallow side-pool and sits herself contently down, letting the cool moisture flow around her as she satisfies her thirst. And as the night moves in, the travelers set up a simple camp for themselves among the palms—relief pouring over their hearts like the spring's water over the rocks. Tonight, they'll rest more soundly than they have in weeks.

3

Time seems to pass so quickly when water's no longer rationed. They spend five days exploring every corner of the oasis, collecting a variety of fruits from the trees and bushes, catching little fish in the crystal pools. They climb the hulking stone that stands at the head of the fountains and peer out over the distant sands, searching for any sign of the desert's end. There's little to be seen. Only the dim shadows of the mountains that stand at the gate of the sands, their siblings far away to the south, and a flat shadow that rises along the horizon to the east—a long, dark stretch of cliffs that stand like an impassible barrier beyond the dunes. It's a wall of stone, beginning a little to the north and extending south as far as any eye could hope to see. At first the southern mountains seem a more likely target. But in time, Tolaiyë finds himself unable to pull his gaze from the cliffs. In time, they begin to call after him.

It's their sixth night in the oasis when Tolaiyë gives up on sleep and wanders to the edge of the trees. He's sitting on a sharp slab of stone to the east of the ponds, watching the cliffs for what could have been hours, when Afai appears at his side. He settles down on the cool stone, barefoot, with a little bowl of water in his hand and a starlight luster to his freshly trimmed beard.

"You're not planning to stop here, are you," he states more than asks, taking a sip.

Tolaiyë smiles at the shadowed horizon. "We were led to find the oasis. But this isn't our destination. Or at least, not mine," he says. He turns to look at his friend. "You've come a long way, and I'll never be able to repay you. I won't insist that you come with me." The thought of traveling alone again is daunting at best. But the voice that calls from the east seems to ebb and echo just beyond reach. So near.

"How far do you expect to go?" Afai marvels quietly.

"To the cliffs. Unless my eyes fool me, that stone wall can't be more than a week's walk from here."

"You're certain those cliffs are the place you've come for, all the way from Ethein?"

Tolaiyë nods. "The longer I wait, the louder the voice calls me. I can't remain here," he sighs.

Beside him, Afai lets a bitter smirk paint his face. "Of all the strange characters I've met in my days, none have been so unique as you, my good brother," he muses. "But if the voice that guides you truly led us to these waters, I've no doubt you'll reach the place you're searching for."

Staring out over the darkened Sand Sea, Tolaiyë doesn't doubt it either. Now that he's come this close, there's a certainty settling at the bottom of his heart that can't be denied. Like the certainty of the dawn, or the unwavering design in the night sky. Something lies ahead—something he's meant to find, *must* find. And only a few more steps will take him there.

Afai drains his bowl in one long gulp. "You'll find it—with or without my aid. But I can't let you go alone either," he says.

"You sure?"

"The Iftav aren't on my back, and this oasis isn't going anyplace. I might as well help my good brother explore the neighborhood," Afai reasons, and Tolaiyë smiles.

Together then.

4

In the hours it took to journey back to their base camp in the woods east of Ontrágo, Talek had imagined countless scenarios in his mind. As he trudged through the thickets, the possible outcomes poured incessantly across his thoughts, some far too wild to be reasonable, others too simple or too dramatic to be expected of the captain. But the reality he and his men discover that afternoon is somehow far worse than any scene the king had imagined. And they find it much sooner than he had anticipated.

The first body appears as they come to the edge of the camp—a hint of gray and red that peeks through the branches ahead.

"Over there!" one of the soldiers calls out, pointing stiffly.

The body lies chest down, pale face turned toward the north. A young man who hadn't served long beneath the captain. Dead. They turn him over, searching for wounds. But there are none to be found. Talek kneels beside the fallen soldier, thumbing the sheathed dagger that was lying in the leaves beside him.

There's an odd thickness to the silence that grows between the trees. It's the sort of silence that seems to frame and magnify the sound of every breath, every heartbeat, at his temples.

"Search the camp," he tells the others.

The remainder of the captain's men aren't far beyond the first. The king's little troop finds them lying all throughout the camp, some sprawled as if they'd lost their lives midstride, some slumped over beside their still-smoldering fires. Their weapons lie scattered all around. All unbloodied, some blades still sheathed. The captain himself is found sitting lifeless against a tree near his tent, without a single wound visible on his bulky figure. Talek feels his jaw tightening as he steps through the scene, hearing the gasps and cries of his soldiers as they discover their fallen friends. They're dead, all of them. The captain and his men never left their camp. And they were likely killed long before Talek's army reached their position north of Ontrágo.

It takes all afternoon to bury the dead. And all afternoon his soldiers debate angrily over the deaths of their brothers. Some say the savages of Ontrágo must have known all along, must have snuck into the camp by night and poisoned the food. But the son of Rand isn't so certain. He can feel the lack of answers burning circles in his thoughts. How could the westerners have done this without being seen? How did they manage to slay only the men serving under the captain? And how is there no sign of injury, no sign of real struggle? The questions are more than anyone can answer now, and the answers aren't here.

They say death lingers in the places it visits. Talek and his small team set off toward the east as the sun sinks again in the west, hoping to put as much distance as possible between them and the site of the massacre before the night falls. Wondering all along the way what they'll tell the families of the fallen soldiers— of the scene they won't soon forget.

5

The sun is high in its throne, casting its heat into a warm wind that whips and plays along the stone edges. It took only six nights to reach the foot of the cliffs from the eastern edge of the oasis. They could've camped one last day to avoid the morning sun, but Tolaiyë was restless. And now that he stands beside them, he can't seem to take his gaze from the towering cliff tops. They rise to meet the sky like ancient guards at attention, sheer and unyielding. But their westward face is full of wide grooves, natural steps, and slanted planes. Paths to the top.

They take their supplies on their backs and unharness Kyn from the wagon. The cliffs are no place for wheels. Tolaiyë begins finding his way up from the desert floor as soon as his shoulder pack is secured. Afai follows soundlessly behind, guiding Kyn along the narrow bends and mild steps. The most accessible route takes them slightly southward along the cliff's face. And the great expanse of the Sand Sea grows wide before their rising view. In time the stones and trees of the oasis can be seen as a wavering shadow in the western dunes. The single blemish in an otherwise entirely golden sea.

After nearly two hours of climbing, Tolaiyë scrambles at last over the final step and onto the crown of the cliffs. The view that awaits him there steals the breath from his lips.

"What do you see?" Afai's voice comes drifting up from below.

Tolaiyë struggles for words. The land atop the cliffs is a world entirely apart from the desolate sands below. A place as green and alive as the woods of North Emér—cascading hills blanketed with trees and vibrant prairie grasses, a sparkling lake that shimmers through the leaves ahead. A hidden paradise.

"It's—"

Tolaiyë's only begun to find his breath when something more catches his eye. An entity that suddenly hovers in the air directly before him and glows with a dazzling brilliance. A being like a scepter, with a single eye at its top. The creature from the sandstorm. And it speaks again.

"Child of gods, the time has come," it whispers. A voice Tolaiyë's heard for ages. The voice that's called him here since before he left Ethein. "The duty to which you are called, the calling of those in the heavens, lies before you. To protect the free will of the children, to stand as a messenger before them, and to present the fate of Claya at the footstool of the goddess. That it and all its realms may become whole and eternal."

He's heard it before, hasn't he? At some time and place no longer entirely recalled. He's certain of it. These are words he was always meant to hear.

"Do you accept this call?" the scepter questions, and it seems as though all the world falls away behind its words, like the endless sands beneath the cliffs. And the peace that floods Tolaiyë's heart is beyond his ability to define.

"I accept," he answers.

"Reach forth your hand."

The white light that bursts from the creature's presence when Tolaiyë extends his open hand burns as brightly as the morning sun. All else fades away behind its consuming glare, erased behind the blinding whiteness.

6

The arai typically sleep under the cover of tents and tarps when they're away from the shelter of their wooden homes. But tonight, their supposed king and his twelve men rest with only the forest canopy overhead. They travel light, for arai men. Their night guard fell asleep long ago, and Onei stands only a few paces away from them, watching. She watches their bare, dreaming faces; their small eyes; their narrow noses. Wondering.

"Why were they all slain? Was it really necessary?" she whispers.

Nearby, her fellow scout shakes her head. "Don't grieve over these arai, Onei. These are an evil kind. The Iftav have stopped their victory over the peaceful arai of the western lands. Now we can leave for the northwest knowing the friends of the Shardehn are at least momentarily safe," she murmurs.

"But did they *all* really need to die?" Onei twitches her broad ears in thought, gazing again over each of the men's faces. "And why do they seem so eager for conflict?"

Hylveh's scarcely listening. She settles down on a lower bough of a nearby tree with her back to the thick trunk. "Let's rest while we can. I'll take the first watch," she suggests.

Onei sighs. She and Hylveh have followed these men from the time they left the grave of their fellow soldiers. Two days, now. And in those two days the men have hardly spoken to one another. All but their king walk as if their bodies weighed almost more than their feet can carry. Slow, heavy. Likely burdened by the scene of death they've left behind.

Was it really necessary?

Onei's heart twinges at the thought. It's true that the men of Rand have become a greater pain with each passing year—many of them creeping out of their military ranks to form gangs in the woods, attacking and plundering unsuspecting travelers from other settlements. The Iftav disregarded them at first. But in recent years the stench of the so-called soldiers of Rand has grown too foul to ignore. They harass other arai, and their filthy camps pollute the land. Their riotous, drunken gatherings shock the stillness of the woods and scatter valuable prey. These days, it isn't uncommon for the Iftav scouts to silence them on occasion—quietly disposing of a little thieving gang that happens to stumble into the hunting paths. And the disappearance of a few scoundrels here and there has only ever benefited the clans of North Emér, voránjevin and arai alike.

But to slay an entire small army?

The Iftav have never interfered so dramatically in the affairs of the arai. And though she fights to convince herself otherwise, Onei can't seem to shake the sinking suspicion in her chest that she knows who was behind it. This is going too far. She *must* confront him.

She gives one last glance over the scene before turning away. Hylveh's right about getting rest. The night's short, and the afternoon hunt was admittedly exhausting, with the men's loud stomping frightening all the prey in a wide radius. But there's suddenly a sight beside her that stops her in her place.

One of the arai men has opened his eyes.

He sits frozen in place, staring breathlessly back at her. He's smaller than the others, with smoother features. Younger, maybe just a boy. Just a child! A child pulled into battles, forced to bury his kin. His small eyes are opened as wide as they seem able. Terrified. It's the gaze of one who may have never seen a voránjevin face before, and it momentarily captures Onei. Such blameless eyes . . .

A sudden stirring erupts nearby and interrupts the moment—and all at once Onei finds herself wrapped in a shawl or blanket with strong arms closing in all around. Another man. His hands grab frantically through the blanket for her wrists, struggling to restrain her, only to fall away with a startled cry when she steals the strength from his grip. Still caught beneath the blanket, she reaches back to lay her palms against her attacker's thick legs and pull the life from the muscles there. The energy slides like hot silk from around his bones, surging into her arms and giving her the strength to yank the tall brute to the ground. She manages to swat the blanket from her head at last as he collapses with a loud curse to the earth.

But there are thirteen men camping here. And now all of them are awake.

One of them snatches Onei's arm as she turns to flee, fumbling for a blade at his hip. Another tries to lasso her knees with a belt. Hylveh leaps like a bird of prey onto the broad shoulders of the first, clinging to his chest and tearing just enough strength from his heart to send him sinking to his knees beneath her, choking horribly. Onei fends off the next with a swift attack to his long arms. Now Hylveh sends another man tumbling to the ground. But they keep coming. Shouting, cursing.

"What in—"

"Watch it! They've got a mean sting, the devils!"

"Get the rope!"

And in moments the two voránjevin scouts are surrounded by more hands than they can hope to withstand. Another cloak appears over Onei's head, and despite her most furious efforts, the captors manage to scoop her up in a tight wrap around her middle. Trapped.

7

When the piercing light fades at last, all the sensations of a mortal life seem to fade along with it. The mild hunger in his stomach, the weariness in his bones from the long climb to the cliff tops, the hot glare of the sun—all dissolve away into the past and are gone. And a world of sound replaces them. A world brimming with endless, echoing melodies. The songs of every living heart ringing out at once.

And among them, far out in Claya's plains, one heartbeat that Tolaiyë's longed dearly to find.

He doesn't wait, doesn't think. He turns toward the sound and steps into the wind. The cliffs and the Sand Sea melt rapidly away behind him, and when his foot touches down again, he no longer stands atop the far eastern cliffs, but on a lonely hillside. Somewhere far to the west, where the sun has yet to rise beyond a solemn glow along the horizon. Somehow he's come here, glided across the earth in an instant to the place where the sound of his father's heart rang so clearly only a moment ago. But the hillside is empty. And now that he's come, the sound has vanished.

Was he mistaken? How could Father have been here, so impossibly far from North Emér?

Tolaiyë closes his eyes, hoping to sort through the myriad of heartbeats that resound at his ears. Searching. But the earth is too full of sound. He opens his eyes again, feeling as though he might sink beneath the weight of it all. The scepter who called him to the cliffs appears and drifts silently in the air beside him, turning its single eye in place, saying nothing. The Palarian. Or so it introduced itself just now. A name Tolaiyë somehow expected to hear.

"You will learn in time to find what you seek. This servant will aid you," it whispers to him.

In time . . . How much time does Father have left? And where has he gone, in all the world?

Before he can wonder further, radiant light comes flooding over the grass beside Tolaiyë's own pool of light, glimmering softly in the dew that remains there.

"In stone no hands can find the blood of sorrow."

His full name. A title he hasn't heard for years— one he's never disclosed to anyone at all. And the voice that recites it is one he's heard once before. The angelic woman it belongs to stands an arm's length from his side when he turns to see her. The woman he once saw as a child, and who appeared to him over the waters of Emér. Her countenance is no less glorious than it was then. Now that she stands beside him, Tolaiyë can see the hazel hue within her starlit eyes, and the way her light curls contrast like autumn leaves against the pale sheen of her face.

"Claya stirs with turmoil," she says, looking up to him. "Can you feel it?"

Tolaiyë looks back at her, unsure where to begin. "You . . . you're . . . ," he whispers.

"My name is Éliva. I've waited for you, Tolaiyë. We share the same burden, the same purpose in this world. Now that you've awakened, we can work together. For the good of Claya," she tells him.

Tolaiyë breathes deeply, suddenly unable to stop noticing the tremendous weight that presses on his heart. A suffocating, straining sensation unlike any he's ever known. "Th-this heaviness in my chest. Is it . . ."

"Many hearts weep. You feel the weight of the sorrows of the world," Éliva answers.

Tolaiyë looks back to her. "You feel it too? How long have you borne this?" he asks.

"Many years."

"What can be done?" The thought brings a terrible sinking to his already breaking heart.

Éliva steps to his side, takes his hand in both of hers. "There are some sorrows we can't prevent. The people of Claya must have the freedom to choose their own paths, and there will always be those who choose to bring darkness into the world. But we can strive to help it heal," she answers. "Come, I will show you." She steps up into the air, pulling him along.

The hillside melts away as she guides him over forests and rivers, lakes and snow-frosted mountains. Great cities full of life and color pass by beneath their feet, crisscrossed with cobbled streets and country byways. They pass over more cities, more villages and camps than Tolaiyë could ever dream of numbering, more harbors and ships at sea than anyone could count. All teeming with living souls! All swarmed with beating hearts—full of dreams and hopes, fears and joys, needs and desires. All so much more than Tolaiyë's ever imagined.

When Éliva brings them to a stop at last, Tolaiyë's almost staggering beside her. Drained—as if he had just breathed in the entirety of Claya in a single gasp. They stand in the air above a modest village that hides nestled in the trees below. Subtle smoke rises from the chimneys there, curling and wavering like gray ribbons into the morning sky.

"Táutha, the capital settlement of the people of Rand in North Emér," Éliva murmurs. "The people of these lands follow Talek, the son of Mighty Rand. I've appeared to him many times, warned him many times to avoid war."

"You've spoken with him?" Tolaiyë asks.

"I've tried. But he won't listen. He thinks he's walking a brave and noble path, seeking to bring all the people of North Emér together under one rule. But there are dangers he can't see on the path ahead. I can see that he leads his people to destruction," she tells him. "We must always do what we can to protect the gift of the children of Claya. But we can never force our will on them—to do so would compromise the gift itself. And our call as sasarianë."

Her guardian drifts weightlessly beside his own, soft light shimmering in its eye. It has a somewhat narrower crescent shape to its head, in contrast to the Palarian's wide semicircle. But it's no less exotic. Floating together, they look like the lost instruments of some powerful sorcerer.

The gift. Hearing of it now, Tolaiyë recalls it from long ago. Something spoken of before Claya came to be. A gift to all living souls, given from the goddess herself: the freedom to choose their way, to follow their own will. The gift was established before the beginning of the world. And somehow, Tolaiyë remembers. But the memories come like a torrent of rushing waters over his mind. Startling. They collide over the memories of the life he's lived until now, crashing like rolling rapids across his thoughts. Only moments ago, he was simply a young traveler from North Emér. Now he hears the rhythm of every living heart. Now he walks from one horizon of the world to another in the time that it once took to turn in place.

"Our purpose is to protect the free will of all people?" he whispers.

"And to help Claya reach its greatest potential."

"But what does it really mean? How will we do it?"

Éliva takes a moment to breathe in the cool air, then lets it slide out. "In any and every way we can," she says, and the resolve thickens like mortar between her words.

"What power are we given?"

"We have many gifts. I have yet to find them all. The power to walk in the wind and traverse the world in a single breath, the power to cross between the physical world and the realm of spirits. Power to sense the heart of every living soul, to speak to them in dreams—even heal their bodies, if we choose," she tells him. "And the earth and its elements will obey our voice, if we call to them."

"Realm of spirits?" he questions. It's a concept he's heard of only a handful of times, when the elders in Ethein would gather and tell their tales over knitting and simple whittling.

"The sphere where spirits dwell when they leave their bodies. Mortals who die can be found resting there together, if you know how to search for them." She describes the possibility as if it were entirely ordinary. But it's incredible to imagine.

"Talk with the dead, face-to-face?"

Éliva nods. "I lost my mother and father as a child. But I speak with them now, from time to time."

Tolaiyë holds a hand out before him, staring at the soft glow that emanates from his palm, his fingers, his arm. Like the aura of a god.

"It's coming back to me now . . . a day long ago, when we were chosen to fulfill this role. Shepherds of the earth, with the Farian and Palarian to guide us. It was the goddess who called us. The Mother of Claya," he murmurs. "But everything's still so blurred."

Éliva smiles calmly in reply, and the light of it nearly outshines the morning rays at her back. "Sasarianë are servants of the heavens, sent to bless Claya. It seems like there's no one way to fulfill our purpose. No written instruction either. But the rains and the sunlight need no instruction to bless and prosper the earth. Neither should we," she says, and she reaches again for his hand. "Come! There's so much to be done."

8

The king's accompanied by only a small party of men when he appears at the edge of Kehnin that morning, a few days sooner than was originally planned. And there's a weariness in his dark-ringed eyes that blooms a sour feeling in Echeret's stomach. Something's gone wrong. He goes out to meet them, eyeing their figures for signs of battle.

Throughout all the years Echeret's spent as a friend of Talek, he's never met another man more stubborn. It's a trait the king seems to have inherited from his father—a proud man who took counsel from no one. But unlike his father, Talek has yet to master the subtleties of his temperament. When careful plans don't play out as smoothly as they ought to, the king's face shows it.

"You look as though you've walked through the night," Echeret says.

Talek comes to a stop beside him, pausing to wipe the sweat from his brow. His men continue past them and disperse into the village. Only two wait beside the king, hefting a covered crate on wooden rods across their shoulders.

"We nearly did," he pants, then looks to Echeret. "Ontrágo's secured, but not half as thoroughly as we need."

"A group of settlers? More than the captain can handle? That's certainly uncommon," Echeret replies.

Talek shakes his head, running a hand through his greased hair. "The captain's gone. He and all his men," he says.

"What? Gone? The west knew the plan?" Echeret steps back as his mind suddenly spins in momentary weightlessness.

"*Someone* did," Talek murmurs, staring strangely at the crate his men carry. He gives them a nod, motions for them to continue on into town. Then he leans closer to his friend's ear. "Echeret, my good brother, you've served as my first officer for many years, and as my friend for far longer. I can trust no one more than you. There's something amiss in these lands. I'll need your aid to resolve it. I go onward to the capital. Will you come with me?"

Echeret glances to the crate as it's carried by, then back to the weary king. "We can move out as soon as you wish," he answers.

Talek nods, clapping a hand to Echeret's arm. "Good then. I'll be ready by tomorrow morning. Come, I'll tell you everything."

9

"*Ivéi!*" the filíl's voice comes piercing through the northern trees, flitting like the calls of a bird among the leaves. The morning hunters have just returned. Now they pause with fresh meat in their hands, ears twitching at the sound.

"*Ivéi*! Cousin!"

Hylveh's voice. The breathless call of a scout who's run without rest. Faleth rises from his place beside the western watch point and dashes across the camp. When Hylveh appears through the northern trees at last, he stands waiting to catch her by the shoulders.

"What news from the north?" He spits his words almost too quickly to be understood.

Hylveh trembles between his hands as she struggles to find her breath. "Onei, cousin! They took her! The arai!" she gasps.

A subtle stiffness grips Faleth's figure. "Which arai? Where did they go?" he rasps.

"It was the one they call king, and his followers."

Now the others have begun to gather around, glancing anxiously at one another. A scout of the Iftav captured by dirty arai? It seems almost too wild to believe. Faleth's breaths begin to deepen. "How could this happen? The arai are weak against us!" he questions, cold dread already pooling at the edges of his orange eyes.

"She went among them in the night. Went too close," Hylveh pants. "We tried to fight them when they came after her. But there were too many of them—"

"But *you* escaped? How is she not with you?"

"She was in the middle of them—I did all I could!" Hylveh tells him, and the tears swell like glistening puddles in her eyes. "I barely managed to break away from their dirty hands. Their massive, stinking hands—" The words struggle through her clenched teeth as she rams a slender fist into the nearest tree.

Faleth turns away and steps in a slow circle, hands flexing at his sides. The clan members begin to wonder aloud together.

"Is Onei still alive?"

"Where will they take her?"

Questions pile up in the air as everyone murmurs at once. But their voices all fall silent when their leader steps back into their midst with his gray hand held high.

"Never in all the days of our people in this land has a voránjevin been taken captive by the hands of an arai. Neither have the Iftav ever forsaken one of their own. Onei *will* return to us alive. We'll find the demons that took her!" he shouts, and all the clan raise their fists in unison, adding their voices to his.

They don't delay. By midday they've organized themselves into seven groups and divided supplies. And by evening each band is well on its way to the northeast, moving swiftly with hearts ablaze in their chests. Each moving for a certain settlement of the nasty arai. Each prepared to search every corner and shadow for any sign of their stolen sister.

* * *

The night's already begun to fall when Faleth allows his own troop to stop for rest at last, and he finds himself pacing anxiously at the edge of the camp as the darkness closes. They're headed for the easternmost settlement of the people of Rand, a place where Hylveh knows the king and his men were planning to rest on their return journey. At this rate, they'll reach the village by midmorning.

But is midmorning soon enough?

The uncertainly plagues Faleth's mind. Tormenting. Of all the scouts that could've been taken . . . She's always looked a little too kindly at the arai. He should've insisted that she be a messenger to the west or south, far away from the dirty men of Rand. Far away from creeping eyes and snatching hands. Curse those beasts! Curse the fool they call king! Of all the scouts keeping watch in North Emér, they had to steal away the one most treasured of all. The one who . . .

The bitter spiral of Faleth's thoughts comes to a halt when he glimpses a familiar glow through the leaves—a pure light that streams in white rays between the branches, bright but not blinding. And soft as the waters of Emér on a windless morning. The woman who stands at its heart has the gaze of a thousand stars.

"Why do you come to us here, sasarian?" Faleth asks, level voiced.

"Because I heard a cry in my brother's heart," the immortal tells him.

He looks up into her glowing face. "I go now to find her. Your precious arai won't be able to stop us," he says.

The sasarian kneels down. "Onei lives," she whispers. "They haven't harmed her."

The words send a welcome rush of relief flowing over Faleth's heart. But he hides it carefully away behind the unmoving expression on his face. "Good. They'll have little more chance to. They've already earned their deaths," he growls.

"Faleth, the arai have only acted in fear. They don't understand the nature of the voránjevin people. These men simply fear what they can't understand," she assures him.

But Faleth isn't convinced. "What, would you have us leave Onei to be tormented and slain?"

The woman's long hair slips in soundless waterfalls over her shoulders, and she shakes her head. "I simply ask that you consider mercy. The Iftav have brought enough death to the people of Rand," she answers.

"Haven't they gone seeking death among their neighbors? We've only given them what they desired." Faleth turns in an impatient circle, ears angled back.

"They don't yet seek war with you, only because they know nothing of the Iftav. Brother, you can rescue Onei without taking life. Stop this now, while you can."

"I make no promises here, sasarian," he tells her.

Brother, she calls him. It was his own mother who took her in when they found her abandoned on the shores of the Atayu Sea. Voránjevin people have always taught their youth to respect the sasarian legends. Faleth will do no less. But even so, this being was never his sister.

Éliva returns to her feet. "Onei's been given into the care of the man most trusted by the son of Rand. He isn't like his king. He has a wise and kind heart. He'll let Onei go free. I can see it in his heart," she says.

"I'll step over his lifeless remains to take her, if not," Faleth murmurs, turning back toward the trees where the others prepare for the night.

But a slender hand appears at his shoulder as he steps away. When he turns, the brightness of the immortal's glowing countenance is near enough to blot out the sight of all the woods surrounding it. Her fiery stare somehow projects into the depths of his bitter heart, and where her hand rests he can feel the surge of unending, immeasurable strength—the limitless life energy of a body that can never die.

"Let mercy run, my brother," she says.

Those words . . . how does she know? Faleth wonders, but the sasarian woman vanishes before he can ask. Gone—like a sliver of lightning in the night. And he's left again to himself, standing alone in the darkening trees.

10

Life among the Shardehn's been nothing short of carefree. It's a welcome surprise—something few of the refugees from Ethein had anticipated. Provided with their own space only a short walk from the place where the voránjevin keep their simple gardens, the initially wary Sketzans find themselves enjoying a level of security unlike any they've known. After all, what thieving gang from the east would dare to venture so near to a camp of the mysterious people of the woods, if they were even fortunate enough to find it? Not all families of the western lands are familiar with the voránjevin clans. But none of them are as naive and superstitious toward them as the people of Rand.

For Kadeis, the forest depths have become a haven. A place where the outside world and the troubles that churn within it seem distant, unreal. She's received no word of Kehljen, and some say it's been too long—that her husband must be held prisoner among the people of Rand, if he lives at all. But Kadeis throws the ideas aside. Her Kehljen lives. It's a certainty that rests in the very base of her heart. And though it can never fully dispel the numbing anxiety that plagues her heart, she treasures the assurance that if anyone can find Kehljen, the voránjevin clans can. And if any Sketzans happened to find him first, the people of the woods would be the first to know.

The last message from Tolaiyë came over a month ago, when a scout confirmed that he was headed to the far east with the man called Afai—for some purpose the scout couldn't understand. The thought of it sometimes finds and haunts Kadeis in the night, sending little tides of uncertainty rippling over her heart that are almost too much to bear. Where could he possibly be going—where in all the wide east? But Lídei's never failed to reassure her, each time they meet.

"Your son will find what he's looking for," she always says. And somehow, Kadeis believes her. Until the night comes at last when she no longer depends on hope alone.

It's raining when he comes. The sort of evening Kadeis has always loved to spend beside a warm fire, mending clothes or baking something delicious over the coals. But tonight the rain means huddling beneath the canvases the people have strung up as rooftops over the campsites, with hot coals glowing in kettle lanterns all around. She's sitting almost entirely alone beneath her canvas at the southeastern edge of the camp, sipping a warm drink with her shawl wrapped tightly over her shoulders, unsure what to think of the first rays of light that come creeping along the ground beside her. Have the moons risen already? But the light isn't cold, isn't silver. It's golden white, like the rays of the morning sun. And now it floods over all the scene, lighting the rain that flecks and falls in the dimness beyond her shelter. When she turns to find its source, there's no sunrise, but an angel—a magnificent being cloaked in shimmering robes, with eyes like fire. A being whose face, though made glorious, she could never mistake.

"Mother," he says. He reaches out one hand, a marvelous smile on his shining face.

Kadeis can't seem to quell the trembling in her fingers as she reaches out to touch him. "My . . . my Tolaiyë," she whispers. "An angel, just as I once dreamed, long ago."

"I've only become what you taught me I always could," he answers. The rain falls in a circle all around him, leaving him somehow untouched in the midst of it.

"Have you become a god?"

The glowing man shakes his head. "Only one of their servants. I'm still learning what it all means." He encloses her hand in his. "I can't stay here, but I wanted to tell you that everything's going to be all right. Don't be afraid, Mother. Father's alive. I can hear his heart beating. As soon as I find him, I'll bring him home."

The tears are cascading down Kadeis's cheeks, mingling with the rain that's already speckling her shoes. But she's smiling. "My son, your name suits you well. You bring the gladdest news I've heard in months," she tells him.

Tolaiyë's smile widens, and his countenance shimmers like the night stars. "The people will be safe with the Shardehn. I must go. But I'll visit you when I can, Mother," he says, and he turns to the southeast.

Only a little circle of dry earth remains in the open space before her when he vanishes.

11

The cliffs are painted dazzling orange and gray in the afternoon sun, catching the light like the outer barrier of a massive fortress at the edge of the Sand Sea. At their tops, the wind gusts mildly among the trees. Cool and gentle. Tolaiÿe returns to them in a single step over the curve of the earth.

"Welcome back. I thought I'd collect one of these incredibly juicy yellow fruits for you," Afai calls out between mouthfuls. "But now that you're here, and I see you floating on the wind like that, I realize you may not need things like food anymore. Do you even *feel* hunger anymore?" He sits lazily with his back to a tree, not more than a few paces from the cliffs' jagged edge.

Tolaiÿe laughs, stepping down into the grass beside him. "Even if I don't, it doesn't mean I can't enjoy good food with a friend," he says. "I left without thinking. Have you and Kyn been all right?"

The light emanating from his presence brings a warm glow to the scene, lighting the leaves overhead. The Palarian floats soundlessly nearby, and Afai eyes it keenly as he reaches for another fruit to peel.

"*All right*, you ask?" he gasps. "Have you noticed this place yet, my brother? Everywhere you look—wild fruits, birds and scampering animals, a gorgeous lake with a river running from it—this place is a paradise! It takes much harsher lands to ruffle this beard. Don't forget that I lived alone on the east shore of Emér for years, and survived crossing the Sand Sea on the whim of the craziest man I know."

Tolaiyë laughs, and Afai glances out over the sands to the west.

"By yesterday evening I found myself returning here to the view of the desert. Marvelous, isn't it?" He hands a fruit to Tolaiyë, giving him a sideways stare. "So, are you going to tell me what's happened to you?" he asks.

Tolaiyë takes a moment to search for the right explanation. "I've been given an assignment. It's something I agreed to do long ago, in another life," he says at last.

"Are you . . . immortal?"

"I think so." Tolaiyë looks out over the wide sweep of green land that envelops them. "I can hear the whole earth now. More heartbeats than I could ever number. As a child I could sometimes hear the wind speaking, or the hills, or the trees. But now, the songs are unending—carrying all the thoughts and cares of the world to my ears," he whispers. "It's overwhelming."

"All the hearts in the world? But what purpose would that have, hearing them all?" The mild hues in Afai's widened eyes seem to magnify themselves against the pale grasses.

"I'm still learning. But I think it enables us to help the people of the world," Tolaiyë answers.

"Us?"

"There's another person like me. She was one of the voices that guided us here, to the cliffs."

Afai shakes his head. "Our stories grow stranger by the day, don't they?" he sighs.

Tolaiyë cracks open the thick peel of the fruit in his hand, watching curiously as a drop of its pale juice beads up and slips rapidly from his sleeve, leaving no wetness at all. He looks back to his friend. "Something's changed about you too. I could feel it as I came here. Your thoughts and your eyes turned my way before I arrived. How did you know I was coming?" he questions.

Afai smiles, a gentle laugh on his breath. "I just saw that you were coming. Don't know how else to explain it. Came to me like a daydream. To tell you honestly, I've been seeing all sorts of things since you vanished in a blast of light," he says.

"What sorts of things?"

"All sorts. But the wildest vision of them all came to me the moment you vanished atop the cliff here. I saw a magnificent stone sanctuary, rising from these very grounds. A massive structure with white columns, courtyards, curving stairs—like the palace of a royal family."

"A stone sanctuary . . . ," Tolaiyë wonders. "Do you think it once stood here, ages ago?"

Afai makes a frown, thinking. "I don't think so. So far, I've only seen things to come. Things that haven't happened just yet," he explains. "Do you see things to come?"

Tolaiyë shakes his head. "I hear all the hearts in the world, but I can't say where they'll be tomorrow."

Afai's beard puckers at the edges, making way for his broad smile. He shakes a proud fist in the air before his chest. "Ah, well then, I suppose we've each got our skills. I'll have to be our eyes for the times ahead," he concludes.

"A skill like that could certainly have its uses." Tolaiyë nods. Far away to the west, the sun begins to gather the remaining clouds in the sky like thinning blankets around itself, sinking slowly earthward. The evening nears—the end of a day he began as an ordinary man. Now he watches its dusk as something different. An entirely changed being.

The yellow fruit tastes sweeter than expected. He can only hope the days to come will be the same.

12

He's only barely let himself sink into a comfortable slouch beside the half-built cabin wall for a much-needed rest when the messenger arrives. And Talek can see from the look in the man's eyes that he carries no good tidings. The thought drops a weary weight into his stomach. The people have had enough bad news in the past week to last them the year—and beyond. What now?

"Good king, I come with word from the eastern and northern settlements." The messenger pauses just beyond the king's muddied shoes, giving a slight bow.

Talek tugs a clean rag from his belt and dries the sweat that's gathered along the sides of his face. The day's grown hot. Too hot, in his opinion, for constructing a new cabin. He looks up to the messenger. "What news?"

"Votyón, Kehnin, Leln, and the northernmost settlements—all have sent requests for additional soldiers to keep the night watches," the man tells him frankly.

"More night guards? Why would that be necessary?" Talek asks as he waves for one of the nearby youngsters to fetch him water.

Echeret looks up from his work a few paces away, having just finished notching a new log. The messenger's gaze dodges momentarily between him and Talek's questioning stare.

"In all honesty, I'm not so sure myself, good king. The people say there've been . . . hauntings in the night," he stammers.

"Hauntings?" Echeret's come to stand beside the king, sawdust-coated arms folded before his chest.

The messenger nods. "Knockings, poundings, things moved from their places," he tells them. "Some night guards haven't been found when morning comes. Now others are refusing to take their posts."

"Raiders from the west?" Echeret murmurs to Talek, who struggles to keep anything but a brow-raised look of bewilderment on his dark face.

It seems like an idle, superstitious rumor. But why would so many settlements send word of it at once? And what reason would they have to exaggerate?

"Maybe, though they've never used such harassing against us," the king replies. "Do they think they can frighten us out of our own lands?" He scoffs, taking a long gulp from the water canteen that's appeared beside him. Then he looks to his first officer. "Send an order for three of our soldiers to visit each settlement that's reported this trouble, and to aid as night guards. If the issue persists afterward, have them send us word."

"I'll send the order now," Echeret nods.

"It's odd news you bring, my friend," Talek tells the messenger. "We must show the people there's nothing to fear. My men and I will go personally to resolve the matter in each settlement, if need be."

The messenger bows anew, stepping backward. "Thank you, good king. The people will be comforted. I'll deliver your word at once," he affirms, then turns back toward the village road.

Talek bites his cheek as he watches the man disappear behind the next cottage. Hauntings. In all his years as king, never has such an odd report come to his ears. Knockings, poundings . . . He feels almost foolish sending soldiers to the settlements—soldiers who could very well be used elsewhere. But these are beginning to be odd times. Strange enough for even Talek, the son of Rand, to admit. And if there's a way to put an end to any sprouting hysterics among the people, perhaps it's an effort worth making. Before things get worse.

13

It was nearly twenty years ago when he first met her. In the days when the Iftav dwelt farther north, toward the plains. He was only seventeen years old. A child—but already well known among his father's clan, though he was raised among the Shardehn. Those were the days when the arai were still young in the land, sparsely settled. Strangers to North Emér that seemed so alien to the people of the clans. There were some who seemed captivated by them. But Faleth could never understand it. The arai came with an undeniable reek on their skins. And it was a stench he couldn't seem to stop noticing.

It was only four years after his father's death when he met her. Four years since the day the arai fell from any hope of favor in his young eyes. They became animals to him—selfish beasts who disrupted the balance of the land, deserving no more honor or kindness than that which they gave.

But Onei always saw the world with different eyes.

He was sent with her to gather the meats that hung drying to the north of their camp that morning. Had he been sent alone, Faleth wouldn't have hesitated to take the lives of the two arai boys he found there, stealing the food of the Iftav. But Onei was the first to step into the grove. And there was no anger in her eyes when she spotted them. Almost no reaction at all. He would never forget the terror in those boys' eyes as she caught them by the wrists. They yelped and gasped like such pathetic, helpless creatures. But she took only enough strength from their arms to free the bundles of meat from their tight, thieving fingers. And then she let them go.

"They're likely to come back! You let them run?" Faleth came rushing to Onei's side as the arai scampered off, cradling their limp arms. Wretched thieves! How could she simply let them run?

But Onei only knelt to gather the jerky, calmly stacking it in Faleth's unsuspecting arms. "I let *mercy* run," she told him.

To run has always been the honor of all voránjevin people. They say there was a time long ago, when the clans began, when the power to run wasn't known. When the ancestors had not yet unlocked the power of Hitérian and struggled to live from one day to the next. They say the ability to run is a gift. To run is to live, to thrive, to overcome.

It was nearly twenty years ago when Onei first spoke the words that she would repeat to him many times throughout their life together. She said it as she took the last of the meats in her own hands and started back to the camp, glancing to him over her shoulder.

"Let mercy run!"

14

It's the largest storage barn in Táutha, one of the few among the settlements built tall enough for a full-sized loft. Over the past fifteen years or so it's been used for a variety of village needs. Most recently it keeps supplies for the king's armies: spare weapons and uniforms, dry food storage for soldiers, tent supplies and travel packs—anything the soldiers of Rand might need, locked carefully into trunks and crates. But now it serves another purpose.

The wide alley before the barn door is empty when he comes to it, lit more by the lantern he carries than by the sun's failing glow in the west. For a moment he hesitates, with his hand hovering just over the metal door latch, listening. Then he pulls the broad door gently open, only enough to peer inside. As if it were too dangerous to do more. But the creature inside remains harmlessly huddled in its cage when he spots it—curled with its little knees pulled up to its chest, staring with large, shining eyes.

Echeret takes a breath before stepping into the barn and closing the door softly behind him, securing the lock. The cage sits several paces away, against a wall of stacked crates that reaches nearly to the loft above. The being inside it makes no sound at all as Echeret steps closer, or as he kneels an arm's length away to place a little box of smoked boar and a bowl of water on the ground. But its eyes never leave him—pale, sandy-golden eyes that seem to reflect the entire scene in their wet spheres. And for what seems like an eternity, Echeret can only stare back. Waiting until something in those massive, pale eyes restores his original resolve. Then he leans forward—key in hand—removing the lock on the cage in front of him and taking several steps back. The creature tips its head at the sight, its reddish-brown forehead furrowing slightly as it glances to the open cage door, then back to Echeret. Now it comes crawling slowly, soundlessly out. It stands scarcely as tall as a child—with limbs equally thin but covered in fur. A simple tunic clothes its slender frame, along with a matching wrap that's tied over the shoulders and around its tiny waist. Coarse fabric, the color of autumn leaves.

Kneeling close by, Echeret keeps one hand to the dagger sheathed at his side. Watching. Wondering how such a small creature could have been as powerful and difficult to capture as the king described. They said this one fought off two or three men before it was finally tied down. Maybe in a moment he'll regret his decision to open the cage. But for now, the prisoner doesn't leap at him. Doesn't claw or bite—doesn't attack at all. Instead, it squats abruptly down over the box of smoked boar and wastes no time devouring the meat in greedy mouthfuls.

Echeret lets his breath out. "I assumed you'd eat meat," he murmurs softly, looking on.

The creature pauses its feast to look up at him. "Thank you," she says. She—it speaks with a small voice that sounds undoubtedly female. And slicked with an accent.

Echeret nearly topples backward onto his rear. "Y-you speak? The language of Sketza?" he stammers.

"We voránjevin are not so much beasts as many arai seem to think," the creature tells him, swallowing another rough bite of boar before looking up again. "Our clan was once a friend of the families of Rand. Now your people seek war always." She finishes the last of the meat and returns to her feet. "We would have left for southwestern lands. Would have left the people of Sketza to the rest of their wars. But now your men bring me here. Your people are in danger."

"Danger?" Echeret watches her tiny, pointed teeth. "From the west?"

The prisoner shakes her head. "The Iftav," she says. "My clan. They have little mercy for your people. They will come for me. And I fear what they may do."

"You expect they'll attack this settlement?"

"Wherever they think they may find me."

Echeret shifts his weight, nodding in slow thought. It's just the sort of thing a prisoner might say. *You'd better set me free, or my powerful friends will come knocking.* It's certainly possible that more creatures like her could come, searching for their kidnapped spy. But will they really? For one individual? And if they come, the king's men ought to be more than able to fend them off. Or so one might expect. This single prisoner may've been a troublesome catch. But if her comrades come sneaking again, the men of Rand will be ready.

"It's kind of you to warn us," he tells the prisoner. "I'll be sure to advise our king."

"They will come quickly," she says, pale eyes gleaming in the lantern's yellow light. And there's an underlying note in her words that catches Echeret's ear. A tone beyond the certainty she carries. Something genuine—like the concern in a worried mother's admonition. As if this creature actually *cares*. But why would that ever be the case?

Echeret blinks away the thought. Nonsense. "Our king has asked that I keep you alive. I'll do so, but I couldn't leave you locked in a tiny cage. You can roam this barn," he says. Reaching for his lantern, he rises to his feet. The little prisoner makes him feel like some massive, towering giant. Walking backward, he stops with his hands to the door latch, carefully removing his temporary lock and wondering curiously why the creature makes no attempt to come at him, no attempt to make for the door. If she's truly as strong as the king described, the effort would be easy. But she simply stands motionless, watching him. He turns and slips out the door without another word, locking it swiftly behind him.

15

The setting sun combines with the dying hues of the western sky to create a vibrant blend of color over the hills where he stands. After days of silence, it was here that Father's heartbeat sounded again at last. Here on the hills east of the heart of Emér. But now that Tolaiyë stands among them, the hills are empty, accompanied by only the mild gusting of the evening wind through the grasses.

"I don't understand. He was here. *Seconds* ago," he whispers into the fading light. How can this be?

The Palarian comes drifting before him now, tipping slightly in the air. "Shadows. Between the realms, there are shadows," it murmurs.

"Between the realms? A place?" Tolaiyë looks to his guardian.

"A space that exists in Claya, which is neither the mortal realm nor the realm of spirits," the Palarian explains, pivoting in place. "You have searched the mortal realm for a sound. But it may be only an echo from a place unseen."

A place between the spheres. The thought tips Tolaiyë's mind on end. He's only just begun to learn of the spirit realm, where the unembodied souls of the children of Claya live on, roaming as they please, awaiting the end of days. It exists alongside the mortal plain, lying like an undetected blanket of mist over the earth, constantly interwoven. In places, the barrier between the realms can be thin. But in his experiences crossing that border, Tolaiyë's never seen a gap. And besides . . .

"If there were such a space, how could my father possibly find it? He's only a mortal man," Tolaiyë questions.

"The man Kehljen alone could not. But there are those who once walked these lands who have since gone to shadow. Those who know the way," the guardian answers.

Dark spirits? A subtle sharpness slips into Tolaiyë's heart. What would such spirits want with Father? "Can you show me how to find it, this place between the realms?"

"This servant has yet to enter that place. Even so, it will do what it can to aid you."

Chasing an echo. It sounds impossible. But it's worth trying. Somewhere between the realms, Father's waiting.

16

The men are boisterous—laughing and shoving one another as the chief of the village guardsmen comes stepping quietly to Talek's side. The man carries an odd look in his eyes, never staring in one direction for long.

"Good king, you're certain you don't need my remaining guards to assist you?" he asks.

"Of course not, my brother. Let your guards rest. My men and I will watch over the village tonight," Talek assures him, bringing a firm hand to his back.

The man nods stiffly, fidgeting with the key in his hand, turning it over and over. "Right then, right. Very good," he mumbles with a nod, then holds out the key for Talek to take. "It's the key to the guardhouse, where the lanterns and oil are kept." His stare becomes suddenly solid. "Keep your knives at hand," he whispers. Then he turns and walks suddenly away before Talek can think to react.

They've an odd choice in guardsmen here in Leln.

Hardly one week has passed since the report of "hauntings" throughout the villages was first brought to

Talek's ears. And already the men he sent to comfort the people have sent back their own complaints. Strange sights, they say; havoc and mischief in the night, they say. Some even claim to have lost one of their men. One short week, and Talek already finds himself coming in person to keep the night watch at Leln, a village just about a day's journey from the capital. He and five of his soldiers. Since when did the people of Rand become so uneasy, so quick to tell and believe odd tales?

The strong wind of the afternoon falls away as evening moves in, leaving serene silence in its wake. Perfect. The men shuffle to gather their lamps and oil, then gather around a crude village map to choose their posts.

"A simple assignment for you this time, my brothers. First and foremost we light the street lamp at each post," Talek reminds them. "Then you each patrol your station until we swap. The people of Leln must be at ease tonight." He follows them out of the guardhouse, then heads to the southwest post with a lantern tied sloppily to the back of his belt. Overhead, the stars are only beginning to peer out from their places in the darkening sky. Faint but brightening.

The southwest post is situated toward the far end of the southernmost lane, where a baker apparently stacks wood and barrels of supplies against the back of his shop. Talek lights the lantern that's mounted there, then settles down onto a barrel beside it. Scarcely an hour crawls by before he's pacing along the lane, cursing his forgetfulness. If only he had thought to bring along the written monthly reports from the seven settlements. As dull as they often are, reading them would at least pass the time. And the longer he waits, the more Talek searches his mind for *anything* to make the night move along. And the more he marvels. How do the night guards manage such dull assignments night after night? The empty village lane couldn't be more uneventful.

Until it isn't empty anymore.

He spots it as he's turning at the far end of the lane, about to come pacing back toward the east—a fleeting, swift figure that only appears for an instant at the edge of his vision. But by the time he's turned entirely around, the figure's gone. Only a toppled barrel lid remains, knocked from its place and wobbling on the ground near the center of the path. It spins and bobs for half a breath longer before coming to a stop, flat on the dirt. Motionless. Then the entire lane returns to a still, soundless space, lit in part by the lamp's quivering glow. Talek steps calmly to the place where the lid fell, looking up and down the narrow alleys between the little shops and cottages. No one. He shrugs. It was probably just some rodent.

But then, there's no harm in being certain, he muses. He lights his lantern and sets off on a lap around each of the surrounding buildings, peering carefully in every alley, every shadowed corner. Nothing. Of course. But he's only just returned to the lamp behind the baker's shop when a loud tumbling comes echoing down the lane. A stiff, hollow sound, like wooden crates tumbling over themselves. Talek pauses, listening. But only silence follows.

Fine then, he supposes. It's about time to make the rounds anyway. Might as well check in with each post. He rolls his shoulders to loosen up as he sets off toward the east.

The southeast post is lit but not occupied when he reaches it. He takes a moment to glance around the nearby corners, expecting to find his soldier pacing the area or relieving himself in an alley. But there's no one. He curses. *Boys* they give him. Nothing but boys for soldiers these days. He's halfway to the next post when he nearly collides into Kaif, who comes backing up from around a corner. The young soldier startles like a frightened animal, then spins around, dagger drawn.

"Oh, it's you, good king!" he whispers hoarsely, eyes wide as river stones.

"Something amiss, soldier? Why's there no one at the southeast post?" Talek questions, eyeing the dagger held in the air between them.

Kaif takes a moment to gather his breath. He lowers his weapon and glances around the corner before looking back to the king, forcing a weak smile. "Eyes must've fooled me," he breathes. "Nothing amiss, good sir." His words are still falling from his teeth when they're drowned out by the sound of stacked firewood toppling over into the lane, only a few paces away.

Talek rushes to the spot, yanking his blade from his belt. But there's no sound, no movement, no sign of anyone at all where the firewood lies strewn. What in . . .

He looks back down the lane.

"Kaif—"

Yet the soldier no longer stands where he was. He isn't standing at all when Talek rushes back to find him around the next corner. The poor man lies collapsed on the ground, gasping. Talek kneels beside him.

"Were you attacked? Which way did they run?"

Kaif shakes his head, wheezing terribly. "I-I didn't see," he stammers.

Talek takes his arm, thinking to pull him to his feet. But the man hangs limply beneath his grip, lacking the strength to lift himself at all.

"Great gods, brother, what happened?" the king exclaims. He searches Kaif's chest and back for wounds, finding nothing. And the sight of the captain's fallen army flashes vividly over his mind. No wounds, no blood. A cold rush washes over his spine, though he fights to shake it off. Kaif can't be left lying here. Talek sheathes his blade and reties his lantern to his belt before lifting the soldier from under the shoulders as well as he's able, dragging him straight west. The guardhouse is unlit when they reach it. He helps Kaif flop like a dead man onto the bench there, lighting the lamp beside the door as he slips back out into the night, feeling stiff. The northwest post is nearest. He heads for it with a hasty stride, meeting Dolan as the light of the lamp there comes just into view.

"Was just coming to find you, sir. There's something in the village tonight." The soldier glances around as he whispers, a stern straightness in his voice.

"Have you spotted anything?" Talek asks.

"Not yet—it's too fast, whatever it is. Heard Forn say he captured something, not long ago. But now I can't seem to find him."

"Which post did he take?"

"North central." Dolan points to his left.

Talek slaps a hand to the man's shoulder. "I'll head there now. Kaif was struck down near the southeast post, nearly dead. See if you can gather the others and meet at the guardhouse. We need to organize ourselves."

Dolan nods, then vanishes down the lane. Talek rounds a corner, heading east, stepping swiftly. The alleys and cross lanes grow narrower as he moves toward the village center. And though he watches for movement in the shadows there, the only sound seems to come from above. A soft, pattering echo that follows along the rooftops, almost too silent to hear over the grind of his own shoes on the dirt. A sound that vanishes altogether when he stops to listen. Just an echo, he tells himself. Though he can't help raising his lantern on occasion as he continues on, squinting up the slow slant of the cabin roofs.

The north-central post is occupied by only Forn's canteen, which lies discarded on the ground beside his unsheathed dagger. Talek steps in a circle, glancing down every connecting lane, searching for any sign of the man. Until he hears an abrupt, solid thump at his back. Forn's lying motionless on the alley floor when Talek turns to see him. And the tiny figure that stands in the faint light beyond momentarily freezes his heart in place. A creature no larger than a child, with dark fur and a coarse shawl over its shoulders—and eyes as bright and large as the twin moons above. Something he's spotted once before, the night they captured the creature in the woods. The little figure stands unmoving at first, staring. But now it raises its thin arm to point two fingers directly at him.

"You took her."

The creature can speak. But there's no time to marvel before it comes leaping at Talek without warning, clearing Forn's body in a single vault. It clings to his arm as he reaches for his blade, and immediately the entire limb falls limp at his side, all muscles aflame. A slender hand claps to his chest before he can react, and suddenly his heart and lungs are fleetingly stopped in their places, ablaze with a sharp aching unlike any he's ever known. He stumbles backward, choking horribly, barely managing to throw the beast from his chest with his remaining good arm. Then he's running, shuffling—moving back along the nearest westward lane and rounding corners as quickly as his heaving heart will allow. The air seems to scream through his aching lungs as he pushes onward. And the way is agonizingly long. Just a little farther . . . just get behind a closed door . . .

It's a pure miracle that he reaches the guardhouse at all. He's scarcely let himself fall to the floor beside the bench when Dolan and the remaining two soldiers come bursting in behind him, hastily closing the door at their backs and throwing the lock into place, gasping. The lamp beside the door swings with the sudden commotion, casting dancing shapes and shadows on the walls and ceiling.

"What *are* they?" someone breathes.

Talek struggles to sit up in his place. "Parafa—beasts. From the woods," he rasps.

The men turn to see him and all at once erupt with noise.

"What—good king! Were you attacked?"

"Those devilish—"

"And Kaif!"

"Help the king sit up!"

They gather at Talek's sides, hoisting him up against the wall, bringing a canteen. He takes a gulp and coughs into his good arm in an attempt to clear the terrible sharpness that's formed in his throat.

"The parafa . . . don't fear them, my brothers. I encountered them in the woods west of here. We can defend against them," he pants. "For now, speak of this to no one. We'll need to be careful not to frighten the people."

* * *

Morning arrives as the remaining able men make one last round through the village lanes, weapons drawn. The bodies of the fallen soldiers are gathered into a wagon and covered discreetly beneath a tarp, laid like rolled blankets between boxes of supplies.

How dare they! How dare those wild beasts take the lives of two good soldiers! How dare they humiliate the king with their games, their pretend predator tactics—forcing him to pay off the chief night guard at Leln to tell no one of the casualties they caused, pushing the king and his men to leave the village under the cover of hoods. Wretched beasts, wild animals!

There were rumors when the people of Rand first came into the lands of North Emér. Whispers of creatures lurking in the woods. Strange animals that walked upright and wore simple clothes. Some said the families who settled to the west made friends with the parafa. But Talek never believed the old superstitions. And no one's spoken of them for years.

You took her.

The words the little figure spoke have sounded endlessly through Talek's mind from the moment he heard them. Curse those beasts—they can speak! And they seem to seek after the spy they've lost. Pitiful. They may be more intelligent than expected, but now that they've revealed themselves, they'll soon regret meddling with the men of Rand. The captain and his soldiers must be avenged. It's certain now. Their deaths were the doing of the parafa. Servants of the devils.

That night, the fastest courier available is sent from Kotán, a settlement to the northeast where the king often retires to his private cabin. Sent with a message for the first officer, urging him to come to Kotán to meet with the king at the next opportunity—and to bring the captive.

17

She stands waiting at the edge of the sea as he comes to meet her, the trailing ends of her robes gusting softly in the winds that drive the waters against the shore.

"You wanted to show me something?" he asks as he steps across the sands.

Éliva nods. "Come. Come and see." She holds out her gleaming hand. She leads him into the wind, stepping over hills and rivers, plains and forests. The world rushes by like flowing water beneath their feet. And when it stops, they stand in a grove lit only by the mild glow of the twin moons above. Éliva steps soundlessly through the trees, then kneels beside a child who sleeps in a simple hammock strung between the branches. A voránjevin child.

"Listen with me, brother. Listen to this child's heart," Éliva whispers.

Tolaiyë looks to the voránjevin's sleeping face, focusing on the soft features there until the chorus of heartbeats ringing in his ears can be pushed gently behind, and the child's heart before him resonates more clearly than any other. And he listens. At first, it follows the same rhythmic melody as so many other voránjevin souls. A song like the summer rains, wild and free. Untamed. But in time, another tone can be heard. A familiar chime that Tolaiyë's learned to recognize elsewhere—in the hearts of human beings. But how . . . ?

"Can you feel it? Though their bodies are different, the arai and the voránjevin people are born of the same light. Siblings, in the light of Claya," Éliva tells him softly, looking up into his eyes. "They were once one race."

"One race?" Tolaiyë marvels silently. "But how?"

"A sasarian who came before us created the forms of the voránjevin people long ago, in order to save them from dangers their human bodies couldn't endure. But this truth is no longer remembered in Claya," she explains.

"Few would accept such a truth."

Éliva takes Tolaiyë's hand. "This is something I hope to change," she says. "The people of Rand stand at the edge of grievous battle with the clan of the Iftav. But we can help them both see that they aren't as different from one another as they suppose. They're one family." She presses his hand gently to the child's fur-covered head. "Feel the energy coursing through this young one. In voránjevin bodies, their energy pulses more strongly at certain points throughout the body, like eddies in a stream. They learned long ago to move their strength at will. They also learned to change their physical shape by channeling energy through these points. The sasarianë were the first bearers of the power that makes this possible. But it was given to the voránjevin people as a gift."

Tolaiyë closes his eyes, tracing the flow of power through the child's frame. It winds like a river through the muscle and tendons, flooding around the lungs as they rise and fall, surging through the heart. It seems to spike at the points Éliva describes, creating little swells of energy at the base of the skull, between the shoulder blades, the lower back, and left side. Like little gates in the river's stream. And in the chest, above the heart, another spot stirs. But it's isolated, apart from the powerful flow that connects the other points. Dormant.

"There's a place the strength isn't flowing to," he murmurs, looking to Éliva.

She nods. "The voránjevin people have mastered two transformations, aside from their original shape. But there's one other. One they have yet to discover that will open their eyes to their true origin. Brother, will you help me unlock it?" she asks, and a marvelous shimmer lights the pale, blended shades in her eyes. All around, the leaves seem to echo her excitement, throwing back the golden glow of her countenance.

Tolaiyë looks to the sleeping child, then back to his fellow sasarian. "How?" he wonders aloud.

"We can direct the energy for them. Let this young one stand in place of all voránjevin on Claya's face. We'll bestow this gift to them all. You must only strive to focus on the sound of their hearts. Follow my lead," Éliva tells him.

She touches two fingers to the dormant place above the young voránjevin's heart. Tolaiyë does the same. Within moments, a soft swelling of energy begins to pool beneath Éliva's fingertips, churning in little circles. Tolaiyë senses the flow if it, then sends his own strength to aid it. The power rises steadily, expanding until it overflows and spills into the current that already courses through the child's frame, becoming another curve in the endless river.

Éliva rises to her feet, not taking her gaze from the sleeping voránjevin. "It's my hope that this gift will give rise to a new day among the clans. A day wherein arai and voránjevin can see one another as brothers and sisters."

The hope in her words is as tangible as the dew that's beginning to gather in the near-morning air. But it should last much longer.

18

It's a subtle sensation. Scarcely present enough to slip into Faleth's dreamless sleep and gently tug his mind to waking. When he opens his eyes, it's risen to a warm stirring over his heart. A soft surge, as if someone has just sent a mild pulse of energy coursing through his chest. But there's no one beside him. In the shadows several paces away, those who travel with him lie tucked in their simple shawls and sashes, motionless in sleep.

It may have been nothing more than a vivid dream. But even now, as he sits up to peer through the canopy above, the swelling warmth persists like a young flame in his chest. Something real. And it somehow shifts the entire feeling of his bones—a light, agile sensation unlike any he's known.

Something's changed.

19

A slight chill hangs in the morning air as they come to the barn door with their hands tucked in warm pockets and a cautious lightness to their steps. Few townspeople are ever out at this hour, when the night guards are ending their long shifts. But there's no harm in vigilance.

Echeret's careful to unlock the barn without rattling the latch, holding the door open only long enough for himself and the woman beside him to slip soundlessly inside. Unseen. Within the barn, the morning's rays have only just begun to fall in through high windows, illuminating faint rectangular patches of dust on the earthen floor. Only a narrow sliver of light rests on the captive creature where she lies, curled in her dark shawl atop one of the larger crates. Still.

"*Tawenin*, little friend, this is your chance," Echeret whispers, stepping softly forward.

But the prisoner gives no response.

"Asleep?" Defehl whispers at his shoulder.

He gives her a shrug. "Not sure."

They pause within arm's reach of the creature's loosely tucked arms. Near enough to see her chest rise and fall with each breath. She's still alive, at least.

Defehl kneels down, watching closely. "She's so tiny. This is the face of the parafa? The ones our king calls *demons*?" A mild smirk appears at her lips as she eyes the prisoner—a smile that's captivated Echeret since long before he married her.

"They say she fought off several men with ease before they caught her. Another like her brought several men to the ground before fleeing," Echeret tells her. "But I've had enough time to reason through it all. And I don't think these creatures are the wild animals Talek supposes them to be."

"You certain we should set this one free? How will you explain it?"

Echeret nods. "I can feel it—keeping her captive will only bring us trouble," he says. "I'll think of some story for the king."

Talek's always given Echeret his unrestrained trust. And with good reason. The first officer has only ever intended the best for his king. And he's never disregarded an order. But this time, something isn't right. There's so little known of the parafa, and Echeret can't seem to dispel the sour sinking that's flooded his heart ever since the captive spoke to him.

Your people are in danger.

"She might be ill. You sure we should leave her at the edge of the woods?" Defehl brings a gentle hand to the sleeping creature's arm, watching closely for any reaction.

"I'm sure her tribe will find her." Echeret kneels down, hoping to scoop the prisoner up in his arms.

But a sudden echo from outside the barn walls freezes him in place. The thin squeal of a wagon's wheels. And men's voices. The soldiers who were ordered to meet him here to transport the captive.

Defehl glances toward the door where the men have paused, chatting idly to one another. "They've come early," she whispers.

Echeret curses under his breath and scrambles to create a plan. "They're waiting to meet us. I could try to distract the—"

A knock at the door interrupts him.

"Officer, sir, that you? We've readied the supplies," a man calls in through the wall.

Echeret looks to Defehl, who reaches to open the captive's cage.

"We'll find another chance," she breathes.

Echeret nods, tight jawed. Of all the times for Rand's men to be diligent . . .

The prisoner shows no sign of waking as they lift her from the crate and lay her gently in the cage. Do they always sleep so deeply? It's nearly a day and a half journey to Kotán, Echeret reminds himself as they toss a tarp over the cage and heft it together to the door. They'll have plenty of time for the prisoner's "accidental" escape. Or to plan for one, at the very least. It *must* happen, or Echeret will never forgive himself for ignoring the terrible premonition in his heart. With luck, the captive can be free before her friends arrive.

20

They don't always roast their catches. Most often fresh meat is prepared with salts and herbs that enable it to remain edible much longer than it otherwise would be. But on occasion, when the hunt is bountiful, he's made it his own custom to roast a bit of meat over fire. The flame and smoke have a way of weaving such savory flavors into things. But he's never enjoyed it without her. It's a thirsty, empty sort of feeling to eat roasted meat without her.

"Faleth! News from the scouts to the west!" A virit messenger lands with a puff of air at the edge of the clearing, folding his wings in a quick, fluid motion as he comes walking toward the fire. It's a fairly expert landing for someone who learned to fly only several months ago.

"Four scouts were sent west, correct?" Faleth replies as he gives his meal a careful turn over the fire. "What news?"

"Yes. It was requested that two of them begin their transformation into virit. Taln and Hyln. But this morning they've triggered a different change." The messenger comes to a stop just beyond the warmth of the flames, silvery eyes catching the orange glow.

"A different change?"

"They wanted to try the new placement—the new shifting point that many have begun to discover. We tried to dissuade them, but you know how those boys are."

Faleth smiles softly to himself. Ordinarily, he might be irritated to find that the clan will be lacking two virit messengers in the coming months. But scarcely a day has passed since the strangely sudden appearance of a new energy-shifting point above the heart woke him in the night. Woke *many*. Some say it's a gift from the gods themselves. And the event's sparked an almost unbearable curiosity among the clans.

"I see. Keep a close eye on them as their transformations begin. Give them any amount of shared strength they may need along the way. We've got no idea what needs may arise as they enter this new change. And let me know what you see," Faleth tells the messenger. "Someone must be brave enough to test the new transformation. It might as well be Taln and Hyln."

"We'll be sure to keep you informed," the virit assures him with a slight bow of the head before turning toward the northwest, wings spreading.

Faleth watches as he rises with a few quick steps and a leap into the wind. Wondering. A new form? The clans of the voránjevin people have been changing forms as long as memory can tell, using the key energy points throughout the body. But there's only ever been two forms, aside from the original voránjevin shape: the winged *virit* and the *virkepa*, a finned, aquatic transformation used mostly by clans who dwell along the shores of Emér and the great Atayu Sea. The three voránjevin forms have allowed the clans to master the skies, the lands, and the seas. What new form could possibly remain to be discovered?

No one can guess. But now the answer's on its way.

21

Echeret enters to find the king sitting beside the window with his gaze on the western skies. It's the view he's always seemed to favor—especially in the evenings, when all the colors of the sky grow weary and begin to slump together along the horizon, like mingled drippings from a painter's creation.

"You brought the beast?" Talek speaks to his first officer without leaving his seat.

"Yes, sir."

"Very good. We'll keep it in the storehouse at the eastern edge of the village for now." He taps his fingers idly against the tabletop as Echeret settles into the seat opposite him.

"What news from Leln?" Echeret asks, suddenly aware of the dark shades beneath Talek's faintly red-stained eyes. "Were you and the men not planning to carry on and aid the night guards at several other settlements?"

"Something strange is stirring, my brother. Something we've never fought before." The king takes a slow breath and brings his arms together on the table before him, leaning forward.

"Not rebels from the western settlements?"

Talek shakes his head, slowly running his hands through his frayed hair and down the back of his neck. His first officer's seen it before—the heavy shoulders, the sleepless stare, the hands that seem strangely pale and vein streaked—all as though the king hasn't slept in days.

"Not this time," Talek says.

Echeret watches him in silence, then turns in his chair to face him directly. "Good brother, what happened in Leln?" he asks.

Talek meets his gaze, glancing momentarily to the cabin door. "The parafa," he says, "like the one we captured."

"More of them?"

"They killed two men and injured two others before I was even able to spot one of them."

"Killed! Who?" Echeret's heart nearly drops to the floor between his feet. In all his days in North Emér, never has any man lost his life while keeping the night watch.

"Forn and Hauden. Good soldiers lost for no good reason." The king shakes his head.

"And now? Do any guardsmen remain there?"

"I told the captain of the guardsmen to armor his men, and to have them patrol in pairs. I've sent the same word to the other settlements. We need a plan to rid ourselves of this new pest," Talek murmurs, then looks up at Echeret. "Those demons were looking for the one we took, you know."

They will come for me.

The prisoner's words echo in a cold ripple through Echeret's mind.

"How do you know?" he questions.

"One of them recognized me, told me so. Then it came at me like a raving animal. Three days—*three days*—and I'm only *beginning* to feel my strength return. Somehow the devils draw the very life from our bones," the king tells him, pulling his shawl more tightly across his hunched shoulders. "They're a greater danger to our people than I anticipated."

"If they're searching for the one they lost, why not return her to them? They may let us be if we do," Echeret suggests, testing.

But the king nearly chokes. "Let it go?" he laughs a breathy, restless laugh. "We need to understand these creatures. We need to know their weaknesses, their tendencies. The people are afraid, my brother. We need to calm their fears. I need you to study the creature we have. Keep it alive, but find its weaknesses. And tell me everything you find." He stands, leaning over the table for support. "In the meantime, we'll assure the people that there's nothing to fear. Tell them we've managed to capture one of the beasts and learn its weakness. Tell them we've easily slain it."

Echeret nods, attempting to swallow the bitter sensation that's begun to swell in his throat. "I'll have the announcement sent out today," he affirms. And he rises to his feet.

Talek lays a heavy hand to Echeret's shoulder. "How could I ever manage without you, my friend? You have my thanks. We'll guide the people through these times together."

The king's words have an unpleasant taste in Echeret's mouth as he repeats them to the men who wait beside the wagon outside, instructing one to contact the next available message carrier in the village. And he takes a slow breath. The prisoner's warning seemed idle when he first heard it. But now her words are proving to be more accurate than he ever expected. Unfortunately accurate. Now two more men have lost their lives. How many more will join them while the creatures come searching for the one that was taken? Even after traveling all the way to Kotán, the captive has yet to wake from her oddly deep slumber. And the constant company of assigned guards has made her release impossible to accomplish. Whether she wakes again or not, she must be let go—in some way that the king could only believe to be an accident.

Echeret directs the men to begin toward the storehouse at the eastern edge of the village, bending to heave the tarp-draped wagon himself. He's only begun to feel the broad wheels turn against the dirt when a discoloration in the trees to the east catches his eye. A shadow floating just beyond the shade of the leaves at the edge of the village. A *face*, with massive eyes and ears that hang down toward the jawline. It's one of them. Watching. A wild stiffening shoots suddenly along Echeret's every nerve. He scrambles for his blade, wondering how many of them have come, how long he and the men can hold up. But the trees are empty when he looks again. And no sign of the spying creature remains.

22

"My father says I must select someone to serve as my first officer."

"Already? I thought he wasn't planning to have you replace him for another two years."

They were fishing along the bank of the river Held, where it pours into the lake and the waters grow deep and clouded.

"I suppose he wants me well prepared," Talek answered with a shrug, swinging his line farther out into the current. The largest fish always seemed to hide there, where the riverbed slumped away at a sudden, sharp incline. "Though I'd rather not dwell on it till I have to."

Echeret fingered a roll of fine twine, snipping off just enough to fashion a simple attachment for his angling hook. The old rod he always used lost its hook clasp just days before.

"Not looking forward to it?" he asked through a sideways smile. "I'm sure you'll make a fine king."

Talek sighed. "I'm sure I will too. Just not so fine as my father."

Echeret made a thoughtful frown as he cast his own line into the current. "The way I see it," he said, "the world's full of all kinds of people. Full of all kinds of kings too. And a good king can come in any shape. The Mighty Rand has his shape. But you'll have your own." He sat up from his lazy recline. "It's like my mother always says: 'beauty's defined by more than one flower in the field.' "

Talek didn't take his eyes from the river. But a slender smirk appeared at the edge of his mouth. "Echeret the Wise," he chimed, and he settled himself down to a comfortable seat in the grass. "You do know you're coming with me on this adventure, don't you?"

Echeret turned to his friend, wondering how to look serious. "Talek, you don't mean—"

"You're the only one for the job, my brother. How could I trust in anyone else?" Talek interrupted with a wave of his hand, and Echeret could only laugh at his plight.

"All right, all right, I'll do it. At least as first officer I'd be in a good place to step in and knock you back into your right mind if you ever decide to become a tyrant."

"Very good. It's settled then." Talek gave a content nod. "And so the downfall of our young nation is underway. And now I won't have to watch it alone."

Echeret laughed again. This time genuinely. Talek was always so convinced that a good king must outperform his predecessor. And as anyone would agree, the deeds of the Mighty Rand simply could not be outdone.

"Oh come on—I bet we can keep things from falling into total chaos for at least a *few* years, wouldn't you say?"

They stayed beside the river for the greater part of the morning that day—as they often did during the midsummer months. Catching fish for their lunch, laughing idly about the latest word around the settlements. It was an entirely ordinary, uneventful summer day, thirteen years ago. But a day that's always remained oddly clear in Echeret's mind.

23

Beasts, they say. Wild beasts that they've learned to slay, they say. The rumor floats and catches like fire in the leaves, the forests, the hills—burning in the ears and hearts of every Iftav who hears it.

Demon arai, foul arai! They say they've discovered the weakness of the beasts, say they've managed to kill them. But in all the clans there's only one voránjevin unaccounted for. One who was unexpectedly stolen away. One who's long been known in her clan for her kind and gentle heart. One who remains unfound despite weeks of scouring the reeking arai villages, who was always most dear to the heart of the amber-eyed leader of the Iftav. And word of her death lights a fiery rage in his soul unlike any the land has known.

All throughout the forests of North Emér the Iftav come gathering. They come creeping with vengeance in their bones, with hot hunger in their blood.

Cursed, disgusting arai! They've toyed in these lands long enough. Now they'll find their rightful place. Now they'll know who to fear.

24

The soft light that glows from the heart of the earth is faint here, casting gentle hues against the uneven shadows. Here the voices of the world waver in and out of earshot, ringing subtly in hidden corners all around. It's taken days to find this place. A place where the realm of spirits meets that of the living. Tolaiÿe walks through the subtle tides of light and shadow there, stepping over the barrier between the realms, hoping to find the gap. He must be so close to the space the Palarian once mentioned—the space between the realms. It *must* be here. But even so, searching for it feels like pushing against an invisible film. Confusing, exhausting. If such a gap exists, how can he possibly enter it?

When he tires of searching and returns at last to an open plain in the living world, Éliva stands waiting.

"You search for something neither of us has ever seen. Few have seen it," she says.

"Forgive me. The world needs our attention. I shouldn't spend so much effort searching for my own father," Tolaiyë tells her. "When the sound of his heart echoes out from between the realms, I can't seem to turn away. I'm getting closer."

Éliva steps soundlessly to his side. "Finding your father would do more for Claya than you know. I didn't realize it until now," she says, turning to gaze out at the rising dawn. "When I was still very young, I once met a strange spirit in the woods. I thought he was just a man. But now, I think I know who he was. Who he *is*." She looks back to Tolaiyë now, brilliant eyes taking on an almost golden hue in the rising light. "He was one of us, long ago. One of the very first of our kind. He was stripped of his physical form after bringing great evil into the world, and he can never return to the gods in the heavens. But he roams the face of Claya, full of malice. A wandering spirit."

"A sasarian?" Tolaiyë wonders at the thought. Is it possible that a sasarian could turn against the promises made in the beginning? Turn against his call?

"He was. Though he brought shame to our name," Éliva sighs.

The Palarian comes drifting between them. "This is truth," it whispers. "There was one who turned against all, who sought to use his gifts for evil. He has coveted the living bodies of men ever since."

The Palarian's words set Tolaiyë's mind turning. He closes his eyes, remembering. Each time the rhythm of Father's heart sounds, it seems to appear in a dramatically different location in Claya. As if Father had somehow gained the ability to travel as a sasarian would. But how could he possibly do so, in his mortal state? The Palarian once mentioned that dark spirits may know the way between realms—the way to slip into the gap between them. But what would such spirits want with Father? It seemed like an impossible puzzle. Until now.

"Even as a disembodied spirit, a sasarian may still be able to move freely among the realms," he ponders aloud. "Is it possible that this fallen sasarian has found my father? The Palarian says he's always coveted living, physical forms. If he manages to take my father's body . . ."

Éliva nods. "He may be hoping to return to the physical world. The easiest target would be an individual full of darkness and malice. Anger is a blinding curtain that allows dark spirits to creep in where they shouldn't. Your father has no malice. But the fallen sasarian may have another reason for seeking after him," she whispers.

"The man Kehljen walks nearer to the spirit realm than most. It is his gift," the Palarian explains, and Éliva takes Tolaiyë's hand.

"Come! I have an idea. And searching together may take us further."

* * *

When searching alone for the gap between the realms, Tolaiyë's always begun by descending deep into the heart of the earth, where the two realms lie spread like colliding pools of oil and water overhead. Two plains with ever-shifting edges, playing in a continual dance against each other's borders. But Éliva takes a different path. Still firmly gripping his hand, she steps forward into the air. They leave the hill where they stood in the mortal world. The scene warps and slides rapidly all around them, churning wildly for an instant before reorganizing into the very same hill—no longer lit by the rising dawn but by the calm, white light of the realm of spirits.

Éliva pauses after a single step. "Now step backward with me," she says, "but very, very slowly."

Tolaiyë nods. They move together, each bringing one foot gradually behind them. The whiteness of the spirit world begins to sink away from their sight as the physical realm reappears at their backs, rippling and pulsing faintly like a half-remembered dream. But they don't continue toward it. Éliva pauses with her heel still raised, softly shifting her weight forward and back, watching the barriers of the two realms collide.

And then it appears. It's only a flicker at first. Impossibly fleeting. But it widens as they watch, becoming a solid stripe of blackness that whips and flashes occasionally into view, stirring between the blurred and swaying scenes of the spirit and physical realms. The gap.

"There!" Éliva breathes.

The two of them move toward the blackness without speaking. The effort is straining—like walking against gravity, like running under water. The darkness repels them. But they press against it. One . . . step . . . more . . . They press until some unseen barrier seems to give way, and all the surrounding sights fall abruptly away into infinite darkness. Then the two sasarianë find themselves standing entirely encircled with blackness— and silence unlike any they've ever known. Total silence. The voices of the wind and earth, the songs of all the living hearts in the world—none can be heard. The stillness comes like a sudden clap to their ears. *Stifling.*

Tolaiyë glances in all directions before looking back to Éliva, who he can still see plainly. "We've found it. The gap between the realms," he marvels.

Éliva stares back at him as the Farian drifts idly ahead in the darkness. "We shouldn't remain here too long. It seems like the voices of the world don't reach this place," she warns.

They step slowly through the darkness. Listening, feeling the blackness sift and roll like thin mist over their faces. For a time, there's only silence, only nothingness. And when Tolaiyë senses a presence at last, it's scarcely noticeable beyond the shadows. A faint whisper that's nearly masked by the sound of his own heartbeat. He walks toward it, uncertain he'll find anything at all. But there *is* something there. Or some*one*.

Now the presence slinks suddenly away as he steps toward it—a flutter of bitterness radiating soundlessly outward in its wake. The bitterness of an angry soul. Tolaiyë follows after the presence as it retreats. Éliva comes carefully closer from the left, maybe hoping to cut off its path. But whoever hides in the shadows seems to stumble away as quickly as the two sasarianë advance. Fleeing—until the Palarian comes floating to Tolaiyë's side, and a sudden burst of cold resentment comes billowing out from the blackness where the presence stands.

"Traitor!" A hoarse whisper pierces the silence of the scene. A man's voice that Tolaiyë's never heard. But another sound accompanies it, echoing for only a fleeting breath before being muffled abruptly away. A heartbeat he could never mistake.

He rushes toward the voice without hesitation, reaching to grasp whatever being it belongs to—to grasp *Father*, who seems somehow entangled in the shadows there—but his hand closes on empty mist. The presence is gone.

"Vanished," Éliva murmurs.

For a moment, Tolaiyë stands motionless in place. So close . . .

"That spirit has nowhere to hide now. It's only a matter of time before we catch him," he murmurs.

Éliva looks to her guardian. "We should return. Farian, can you help us find the exit from this forgotten place?" she asks, and the Farian's single eye seems to summersault in place.

"Come," it answers.

The mist near its slender body begins to twist and bend as the sasarianë come walking toward it. As if some invisible hand wrenches at the edges of the darkness there, pulling until the light beyond begins to peer sharply through the dimensions. A rift appears in the darkness that draws them in until the shadows close suddenly at their heels and expel them powerfully back into the physical, mortal world. They find themselves standing again upon the very hilltop they left behind only moments before.

But the hilltop feels different now. Something's gone wrong. Terribly wrong.

The sounds of the world come back to their ears in a loud, merciless wave. Colder, more relentless than usual. Saturated with the concentrated sorrow of countless human hearts—wailing, weeping, hopelessly broken hearts. Hearts crying out for the loss of life— mothers' and fathers' hearts breaking with the deaths of their children, children crying out for their families. Hearts blazing bright with courage and selfless zeal as they rise to defend the ones they love, only to be lost. So many lost! A terrible cry of despair drenches the wind and soaks the air, and Tolaiyë falls to his knees beneath the weight of it. Gasping. It resonates from a village in the eastern continent, in North Emér. An entire settlement among the people of Rand.

"What . . . what's happened?" Tolaiyë wheezes.

Éliva stands beside him, staring eastward with tears rolling like radiant crystals down her cheeks. "Many have wrongly died. Even now their sorrow still stains the earth. We . . . we couldn't hear their cries between the realms. We failed them." Her voice trembles.

"But . . . who's done this? The people of Rand have threatened the western villages. But this was no battle. These cries come from the people of Rand alone. From *families*."

No. This was no battle. This was a massacre.

Éliva answers in a whimper, not taking her gaze away from the east. "The Iftav."

25

He's far too asleep to stir when she comes. Too asleep to feel her hand at his shoulder; too asleep in dark, dreamless worlds to hear her whisper.

"Your Onei lives, Faleth. How could you do this? How could you bring such sorrow into the world? I told you she was safe—your Onei lives, Faleth!"

Her shimmering tears are a steady rain over him, spotting along his arm, his tightly clenched fist. But he's too asleep to notice. She closes her eyes, tries to slip into his dreams. But the heln's mind is closed against the world. Sealed. Tucked away where the sounds and sensations of the world can never reach. Hidden, like the cursed gap between the realms.

26

Echeret pauses near the outskirts of the village to tie a dark wrap snugly over his nose and mouth and pull a hood over his head. All around, the other men follow suit. The king stands several paces ahead, already hooded and staring wordlessly onward. They say the hoods and wraps will protect the king from being targeted, should the beasts still linger nearby. But Echeret can't help suspecting that it's all an attempt to ward off the thick scent of death in the air.

It was only yesterday morning when a girl collapsed at the steps of the guardhouse at Leln. They say her face was flushed from running all morning, tears and sweat smearing the dirt that painted her cheeks. She came all the way from Votyón. Alone. Came to beg the people to save her family, save her friends. They say she couldn't have been more than eleven or twelve years old.

Word of the attack reached Kotán by the afternoon. Men were gathered as quickly as possible. But even the few soldiers from Leln were too late. Far, far too late.

Few words are spoken now, as the king and his men come walking to the borders of Votyón a day later. They spread out into the village, moving with slow caution in their steps, looking in all directions. The bodies can be seen before they reach the first houses. They lie like silent statues here and there, blending with the stillness of the trees. Echeret kneels to look closely at the first remains he comes to. It's the body of an old man, lying on his stomach beside a well, with his gray-blue eyes gazing to the southeast. Empty. A younger woman sits slumped against a tree not far beyond. The knife she most likely wielded in her last moments lies in the tall grass between her and the child who lies motionless nearby. So still, so lifeless. The sight brings a suffocating tightness to Echeret's throat and a stiffness to his lungs. He keeps moving.

The door of the first cottage he comes to stands wide open, held in place by the fallen figures of a young husband and wife. They sit close together, sleeping faces nearly cheek-to-cheek, with their backs propped against the door. The man sits somewhat in front—as if he had hoped to stand between his wife and the oncoming threat. To no avail. A sheathed sénsin rod lies across the floor near his feet. It rocks subtly side to side now as a mild breeze finds a path through the open door. So young! They couldn't possibly have been married long. The marriage charms hang like frozen memories from their wrists—delicately crafted circlets full of flecks of colored stone.

Echeret pauses just beyond the threshold. Staring. The world seems to fall to silence, momentarily forgotten. He's seen death before. Seen children lost to illness, seen men and boys die much younger than they ought to in skirmishes with woodland thieves and the western settlers. But this is different. This is an entire village. A community of husbands and wives, mothers and fathers, sons and daughters. These were *families*. Death took these people from within the walls of their homes—came and swept them out of the middle of their morning routines. Harmless, peaceful people. How could this be? How could this possibly be?

Suddenly, the loss of life weighs down like ten thousand boulders on his chest, pulling him earthward, choking the breath at his lips. His hands quake as he leans back against the cold cabin wall, struggling to blink the wet blur from his eyes. There's too much silence here. Too much death. He needs to keep moving.

He shakes his head and sets off toward the center of the settlement, not allowing himself to stare too long at the bodies that lie along his path.

The king's standing alone beside the central watchtower when Echeret finds him. The body of a tall, thick-built man lies at the base of the tower, still partly girded with wooden armor. The ties that would have held it in place have been reduced to little more than torn shreds. Talek holds what must have been the man's knife in his hands.

"Not a single bloodied blade among all the dead I've seen," he murmurs without looking up. He runs his fingers over the flat sheen of the blade. "I can't find any wounds. No bruises, no cuts. It's all exactly as we found the captain and his men." He kneels to lay the knife across the fallen man's broad chest before turning to look to his first officer. "I have no doubt. This wasn't the doing of the western settlers, or any human beings at all."

The king's words carry Echeret's mind fleetingly back to the image of the prisoner—the way her wide eyes seemed to capture him in their bottomless stare.

They have little mercy for your people.

He brings his hands to his temples in a fruitless attempt to calm the sudden buzzing in his mind. Votyón's always been one of the most strongly guarded settlements. Aside from the capital, it's the last place anyone would expect to lose so quickly to an attack.

"Some of these men were armored. They must've been outnumbered. Overwhelmed," Echeret says. He pulls a pair of gloves from his belt. "These good people deserve honorable graves."

But the king isn't looking, isn't listening. Echeret looks up to find him staring off to the south, where the village lanes end and give way to a thick grove of trees. And there's an expression on his face that's difficult to name. Is it rage? Or dread?

What does he see?

"Good king? Have you spotted something?"

When Talek looks back to him at last, the color's gone from his face. "No, no, there's nothing, brother. Nothing. Just . . . thinking through it all," he mumbles.

The other men come gathering before Echeret can ask any further.

"My brothers, a great tragedy has come to us," the king calls out to them. "Before all else, let us aid the men of Leln and prepare decent graves for our kinsmen!"

The burials take time. They dig the graves in the meadow just east of the houses, marking each with the best stones and bricks they can find. Humble words are murmured over the freshly turned earth. Words of strangers, too shocked and unprepared to offer much comfort to anyone listening. But somehow necessary.

The night's coming on as they gather at last for the return journey. And as they turn their backs to the empty cottages, the life and bustle of Votyón slip quietly into memory.

27

"Why does Talek the king ignore our warnings? I know he can see us when we appear to him. But he pretends to see nothing." Tolaiyë settles down with his feet hanging over the cliff's edge, long robes and sashes draping over the stones and catching the wind like thin, glowing banners.

"He's done so for years. Even when I find him alone, he responds to me as if I were a daydream or hallucination. He always thinks he knows what's best for his people and won't take advice. But I've never stopped trying to warn and guide him when I have the chance. If we're patient, he might give us his attention in time. I've done the same for many leaders in Claya, when I've been able." Éliva sits beside him. The evening light always seems to bring out the brightest colors in her long curls.

"And what about the Iftav? Can we not stop them? Talek isn't able to protect his people from them."

"They have their free will," Éliva answers. "We can't force them into anything. But we can offer them a proposition. I know their leader. He may agree to leave the Sketzans in peace if we help them leave North Emér. And it may help if he knows they haven't harmed the one he loves.

"We can offer an escape for those whose freedom of choice has been compromised," she continues, "should they wish to take it. The people of Rand may be willing to settle elsewhere, although they're also free to reject that opportunity. Consider the voránjevin filíl that Talek's men have captured—she's already had many chances to free herself. But for some reason, she hasn't taken those opportunities." She turns to Tolaiyë now, voice lowering. "Brother, I fear that a greater danger than the Iftav lurks between the realms."

He looks back to her. "The spirit who's taken my father?"

"Yes. If he succeeds and inhabits a mortal body, he could bring great darkness into the world. We must find him and rid him of his ability to take the bodies of men."

"My father must have been struggling against that being all this time. There's no telling how much longer he can fight," Tolaiyë tells her. The thought sends a bitter ripple through his heart. All this time . . .

"He's strong to have resisted for so long," Éliva assures him. "There's still hope."

"The power is given you to free Kehljen." The Farian's mild whisper comes drifting to their ears. "But the one who holds him captive will have no rest. If you tear him from his target, he will immediately seek revenge upon those nearest you."

Tolaiyë looks over his shoulder to the guardian's glimmering eye. "Those nearest to us . . . But there must be some better way to find him, without putting anyone at risk," he says.

The Palarian provides the answer. It floats idly in the air just beyond his knee, entirely unfazed by the massive distance to the desert floor below. "There is a way," it confirms. "Each of you has your haven. A place in the mortal world wherein you can retreat for rest, where darkness cannot enter. These cliffs are your realm, Tolaiyë. Within its borders, the darkness cannot follow."

Éliva straightens her back. "The sea is my haven. But if yours is here . . ."

"I'll build a sanctuary here for the refugees of Ethein." Tolaiyë smiles to himself, imagining the faces of his people as they set eyes on the paradise atop the cliffs. "A place free of the soldiers of Rand, protected against the fallen spirit. But the way is long. I can only hope they'll agree to come."

"When those you wish to protect are within your realm, these servants will give you the name of the one in darkness." The Farian glides softy to Éliva's side as it speaks. "With his name you will speedily find him. All spirits turn toward the sound of their own name."

"I'll go now to tell my mother." Tolaiyë rises to his feet, about to step into the wind and vanish over the land. But a subtle presence catches his attention. He turns to spot a familiar red-bearded man sauntering toward them through the grass.

"What news do you bring, good friend?" he calls to the man.

Afai gives a simple nod. "I know you need to leave. But before you go, I need to tell you. I've seen something." He comes to a stop several paces away.

"Something to come?"

"Yes, though I'm not sure how long we have before it becomes reality."

"What did you see?" Éliva asks.

Afai looks down for a moment, thinking. "I saw a man among the people of Rand. One who walks near the king. He stood at the edge of a windswept plateau that overlooked a vast prairie, with all the families of his people gathered behind him," he says. "Watch for that man. I think there's a role he needs to fulfill."

Tolaiyë nods. "We'll watch for him. Your visions have never lied," he says.

"Not yet, at least!" Afai grins. "And one more thing. His common name. They call him 'Hidden.' "

28

The knock comes unexpectedly at the door of the village hall, loud and firm, at an evening hour when messengers rarely come knocking. The sound mildly startles Echeret where he sits sifting through letters from the chief guardsmen of the settlements. The king hardly seems to notice. He's sat at the table beside the fire for ages now, staring into the orange blaze and saying nothing at all.

"Who comes?" Echeret calls out.

The answer comes sounding back through the thick doors of the hall. "Messenger Veleht, with a return message for the king. I come with Paldein of the western families, chief elder of Hadón."

Veleht. The messenger sent to the west only seven days ago. Echeret glances to Talek, who looks up at last from his thoughts to give a silent nod. Echeret rises from his seat to heave the hall doors partly open. The square-jawed man who steps in behind the messenger wears a long shawl—garb commonly seen among the village leaders in the western settlements.

Veleht tips his head to the king. "Good king, in my journey westward I was directed to Paldein. He's insisted that he bring his message to you in person."

Talek turns in his chair to face his guests, eyeing them carefully. "Very well," he says, and he motions for them to speak.

Paldein steps forward. "Talek, son of Rand," he begins, "your messenger has told me of your troubles. I come to deliver a treaty in the stead of my fallen brothers, with the hope that we might end the grief between our lands.

"Long have the people of Rand sought to bring the western families into their rule. But we in the west have only ever defended what is our own. Death has come to your people. Our men had no part in this. They would never commit such murder. We don't know who your attacker is or where they hide. But you won't find them among the western settlements."

For a time, Talek only stares back to the older man in silence. Then he stands, extending his hand. "My good man, you've confirmed what I already suspected. The evil in Votyón was not the doing of any Sketzan, east or west. Neither did my soldiers take the lives of your messengers," he affirms, taking Paldein's broad hand in a firm grip. "You have my word. The men of Rand will no longer strive to take command of your lands. I'll write the order tonight for my soldiers to return Ontrágo into the hands of its people. We can no longer afford to waste our efforts battling our brothers to the west. May you return in peace."

The older man gives a gracious bow. "Many thanks, on behalf of all families of the western villages," he murmurs.

Talek looks to his messenger. "Veleht, please show our guest to a suitable shelter for the night. I should have the order ready by morning."

"Yes, good king!"

Echeret closes the broad hall doors behind the two men as they leave, wondering soundlessly to himself. Never before has the king so readily backed out of any significant plan—let alone his long-held desire to unite North Emér. Now, in only a handful of words, the entire westward conquest is suddenly undone. It's an oddly abrupt change for the king to make. But likely a good one. Well enough, Echeret tells himself. These days, the soldiers have greater troubles to occupy them.

The king's already settled back into his chair with his chin resting over interlaced fingers. A restless frown furrowing his face. "I knew it. It was the beasts. It was them all along," Talek mumbles to the tabletop. "The people are afraid. We only have one choice."

His first officer sits across from him, arms folded. "One choice?"

Talek's eyes flick up to meet Echeret's. "We must make our lands safe again. There's an enemy that must be driven from North Emér," he says.

"We still have so little knowledge of how to battle this enemy. We don't even know where they're coming from, how many of them are out there. But we know they reacted when we took one of their spies captive," Echeret reasons.

But the king sits up in his chair, letting his hands drop to the table. "Again with this—what, you want to release it? And when the deaths don't stop, what then, my brother? Don't you see? It was the parafa who slew the captain and his entire camp the morning we moved on Ontrágo. The beasts have slain us in secret, using the western families as their cover. They've been after us for much longer than we've known. Returning the captive would only deprive us of our only chance to study them closely," he refutes, reaching for the drink in front of him that's likely gone cold. "What have you learned from that creature?"

Echeret sighs. "So far not much more than you've already observed. She finally became conscious again this morning. Her kind call themselves 'voránjevin.' They eat meat and live in somewhat nomadic clans. They've stalked these lands for many generations, hunting and surviving using some sort of ability to steal strength from their prey. And at least some of them can speak our language," Echeret tells him. "They seem as vulnerable to weapons as we are—just more difficult to pin down in a fight."

"It spoke to you? What else has it told you?" The king's eyes grow briefly wider as he tips the drink to his lips.

"That our people are in danger as long as we keep her imprisoned."

"Of course. I should have known," Talek scoffs. "Don't be too quick to listen to that beast, my brother. And we can't let it hear anything it shouldn't. It may be best to avoid speaking with it at all. These parafa are full of crafting, scheming . . ."

"Talking with her may help us understand the enemy's motive—"

The king nearly breaks his clay cup as he brings it sharply down. "I will *not* speak to the beasts who've slain an entire camp—an entire *village*—of my people!" His voice rises to a startling volume, bouncing and rebounding off the thick log walls of the hall.

Echeret stares back at him, unsure how to react at all. Since when was the king so outward with his emotion? So uncontrolled?

Talek breathes, bringing his fist to his lips as he stares back to the fire. "I may be losing my mind," he almost whispers. "I've had visions. Seen shining figures, like angels. Telling me not to seek battle with the beasts. But I refuse to sit idly while my people are hunted. I must fight."

Visions?

Echeret watches him. Talek's eyes are sleepless, always shifting. They have a new gaze—one that's gradually replacing the once stern and fearless stare for which the king's come to be known. It's shaken him, all of it: the destruction of the captain's army, the attacks at Leln, the massacre at Votyón . . .

"Good king, the hour is late. You should rest. We can make plans in the morning," Echeret whispers.

Talek shakes his head. Slowly, wearily. "They called him 'Rand' because his rule would extend over the face of the world like the waves of the sea," he murmurs. "They called him 'Mighty.' But my father never faced such struggles as this. Such death."

Echeret leans forward in his seat, looking closely at his friend. "You and I both know that it's the greatest struggles that build the greatest kings," he says, and he rises to his feet. "Our people will make it through these times. Just promise me that you won't try to win this battle alone."

The king nods, letting a fatigued smile appear on his face—nearly returning his countenance to the Talek that Echeret's always known.

"Together," he says.

* * *

The captive is standing, staring calmly out the little window of her prison. Echeret closes the outer door behind himself as he enters the stone keep, and pulls an old crate from the corner for a chair. He settles down only an arm's length from the bars that run from the ceiling to the earthen floor of the keep, dividing it down the middle. This storage shed has served as a prison before—for the occasional thief or dissented soldier caught in the woods. Though never for long. The entire structure's hardly wide enough for four men to stand shoulder to shoulder.

The night chill is moving in. Echeret sets his lantern beside his foot, watching the way its light casts yellow swaths along the walls, chasing the darkness with stark contrast. The prisoner looks out at him through the bars, silent—half of her furred face darkened by the shadows.

"The night is deep." She speaks. An echoless sound.

Echeret leans forward to rest his arms on his knees, looking up at her. "Glad you haven't fallen unconscious again. Is it common for your kind? Sleeping for days?" It's a question he forgot to ask when she first awoke. And the answer could prove useful.

"We voránjevin depend greatly on each other for shared strength. It helps us overcome all illnesses," the captive replies.

"You've fallen ill, then?"

She shakes her head. "Only very weak," she says. "I sense there's been a shift in the flow of strength through my bones. Without the aid of the energy shared among my people, it must have drained me. I've never felt so feeble."

"The king insists on carrying the key to this prison himself. Or I'd open it for you now. But don't worry. Our chance will come again soon," he tells her, and he lets his forehead sink into his hands. "You were right, my little friend. The people of Rand are in danger. Something terrible's happened."

The creature steps closer, gripping the metal bars before her as she stares back. "Was . . . was it my clan? Did they harm your people?"

Echeret looks briefly down at the palms of his hands, swallowing the stiffness in his throat. It was days ago, but the heaviness of the carefully wrapped bodies still seems so fresh in his palms. And the weight of the shovel he used to bury so many of them. It's a cold, coarse heaviness in his hands that seems to pull at the life in his breath. "We had no time to react," he says. "An entire settlement. Gone. The old, the young—all of them slain."

Behind the bars, the prisoner's great tannish eyes become wider than Echeret would have thought possible. And they become suddenly cloaked in shimmering, silvery wetness. "*Efyth leu saha* . . . no . . . how could he do this?" she breathes, little hands beginning to tremble.

"You know who did this? Do you know why?" Echeret asks, quietly surprised by the emotion in the creature's face. Real emotion, real *pain*. But why would she care if the Sketzans suffer loss?

"No other clan among my people would do this. Not ever. It was the Iftav," she whispers, shaking her head. "My clan has counted the misdeeds of the Sketzans for many years, though I've tried to persuade them otherwise. But to slay so many . . ." She breathes deeply. "Maybe he thinks I'm dead. It's been too long since I was captured."

"He?" Echeret questions.

"The one who leads the Iftav. Few know him as well as I do. And few carry as much contempt for your people as he does. He blames your people for the death of his father. If he thought I was dead, there's no telling what violence he might justify." She shakes her head again, her broad ears angling backward as she smears the wetness from her eyes. "And your king? What will he do now?"

If he thought she was dead. The king's recent announcement to the settlements rings faintly at the edges of Echeret's mind. It was declared in every village that the king's men had managed to slay a captive parafa. But is it possible? Possible that the creatures somehow heard?

"The king thinks he must seek out his new enemy and drive them out. But I honestly believe that such a plan will only bring more death to our lands," he answers.

"Your men can't fight them. We must find another way. If I could just talk with my clan. . . . I must escape this prison."

"I'm sure I can get the key to this cell. I'll—"

His words fall away when the prisoner reaches her skinny arm out between the bars, letting her hand grip his. "They call you *Echeret*, 'hidden.' I've heard the others call you this. My name is Onei," she says, and her voice wavers. "Echeret, I'm sorry for everything. I should have returned to them when I had the chance, the day we met. But I was angry. Angry with *him*. Maybe I could have prevented all this death, all this sorrow. How will you ever forgive me?" She tightens her grip. "I can see that you aren't like the other arai here. There may come a time now, very soon, when you will meet the Iftav. I want to give you something—to protect you."

Echeret stares speechlessly back, mildly aware of an odd, buzzing sensation in his hand where Onei's palm and fingers rest. Something to protect against the attackers? A secret weakness?

"Listen carefully," she tells him. "Remember these words: *sielil dehvt hiri.*"

It's a phrase unlike any he's heard, in a language he doesn't recognize. The language of the creatures of the woods.

"Si . . . e . . . ," he mumbles, trying pitifully to pronounce it.

"*Sielil . . . dehvt . . . hiri.*" Onei repeats the words over, slowly, watching him closely. "Practice it until you can never forget. These words will protect you."

"What does it mean?" Echeret asks.

"Let mercy run."

29

It was many summers ago when she nearly left the Iftav. Her father's kin were leaving for the southwestern sea, and she'd imagined for ages what the sparkling shores might look like with the rising dawn. It's been spoken of through the generations— the place where the voránjevin people first arrived from over the sea. Long ago, when their numbers were few. Before the clans came to be. A time of new beginnings.

She was waiting for him atop the steep hill at the southern edge of the camp that night. Only several days before her planned journey to the sea. It was a warm and windless night, and the stars had only just begun to appear as scattered, random sparkles across the eastern sky. She was distracted by the blending hues of the evening sky, was gliding far away in her thoughts, when he returned from the hunt. The heln with eyes like the morning sky when it sets ablaze with the coming of the sun. The one whose warmth and touch she would miss more dearly than any other when she left.

"Seems the rain's missed us." His voice came unexpectedly to her ears, echoing up from the foot of the hill. He was staring up at her with the same serene gaze that had always fascinated her soul and poured peace like a lullaby into her heart.

"Back already? The night's still young!" she called down to him, leaning to see him over the thin tips of the grass.

"The woods were alive tonight," he told her, "an easy hunt."

Even now, she can still recall the way his gaze never left her as he came up the hill to meet her that night—the way she found herself entirely consumed in every feature of his calm face. He climbed the hill without saying anything more. Slowly, until he was kneeling directly before her, bringing his forehead to hers. And his hand was warm on her cheek. Stirring with strength.

"Onei, stay with me."

It was many summers ago when she nearly left the Iftav forever. Eleven summers ago when Faleth, son of Drinehn, asked her to stay.

30

No one seems to chop vegetables with swifter, cleaner skill than Mother. The blade becomes part of her arm, delivering perfectly angled slices with each downward stroke. She must be preparing a stew. Tolaiyë descends from the winds to find her busily chopping fresh greens atop a makeshift table with several other men and women from Ethein.

"Mother."

Her smile is marvelous when she turns to see him—seemingly unaware of the gasps and wide-eyed stares of her fellow villagers. "Tolaiyë, my sweet child!" she exclaims.

He gives her a mild bow. Behind her, all the faces in the grove turn to watch the shining man, whispering and marveling.

"Mother, North Emér is falling into dark times. The people of Ethein will no longer be safe here," he tells her.

"What's happened?" She searches his gaze.

"The men of Rand have brought war upon themselves with an enemy they can't fight. And a greater threat stalks very near now—a danger none of the nations of the world are aware of," he explains.

"And your father?" she asks.

Tolaiyë takes her hand. "Mother, don't be afraid. We've found Father. He's been held captive by a dark spirit. We know how to set him free. But once the dark spirit is cast out, the people of Ethein will be endangered. We need them to move to a safe place."

"Oh, child . . ." Mother's grip becomes tight on his hand as the rain rises up in her sky-colored eyes. "Where must we go?"

"There's a place where the darkness can't follow you. Mother, you must lead the people to the far east, beyond the Sand Sea."

"So far! But what lies beyond the sands?"

"A sanctuary for our people," he says. "I'll show you the way. I'll be your guide and protection in the desert. And the Shardehn will protect you until the borders of North Emér."

A single tear escapes from Mother's eyes as she looks into his. She turns to glance fleetingly to the faces of those who look on. Some are whispering, calling Tolaiyë an angel, a god. Others have dropped everything in their arms to stand silently with their hands over their hearts.

"We'll spread the word and ready the people as quickly as we can," Mother whispers, looking back to her son. "Do whatever you can to bring your father home to us, Tolaiyë. Bring him home!"

"I promise I will, Mother," Tolaiyë tells her, and a familiar rhythm comes resounding faintly through the realms as he speaks. A sound that never lasts long. "I must go, but I'll return to guide the people when you've begun your journey."

Mother nods. "Go, child."

* * *

This time, he finds it without delay—the flickering edge of blackness between the borders of the realms. The gap. He's only just pressed forward into the darkness when the presence there shrinks hurriedly away, slipping further into the shadows. He chases after it. Now the presence darts sharply to the left, and Tolaiyë turns to intercept, reaching out his hand. And for a moment, one fleeting instant, the darkness ahead grows suddenly thin. The face of a man becomes momentarily visible, staring back at him with a calm, weary gaze that he could recognize anywhere.

"Father!"

But the shadows that shroud him pull him abruptly away. And the presence is gone.

No!

Without thinking, without entirely knowing how, Tolaiyë grips the darkness in his outstretched hand. It twists and warps beneath his grasp until the white light of the realms comes piercing through, tearing a hole in the blackness. He stumbles back into the physical realm, where the sound of Father's heart echoes like a village bell over the hills, far away. South, where the Emér and its rivers have never reached. Tolaiyë follows it. He arrives within a single breath— appearing in a barren, stony land, edged by jagged mountains that rise along the southern horizon. And he listens. But the echo's already gone.

Part Four

1

"Faleth!" The voice comes hiccupping down through the trees, swelling louder and then softer as the wind competes with the sound in uneven gusts. "The change is complete! They're waking!"

Faleth stops in his place to gaze up through the canopy. He isn't far from the camp. Close enough that he'd count it odd to see a virit messenger sent to him rather than someone on foot. Unless the news is urgent. The young virit circles overhead several times before sweeping down onto a high bough in a rush of leaves and fresh wind.

"Faleth! My sister, Hylveh, calls for you. Taln and Hyln are waking! The change is complete. You need to come and see," she pants.

Taln and Hyln, the two young helns who chose to ignore their orders to change into virit, and instead toyed with the new energy-shifting point that was recently discovered. They triggered a transformation in their bodies that no one's ever attempted before, nearly a month ago. What could they possibly become?

"I see. I'll come immediately," Faleth calls up to the messenger.

* * *

Hylveh motions frantically for him to come closer when she spots him at the edge of the camp. She stands beside the cocoon-like shell that holds one of the sleeping voránjevin boys, with a dampened cloth clutched tightly in her fist. As Faleth steps closer, he can see the fogged silhouette of a figure moving slowly beneath the shell's surface, turning and shifting its limbs like an infant in its mother's womb, about to be born. But this is no infant. The cocoon is larger than any Faleth's ever seen. He can only guess at the size of the transformed voránjevin inside.

"Which one is this?" he asks.

"Taln," Hylveh answers.

"Seems like they've become something much taller than usual."

"Both he and Hyln ate like starving animals before they began the deep sleep. I'm not surprised."

A small crowd gathers near the massive egg, waiting, watching. Anxious to see what strange new creature it hatches. A child sent for a satchel of water has only just returned when Taln suddenly moves more dramatically in his shell. He gives a low, wet cough. Awake. His broad hands become abruptly visible against the film that covers him, pressing until his fingers tear through into the open air. Long, pale fingers. Faleth steps forward to grasp Taln's hand, helping him sit up as the others move in to help carefully shred away the wet remains of the shell.

And then the entire grove is shocked to silence.

Some standing nearby back slowly away; others freeze in their places, round eyes unable to pull away from the newborn creature before them. Taln gasps deeply as he moves onto his hands and knees. Aside from the dark swaths of hair that have grown atop his head, his tall, bulky body is entirely bare. His ears have become shrunken and upright against the sides of his head, matching his notably smaller eyes.

"Taln, do you have the strength to stand?" Hylveh asks him softly as she presses her hand to his lower back, sending a soft flow of energy into his spine.

He takes a moment to respond, blinking again and again at the ground. Then he nods. He brings one foot forward, taking a massive breath before rising to his feet in the center of the crowd. His shoulders stand dramatically higher than any of the heads that surround him.

"I-I've become . . ." Taln searches for words as he inspects his own limbs, touches his bare face— almost startling himself with the deepened rumble of his new voice.

Looking on, Faleth's helpless to dispel the wild grin that spreads along his face. Is it a dream? Could it possibly be?

"You've become—but how?" Hylveh's dark eyes have widened as far as physically possible. "An arai! Taln, you've become an arai!"

"How is it possible?"

"An arai!"

"Exactly like them!"

All who look on begin to wonder and marvel aloud. It can't be, and yet it is—a voránjevin heln hidden in the form of an arai man. A voránjevin who can go entirely unnoticed among the Sketzans, who can walk among them as if he belonged. The arai would never know the difference.

Taln catches sight of Faleth now. He kneels, the tips of his wet hair falling over his eyes.

"Faleth, my apologies for disregarding your request to change into a virit," he says.

Faleth laughs, stepping closer to place his hands on the young man's shoulders. "There's nothing to be forgiven," he assures him, then turns to those gathered around. "My friends, give him water. Help him clean the blood and sweat from his new body! This is a great day for our people. This is a triumph we won't soon forget." He steps aside as the others come hurrying with water and rags, suddenly reminded of their duties to the newly awakened.

Hylveh leaves her post to come rushing to Faleth's side. "Can you believe it?"

"I couldn't have hoped for better," he answers as he turns to leave the grove.

Hylveh moves to stand in his path. "*Ivéi*, cousin, let me start the change. Send me into the villages of the arai with a body like theirs. I can travel among them in the light of day. I can find where they hide their king," she whispers.

There's a cold urgency in her eyes when he turns. Hylveh. The daughter of his father's sister. She speaks the language of the Sketzans as fluently as Onei did, and has always impressed the clan with her ability to track the rumors that float among the arai. She's always displayed an unmistakable vigor and tenacity for the welfare of the clan. It's a trait that's well known among the Iftav—and especially strong among the family of Drinehn.

"It'd be difficult for the clan to get along without your skills for a month," he tells her.

She grips his arm. "But disguised as an arai, I could do so much more," she urges. "Those *directly* responsible for Onei's suffering could be found!"

Faleth brings his teeth together. It was immensely satisfying to destroy the village that took the life of Drinehn of the Iftav. No doubt the arai scum have found the damage by now. But the men who took Onei still run free—hiding like rodents in the bush. Hylveh's right.

"Only you knew Onei as I did. Help me avenge her."

2

The vision comes to him at the most silent hour of the evening. That time when the cliffs are lit by the reflection of the setting sun off the desert sands below, when all the grasses seem to still their dance. It comes like a dream—drops like a sudden, vivid curtain before his eyes. But he isn't sleeping.

The face the vision brings into sight is a familiar one, though it's a face Afai hasn't seen in many, many years. The face of the king, son of the Mighty Rand. Now he sees the king lowered to his knees. Unarmed, with rage like dying embers in his eyes. He's surrounded—not by his men, but by the shining eyes of the people of the woods. Voránjevin hunters. One of them steps forward. A silvery-gray voránjevin with a dark sash and eyes the color of flames. He brings his hand to the king's chest—

Then the vision's gone as abruptly as it came, and Afai finds himself sitting alone, gasping in his open tent. It was a dream—but more than a dream. A vision with the weight and consequence of a memory, as if it's already occurred. Or *will* occur. Soon.

3

The woods just southwest of Votyón have always seemed uncommonly dim to Talek, ever since he first passed through them as a child. The trees here love to huddle their branches close together, whispering secrets to one another. Of all the woods surrounding the lands of Rand, none have become so notoriously dangerous. More than a few huntsmen and travelers are said to have vanished in these groves— sometimes leaving behind only a dropped dagger or torn shawl. Or nothing at all. For ages, no one could explain it. But after all that's happened in recent months, Talek doesn't doubt that the parafa are to blame.

Today, the king and a handful of his men come searching the forest for any trace of the beasts. Echeret was sent to interrogate the captive about the location of its foul nest. But it would only speak to him in riddles. *Always moving, never camping in one place for long,* it told him. Of course! Of course the murderous parafa would seek to make themselves into something mystical, unknowable to the people they love to haunt. After all, there are few things more terrifying than the enemy that can't be found, can't be seen or understood. But Talek isn't fooled. The beasts are little more than animals. They must gather *somewhere*. And the men of Rand will find the place. For now, they'll investigate what clues they have.

Talek's armored them as well as he could—though many were reluctant to don the wooden chest plates. The soldiers of Rand have long been proud of the quickness of their blades and sénsin rods. In their eyes, relying upon armor seems fearful—even cowardly. But now they face an enemy unlike any they've battled before, and their king hopes silently that his men will be as quick in combat as they believe themselves to be. Or quicker.

"Signs of footsteps leading south," one of the men calls softly through the leaves. "Hard to follow. Curse the light-footed beasts."

"This way!" another calls out from the south. "A survivor!" Kaif's voice.

Survivor? On all sides, the men pause to glance at each other through the trees, trading confused faces.

"A Sketzan?" Talek calls back.

"A Sketzan!" Kaif's words muffle oddly as he moves away through the foliage to investigate.

Talek rushes toward the sound, swatting branches from his path until Kaif comes into view. The boy he's helping sit up against a tree couldn't be more than sixteen years old. He's thin, with clothes resembling little more than dirt-stained rags. Talek kneels beside Kaif, looking the boy over.

"Where are you from, brother? What happened here?"

"Where are you hurt?"

They ask the stranger together, but the boy only shakes his head, breathing deeply. Cold sweat sleeks across his slender face and gathers like dew along his neck. He raises his weary hand and motions for them to back away.

"Go," he rasps. "Go now—they . . . are coming. . . . They . . . they are . . . already here."

They. Talek and Kaif exchange glances. Behind, the men draw their weapons, turning to peer in all directions. The boy must be too weak to run.

"We can't simply leave you to die. Come now, we can outrun them, get you to safety," Kaif whispers as he moves to his feet, extending a hand.

The stranger rises on trembling legs. "We can't . . . we can't run . . . ," he breathes. "I told you . . ."

Talek rises and pulls his own dagger from his belt before looking back to the wounded young man.

That is, the boy who seemed wounded a moment ago. Suddenly, the stranger stands with a straight back. The quaking in his knees and shoulders ceases entirely, and the look of fear and desperation on his face gives way to an almost emotionless stare.

"They're already here," he says.

Then, without warning, before anyone can react, the boy grips Kaif's arm and reaches under the loose wooden armor to clap his other hand to the soldier's chest. Kaif can scarcely let out a startled cry before he falls limply to the ground. Watching from only a single pace away, Talek finds himself momentarily stiffened in place—unable to blink or shout, unable to make any sense of the sight before him. He should run to Kaif, should fight.

But what exactly is he fighting?

"Kaif!"

Dolan moves first. He comes barreling through the bushes nearby. "Ungrateful traitor! You dare attack a man of Rand who offered you kindness! Have the parafa taken the senses out of you?" He takes the stranger firmly by the arm, giving him a jerk.

"Dolan—" Talek tries to interrupt, but the man takes no notice.

"No explanation for yourself? We'll take you back tied up like a boar if we mus—"

He moves to restrain the boy's wrists, but something interrupts the motion. Dolan's entire frame becomes suddenly rigid—back arching violently as a hoarse gasp escapes his lips. Then he falls lifelessly backward into the leaves. And another young man now stands in his place, staring blankly down at the soldier he's just slain. This stranger looks to be the same age as the first. A dark-haired boy dressed in the ragged uniform of a guardsman. But this is no guardsman. Now the two slender strangers look up at Talek.

Run.

The instinct flashes across his mind, jolting like static through his now-racing heart. There was a time when the king would never flee from a fight, never run from an enemy who's slain two of his men before his face. There was once a time, not long ago, when Talek, the son of Rand, had nothing to fear but a bad harvest, a harsh winter, or the occasional rebellious soldier. But those times have gone. Today, a new fear is born in the secluded corners of the king's heart, and his feet seem to move before he can think. He turns and dashes madly through the trees, cursing at the branches that snag and catch at his clothes. Not caring to look back.

"Stay back!" he calls out frantically to his men. "Regroup!"

But it's too late. The shouts of his soldiers begin to ring out in all directions.

"You—!"

"They're here, the parafa!"

"More of them!"

"From the southwest!"

Talek searches frantically through the trees for the figures of his men as he runs, catching only fleeting glimpses of their heads or shoulders as they race through the gaps in the leaves.

"Turn back! To the east! Retreat to the edge of the woods!" he shouts breathlessly. A group of soldiers appears to his left, running with weapons in hand. Others join in behind.

Kaif! Dolan!

Bitterness erupts like molten stone in the king's heart as he rushes onward. They hadn't fastened their armor. But how could they have known? What exactly did they just encounter, deep in the southwestern woods? Men who dissented from the people of Rand, who joined the dark ways of the beasts? Since when did young men learn the life-stealing black magic of the parafa? Were they men at all?

A total of thirty-two soldiers manage to regroup at the forest's edge, moments later. Thirty-two out of the forty-five who came together. Talek lets his breath pave deep paths into his chest as his men curse and spit at the trees.

Don't let them shake you, he tells himself, fighting to contain the tremor in his hands. The men need a strong king.

"My brothers, I've got no idea what we just witnessed. But men have been lost. Let's not lose them in vain. Secure your armor. Don't let the devils get their filthy paws beneath it. This time, we stay together."

4

She finds him returning alone to the camp as evening falls. A gray figure moving almost soundlessly among the greens and browns and subtle shadows of the woods. Like a ghost. He doesn't seem to notice the sasarian woman standing in the leaves nearby, watching.

"When will it end, Faleth?" she asks.

He stops abruptly in his path at the sound of her words, bright eyes turning to frame her in their cold gaze. Saying nothing. He stands in a gap between two ancient trees, where their hard roots have coiled and woven together like serpents at his feet. He's small beside them—a single, tiny creature beside the timeless columns of the forest. How is it that one creature could bring so much sorrow into these lands?

"Has there not been enough death? How many arai must lose their lives to the Iftav before your thirst is quenched?" Éliva questions him.

"The stench of the Sketzans will never cease to offend our senses," he tells her.

"And so you seek to murder them all? Hunt them like animals? Faleth, Drinehn's sacrifice was long ago. The families you haunt are not your enemy." She steps directly in front of him. "We gave your people a gift. A gift that would enable you to see that the voránjevin and the arai are not so different as they suppose. The children of Claya are one family."

"We are *nothing* like those fowl creatures," Faleth growls, and the silvery hairs along his neck stand sharply on end. "We'll deal with them as we please. The ability to mimic their appearance just makes some things easier for us—"

"These arai have done nothing to deserve the sorrows you've brought them," Éliva insists, but Faleth tips his head to one side, unconvinced.

"Is that so? And why would you care? You never did live among your own kind."

"I'm called to serve them all. All creatures have a right to live free," Éliva tells him, and she kneels to look more closely into his eyes, speaking softly. "If you hate the arai so dearly, why remain in these lands? The world is vast."

"I refuse to turn my back when the men who made Onei suffer roam free," he whispers back.

Éliva shakes her head. "And if the people of Rand were to leave these lands, would you still seek to destroy them?"

"We would love to see North Emér free of the foul arai. But until that happens I'll give you no promise."

"We will offer to lead the son of Rand and his people to a new land. But if they choose to do so, the Iftav must covenant to let them go in peace. No more killing. If you break the promise, the sasarianë will reclaim the power that was lent to your ancestors. And the Iftav will be known for all generations to come as the clan who is bound to a single physical form."

Faleth takes a moment to stare into each of Éliva's waiting eyes. A long moment. "Fine then," he agrees at last. "If they ever truly leave."

"And those who settled to the northwest? If the people of Rand agree to inherit a new land, will you swear to leave the western families in peace?"

Faleth stares silently back at her, thoughts stirring and coursing like boiling waters behind his gray face. "Just get rid of the scum of Rand if you want to protect them," he answers, and he steps around her, continuing on his path.

Éliva turns to watch him go. "Onei still lives. I've tried to tell you," she calls after him. "You slay the arai for a crime they never committed."

The voránjevin pauses midstep, and Éliva can hear the sudden leaping in his dark heart. Maybe he's about to turn around, about to ask where Onei is—but Éliva doesn't wait to see.

* * *

"It was a gift. I thought the ability to temporarily return to a human form would help them see beyond their prejudices." She paces slowly along the jagged edges of the black stones as she speaks, arms wrapped tightly against her shoulders. "But they've only used our gift for murder."

"The Iftav have done so, and the Iftav alone. Don't forget the other tribes. There's no telling what future they may make for themselves with the ability you've given them," Tolaiyë assures her from his place a short way uphill, where the ebony boulders rise out of the earth like massive, merciless teeth. Perfect seats for a westward view of the sea below. They've come to the Black Shores, far to the west—a place as far from the lands of North Emér as they could possibly find. They've come here to think.

Éliva pauses her steps. "We can't force the Iftav to do anything, but we can help create compromise and peace in North Emér."

"You told me once about the way your predecessor stopped the dark spirit we've been chasing," Tolaiyë says. "That she stopped him because he was once a living man who brought evil into the world. Can we not put an end to the Iftav for all their murders?"

"No, my brother. We can intervene when a fellow sasarian falls to corruption and misuses the power we're given. But the Iftav are mortal children of Claya. We aren't their rulers. We can't rob them of their freedom. But if they accept the terms of the offer I gave them, they accept the consequences of their choices as well. We can deliver the punishment they agreed upon if they break their promise," Éliva answers. "It's true that the power to destroy is in our hands. But to misuse our power is to give it up entirely, as the sasarian of old."

"But what good is all the power in the world if it can't be used to stop murderers?"

"That's the difficulty of our position. Claya's a broken world—broken in many different ways, depending on who you ask. And everyone hopes to mend it. Consider North Emér. The happy society of the western families was broken by the constant threats of Rand and his followers. The people of Rand have long hoped to mend their broken kingdom by bringing the western families into their fold. Now they hope to mend their torn world by somehow abolishing the Iftav who torment them. But in the eyes of the Iftav, the presence of the people of Rand is the flaw that needs mending. The Shardehn mourn the corruption of their sister tribe, and even now are counseling among themselves, wondering endlessly how to mend the growing rift between the clans.

"Must I go on? All life on Claya is imperfect. Give freedom to the imperfect, and the result is a world that needs constant mending. But take away that freedom, the ability to choose one's actions and reactions, and you have no world worth living in. It's the unfortunate truth that there are always people who use their freedom to bring darkness into the lives of others—no matter how many laws and governments may exist to discourage it."

"Then how is it done? How do we truly fulfill our purpose in this world?"

"I've strived for years now to bless the people of Claya. I've done anything I could think of to free lives from bondage, to prevent wars, to help peace endure among the nations of the world. But there are times when my interventions seem to have little use. And I can't seem to escape this thought . . . this thought that I've only ever toyed at the edge of our potential. That our true purpose has yet to be fulfilled," she says.

"Our purpose . . . ," Tolaiyë murmurs. "I remember the words 'to protect the freewill of the children, to stand as messenger before them, to present the fate of Claya at the footstool of the goddess—' "

"—That it and all its realms may become whole and eternal," Éliva finishes the line. "How do we *truly* accomplish that? The heavens have given us this purpose, and given us countless abilities in order to fulfill it. But we're left to use those gifts in whatever way we see fit—to find our own path."

The Palarian drifts near Tolaiyë's shoulder. "The gift of freewill is given to all—the sasariannë themselves are no exception. You are the hands of the goddess on this earth, trusted to influence the world for good, in whatever ways you can. These servants are here to guide you, if you will ask," it whispers.

Tolaiyë looks to it, wondering what mysteries the creature may know, if he only knew what to ask. "Where do we begin?" he asks.

"By considering all you have, which you are able to give back to Claya."

"All we have . . . ," Éliva repeats. "Talek's people face destruction because of the Iftav. We could give them a new land, away from their enemy. But where?"

Tolaiyë stares out to the gray sea, letting the question roll like the tide in his mind. The waters here are fiercer than those of Emér. A new land? Of all the lands of the Glesian continent, those that surround the Emér and its rivers are the most desirable. But only the inland sea's southernmost edge would be far enough from the haunting scouts of the Iftav. A barren land, riverless—almost entirely void of trees.

Unless . . .

5

All the settlements of Rand are aflame with rumors. Full of fear, full of uncertainty. Some say the beasts of the woods have possessed the bodies of men they captured. Others say they've learned to control the minds of their captives, sending them like puppets to do their bidding. All have their panicked theories—and none sleep without a weapon at their side.

Whispers tell of a terrible encounter in the southwestern woods—of the king and a band of forty-five soldiers who pressed bravely forward in search of the enemy's hideout, only to be scattered and slaughtered. Four times the men charged with their weapons held high. Four times they were driven back. Until only eighteen of the forty-five soldiers remained. And the bodies of their brothers remain unclaimed in the woods.

* * *

Tolaiÿe finds the king alone in a cabin in Kotán, sitting with his head in his hands and nothing but the dim flicker of a dying fire to accompany him. The sasarian's presence sends soft streaks of white light into all corners of the room. It lies like frost over the floorboards, chasing the shadows and blending warmly with the orange glow of the fire. Talek doesn't raise his head until the light's begun to climb his ankles. His face bears the dark outlines and sharp shadows of a man deprived of sleep. A look magnified by the wild fray of hair atop his head. Now his restless stare widens as it catches sight of the sasarian visitor.

"Y-you again," he whispers. "I'm losing my mind, aren't I?"

Tolaiÿe shakes his head. "Talek, I come to aid you and your people, if you wish it," he says.

"Are you some kind of being from the heavens? Some kind of angel?"

"We're simply servants of the goddess, sent to protect the freewill of all people."

"There's another like you," Talek tells him, shaking a finger in the air as if he were struggling to remember. "A woman. She always tries to warn me, tells me to avoid angering the beasts, but it's too late now. You've come too late to warn me."

"I don't come to warn, but to offer you an escape," Tolaiÿe replies.

The king brings his hands to his temples. "Some say these lands have been cursed," he says.

"The clan that haunts your people will give you no rest so long as you remain here. But the lands of Glesia are vast, my brother. We can lead the families of Rand to a new home. A place where your enemy won't follow," Tolaiÿe tells him.

Talek looks up. "You propose that we give up our homeland? Our inheritance? My father, Rand, and his people sacrificed all to come here, to build their kingdom. And now we must leave it to the hands of the beasts that torment us?"

"The people of the woods are fiercely loyal to their promises. Even the clan that seeks your death," Tolaiyë assures him. "If you leave these lands, they'll covenant to let you go in peace. But so long as you remain, they'll give us no promise."

The king's gaze drops to the floor as he takes a slow breath. "And so we must conform to the will of the offenders? Bow to the demands of a heartless enemy? I can't. I can't." He shakes his head. "The people of Rand are not so easily frightened into submission. Leave me be, messenger—whether you're real or some imagination of my weary mind—leave me be. I need time to plan the battles ahead."

Tolaiyë opens his mouth, about to say more, but the son of Rand turns himself to the light of his fading fire, eyes shut, heart closed. And the sasarian finds himself somehow unseen—invisible, despite the radiance that streams from his countenance and chases the darkness of the room in all directions. He turns to vanish into the night. And in the fleeting instant before the wind carries him away, the subtle presence that waits outside the cabin wall becomes suddenly obvious. A man with the colors of Rand in his woven shawl and the shadow of a sheathed sénsin rod at his back. A man standing just outside the light of the cabin window. Watching.

6

"Little friend, you need to leave this place. I've got the key at last. I'll go out first, talk to the guards outside to distract them," he whispers as he fumbles with the lock on her prison door. "Do what you must to escape the borders of Kotán, but please don't take any lives. I trust you won't need to."

The morning's still dark when he comes rushing into the cramped stone prison. Behind the bars, Onei rises slowly to her feet, heavy eyed.

"Thank the heavens," she whispers.

The rusting hinges of the prison bars let out a mild squeal as Echeret pulls them open and crouches low to the cold floor. "The king's just refused the help of some higher power that offered to rescue our people," he breathes. "He plans to fight your clan to the end. I fear a great deal of death lies in the path ahead. Go now, while you can. Maybe you can talk to your clan, help bring an end to the killing."

"Higher power?" Onei steps out beside her friend, wondering.

Echeret shakes his head, shrugging his broad shoulders. "These are strange times. I'm not sure how else to describe it—not even sure if it was real. But there's no time to wonder. Only time to act. Now you're free to return to your clan. Please, help us end this violence."

"And what will you do?"

"Whatever I can to protect the families of Rand."

Onei glances fleetingly to the prison's exit before looking back to him. "Echeret, I can't abandon you. There's too much death already. And I'm certain my clan is full of anger. Even if I return alone to them now, they'll continue to slay your people. We must make an agreement. My people and yours. The Iftav do not break their oaths," she tells him. "Tell your king that I will walk before him and his men. I will be his speaker to my clan. We can make a treaty."

Echeret gives her a bitter smile. "The king's reason is leaving him. He won't listen to any plan you propose," he says.

"But we can try! Can we not try? I can wait here so he won't be intimidated. If he refuses, I'll flee to my people and do what I can to persuade them alone," Onei urges, staring up with new alertness in her dark face.

Echeret lets a slow breath ease out of his chest. "I'll try to talk to him."

7

They come with long shawls and embroidered sashes draped over their shoulders as the sun rises high over the canopy—come with the slow, solemn steps of a funeral parade. They arrive with gathered hands and bowed heads at the camp of the Iftav, only shortly after the morning hunt. Walking in unison. The elders of the Shardehn. Faleth goes alone to meet them at the edge of the grove.

"Mother," he murmurs. She stands among them, wearing an emerald sash. He tips his head to her before looking over the company. "What brings the Shardehn so far to the east?"

The eldest among them steps forward. An aged heln with fur the color of a star-speckled night sky. "Even a peaceful clan would fight and kill to protect its own when absolutely necessary. But we will never be the instruments of senseless murders. Not the Shardehn," he declares.

"We never asked for your help," Faleth answers.

"The truth can't be hidden or ignored any longer, my son," his mother tells him softly. "The Iftav have had part in the deaths of the arai for far too long. I should have known."

Faleth tests the tension in his teeth as he stares back, subtly shifting his jaw to one side. Have they turned even his mother against him? "Have you come to stop us from purging the land of those who wronged our people? Some have chosen to forget the crimes of the arai against us. But the Iftav will not forget." He keeps his voice level.

"Word of your acts is spreading throughout the clans. We won't battle against our brothers and sisters. But we can no longer stand beside them," the dark elder answers. "The messengers of the Shardehn will no longer carry any word for the Iftav. We will share no more of our winter stores, will allow no more companionships with the sons and daughters of the Iftav." He raises a single hand in the space between them, palm forward. The symbol of an oath. "If the Iftav turn away from their murders, perhaps someday we can accept them again into our families. But until then, you have no place among us."

Their words fall like downed trees to the forest floor. Solid, irreversible. Never in all the days of the clans has any tribe turned its back to another. And now . . . The outrage fails to find any words in Faleth's heart. And so he simply stands in silence, fists clenched, as the elders of the Shardehn each raise their palms in agreement. And as they each turn back to the west, vanishing again into the shadows of the forest, only one tarries. Her violet eyes sparkle with moisture, like the rare stones children of the seaside clans often search for after rain. But her face is calm.

"I once lived with those I loved most. I was once a wife and a mother, never alone," she whispers to him. "Now I'm alone again. Alone among my people." Her stare lingers for a silent moment longer. Long enough to torque the raw numbness in Faleth's heart.

Then Lídei of the Shardehn pulls her sash more tightly across her chest as she turns away, saying nothing more. It's the emerald sash once proudly worn by Drinehn of the Iftav.

"Goodbye, mother," Faleth breathes at last. But she's already gone.

* * *

"*Araikeus?* It's not the most elegant name. Though it seems like our ancestors never worried much about elegance when they named the transformations they discovered," she says. The afternoon sun bounces off the reddish-brown hair that now clings in loose, damp curves around her pale face. The face of an arai woman. She slips her arms into a simple wrap tunic, tying a knot at her side.

Araikeus, "fake arai." It's the name the others have coined for the new form. Faleth frowns at the sound of it. She's right. It's an ugly word. But maybe fitting for the form that mimics the foul arai.

Hylveh wraps an old shawl over her shoulders. Clothes from one of the arai villages, snatched from the dead. It's taken her nearly five weeks to wake in this new body, and despite her short hair, she looks enough like an arai in her new form to put a sickening twist in Faleth's stomach.

"What would you call it, then?" he asks her.

She looks up with her lip pushed out in thought, red-hazel eyes catching the afternoon light. "Something that fits with the names of the other forms. Something simple, like *virsevin*," she says. " 'Biggest body.' Can't be much simpler than that."

Faleth hands her a water satchel. It hangs on a loop that ordinarily fits loosely across a voránjevin chest to rest at the hip. Now it's hardly wide enough to fit her waist. Maybe her name for this form is accurate.

"You may need more tact than we've used before. I doubt they understand that we can take their shape. But they know something's amiss," he tells her.

"I've watched the arai all my life. I know how they act," she assures him, and she tips her chin impatiently—the way he's seen so many Sketzan women do.

The sight sends a cold spark down Faleth's spine. He resists the urge to bare his teeth. Hylveh's a talented filíl. She'll have no trouble fooling the arai.

"Go. Find where the cowardly king hides. And listen for any word of my Onei."

She looks back at him as she turns to the east, gaze calm. She nods. "We'll either find her or avenge her," she assures him. "Of that I'm absolutely certain."

8

The people of Ethein have come far. In nearly two months' time they've managed to come from the borders of North Emér through forest and plain, over hills and dales to the gate of the Sand Sea. And now, as they prepare to continue their journey by moonlight, the time has come. A home must be prepared for them.

The sun's still setting in the far west, casting its orange and yellow rays over the sands as Tolaiyë descends over them. Ahead, the cliffs glow like towering gray fortresses over a golden sea. A place told of in songs, a place that's always remained wild and unclaimed, void of all human presence. Now, new songs will be written.

The ability comes from somewhere ancient in his bones. As if it always existed within him, dormant. Untapped. All these years, the earth has spoken to him. Now he'll speak back. He holds his arms out wide from his sides, closes his eyes, and whispers—murmurs to the stones that lie asleep deep in the heart of the cliffs. To the sands and clay that lie atop them, to the soil.

"*Rise!*"

The stones rise at the sound of his voice, shedding away their rough, jagged edges. They rise from the depths like a rolling, backward avalanche. Churning, shifting—cleaving and colliding until they're smoothed and carved with straight edges. They form foundations, walls, arches, and great columns. They come together as corridors, courtyards, and broad stairways. They move at the sound of his voice until the cliffs no longer stand empty, but crowned by the white and gray walls of the massive stone sanctuary that now stands atop them. A new home for the people of Ethein.

9

The morning's giving way to the heat of the day when Talek the king agrees at last to hear his prisoner speak. He comes to the little stone shed with a stiff stride and a hand hovering over the sheathed dagger at his hip. A straight-mouthed, cheerless expression hangs over his face as he accompanies Echeret through the door. A look that only hardens at the sight of Onei standing silently behind the bars of her cage. And for what seems like an eternity, he stands, staring wordlessly down at her.

"I'm told that you want to speak to me," he mumbles at last.

"Yes. I can help your people," Onei whispers.

A mild twitch appears at the corner of the king's eye at the sound of her voice. "What plan do you propose, beast?"

"I'll go with you and your men, walk before you to meet your enemy. I know their leader well. I'll persuade them to make a treaty of peace."

Talek gives a slow nod, moving to sit on a crate beside the bars. A five-day scruff darkens his jawline, gray flecked and unkempt. It's an uncommon look for a king. "How can I trust you? Why would you care to aid our people?" he questions.

"I find no joy in the death of your people. The one who hunts you has motives of his own," Onei tells him.

"What would you have our enemy promise?"

"I'll make them swear to end the killing. No more Sketzans would die."

"Would they covenant to leave our lands?"

"I can try to persuade them," Onei assures. She steps closer, tannish eyes aglow. "Let me help you. My people always keep their word. This battle needs to end."

The king nods again, watching the dirt-covered floor. "Yes, it does need to end," he murmurs, and he looks back to the creature behind the bars. "I'm just not sure that you and I have the same definition of victory." He rises to his feet and steps out into the daylight without saying another word.

Echeret follows him out. "Good king, I think the prisoner speaks honestly. Will you not consid—"

Talek stops abruptly to face his first officer. "Consider what, my brother? Consider going on a whim, making agreements with the same creatures who've slain our people without a thought? Consider believing the words of a beast that has every reason to seek its own freedom, every reason to walk us right into the hands of its murderous clan? Should I consider taking that risk?" His voice is coarse, restless.

"Our people deserve every chance to survive. Is it not worth the risk if they have a chance to live on? Send me—the people of the woods don't frighten me," Echeret urges.

But Talek only peers at him through the corner of his sleepless eyes. "Is that so, Echeret?" he whispers. "You *trust* that creature, is that it? Tell me, how can we possibly trust it?" he asks, and his complexion suddenly shifts—moves from weary irritation to a stern, unwavering stare. "You've been talking with it, haven't you? They've gotten to you, brother. They've convinced you to believe in their false promises, haven't they?" His pointing finger rises subconsciously in the air between them as he speaks.

Echeret shakes his head. "Talek, I only care that the families of Rand are not all slain in this senseless slaughter. We have yet to find any way to truly fight our enemy. You say we'll defeat them, but they slay us like we're boars on the hunt."

"But we'll fight and survive all the same!" the king shouts in reply. "How dare you lose faith in the strength of our people, the mighty people of Rand!"

"If you continue to seek battle, our people will only continue to lose their lives. This is madness. *Madness!*" Echeret bellows back at him, hardly able to believe the wild glare in Talek's eyes.

Now the king lifts his hand to eye level, pointing directly to his first officer's bewildered face. "If we must die in this fight, then we'll do so honorably. One who isn't willing to give his life for our nation is not worthy of it."

Talek turns to the soldiers who stand beside the prison. "Men of Rand," he cries, "this man has conspired with the enemy of our people. He's *betrayed* us! He can no longer be welcomed among us. Get rid of him."

For a moment, Echeret stands motionless in his place. Conspired? Betrayed? The king's words come collapsing in like tumbling boulders against his unsuspecting ears. He shakes his head in disbelief. "You've gone mad, my friend. This is madness," he whispers, and he turns toward the village. Maybe the chief guardsman will talk reason—

"You heard me! After him, *now*! I'll accept no more disobedience from among our ranks," the king spits to his men.

Footfalls come thudding through the grass, and Echeret turns in time to see a young soldier advancing after him. Stone faced, blade drawn. He swings his weapon in a sharp, sudden swipe from the left—an attack Echeret just manages to parry as he unsheathes his sénsin rod from the slender metal case at his lower back. The soldier scowls as the rod's burning surface lands against his upper arm, searing through the sleeve of his red and gray uniform.

Now the other men are closing in.

Echeret sends one final glance toward the stone prison, catching sight of the king where he stands staring coldly back. Talek, son of Rand. A friend Echeret's known from boyhood, a leader he's accompanied to skirmishes and councils, a comrade he's toiled beside to build homes and dig wells throughout the years. Someone he once knew. But the man who stands staring back at him now is somehow changed—as if the Talek who once existed was chiseled down and swept away like dust from the village lanes, leaving only a stranger in his place.

"Get the others and put the beast in a cage we can transport. We're leaving for Tol tonight," the king mumbles to the soldier who remains at the prison door as he turns away.

And the man who once served as his first officer doesn't wait for his gaze to return before slipping into the cover of the trees.

10

S he tugs her mildly dirt-mottled shawl from her shoulders as she comes into the courtyard near the center of the village. It's a place that apparently every Sketzan settlement has near one of its wells, where the people come to wash their clothes and blankets in little stone troughs. In the four days Hylveh's spent wandering the villages of the arai, she's often found the wash yards teeming with life and conversation. But today, only a handful of women stand at the troughs, with their hands buried deep in soaking fabric, as she comes near. They chatter idly back and forth as an older man draws water for rinsing. No one seems to notice the scarlet-haired newcomer as she bends to press her shawl into the cold waters.

"You won't wait until next spring?" One woman raises an eyebrow to another as she stoops to press the wetness from a ragged pair of trousers.

"No, no," the other replies, frowning sternly at her own pile of work, "we'll leave for the north once we've cleared our garden. My girls've become too frightened to sleep these days. The old kingdom was good enough to our family. We'll do well enough again—or at least be free of the terrors that haunt these lands."

"I pray these times will pass before my son is old enough to remember them," a third woman sighs.

"Rand and his men led us bravely through many a hardship, in his day. I'm sure his son the king will do the same," the first woman assures her.

"I once supposed the same. Now I'm not so certain," the aged man beside the well interjects. "They say the king's cast out his most trusted officer, accused him of betrayal."

"You mean the son of Hauten and Ilei, that strong soul?"

"Cast out? For what sort of betrayal?"

Several women question at once, but the old man only shakes his head in dismay, thin beard twitching in the mild breeze. "Haven't heard. But any who know him say that the first officer's always been an honest man. It's a strange danger that lurks about us, and the king's made little progress against it," he murmurs.

"I heard only just this morning that the king's left for the northern outpost with only a few soldiers, carrying a captive beast along with him," a fourth woman speaks up. "Now why do you think he'd choose to keep one of those dreadful things around?"

"A beast?" someone asks.

"Yes, one of *them*. The parafa responsible for the massacre at Votyón, and all our troubles these many months. I suppose the king may still be searching for their weaknesses. Or looking to set up a bait."

The women continue on, debating amongst themselves about how big the parafa must be, what sort of terrible features they must have, but Hylveh doesn't notice. Her hands become momentarily stiffened in the chill folds of her dripping shawl—frozen by the words that have reached her ears. A *prisoner*. One of *them*.

Onei!

11

The sands are often still when night comes. Silvery waves frozen in place, sparkling back the mellow gleam of the twin moons like the shattered remains of all the world's crystals. A breathless ocean.

But tonight, the sands refuse to rest. Their sleepless voice can be heard hissing in the east well before the sun's final burning rays have vanished beneath the western skyline. And a shadow rises in the wake of dusk. First like a mist—then a thickened cloud that rolls and tumbles over the dunes. And now, as the people of Ethein have just collected their tents and begun the night's walk, nearly all the eastern desert lies shrouded behind an immense dark wall. A storm, raging westward. The families slow their steps at the sight of it, turning to glance at one another with silent, widening eyes.

It comes quickly. The winds are like fluid stone when they reach the huddled travelers—beating mercilessly down on pull carts and cattle, pummeling hunched shoulders and uncovered heads. Biting, stinging. Assaulting from every angle . . . for a fleeting moment. Then, more suddenly than it arrived, the attack ceases—replaced by a mere whisper of air that whirs softly over the scene.

The bent figures of the caravan are hardly distinguishable from the silvery-smooth slope of the dunes when Kadeis uncovers her face. All still, all cloaked in gleaming sands. But now the people begin to stir, blinking the storm from their eyes and shaking the desert from their shawls. Raising their heads to the odd silence that now surrounds them.

The storm hasn't ceased. But its winds whip like dark silk on all sides, parting flawlessly around the bewildered people of Ethein—leaving them entirely untouched at the heart of the raging sands.

"Thank the heavens—we're saved!"

"The storm . . . how . . . how could this be?"

"A miracle!"

The people have only begun to whisper and marvel together when Kadeis spots a familiar silhouette coming toward them through the wall of sands. A golden figure shrouded in brilliant, radiant light.

"It's him," she gasps. "It's my Tolaiyë, my angel son. The sands obey him."

The angel's bare feet leave no prints in the sand as he comes, and he enters the calm at the heart of the storm without a hair out of place on his glowing head. "Mother, I heard your heart racing," he tells her. "I came as quickly as I could."

"You've saved us, my child. You have the thanks of all your people." Kadeis tugs the kerchief from the unraveling bun on her head, letting the sand fall idly from her braids. "The Sand Sea was warring against us."

"There's no need to fear. The oasis isn't far now—only another night's journey. You can rest there as long as you need before crossing to the cliffs, where your sanctuary awaits," Tolaiyë assures, and the people of Ethein gather in, eyes dazzled anew by the glowing being that stands among them.

Only one of the children has the courage to approach him, and she reaches out her hand to touch the shimmering edge of his robes—but the angel vanishes before her fingertips. Gone. And the storm leaves with him. All around, the winds that raged only moments ago fall abruptly to sleep. The whirling sands fall lifelessly to the dunes, revealing the clear, sparkling face of the evening sky. And the night is still.

12

The outskirts of Leln are blanketed with thin mist as they come to it—scarcely outrunning the dawn that's already begun to peer over the eastern trees. The sight of Leln's rooftops comes as a silent surprise to Echeret's weary eyes. Nearly overnight, he and Defehl have managed to complete a journey that would ordinarily require the greater part of three days on foot. There were few other options, with the king's men tracking at their heels, shouting accusations.

Traitor! Conspirator!

How has it come to this? And so suddenly?

It was miraculous that he found Defehl so quickly as he fled Kotán. She's known Talek as long as Echeret—from the days of their childhood, when the kingdom was still in its earliest infancy. But now the first officer himself is outcast, labeled an enemy of the king. Would the wife of a traitor receive any mercy?

The two of them left Kotán without any plan or supplies—simply hoping to slip outside the sights of the soldiers who pursued so relentlessly after them. They fled westward through the night, stopping only on occasion to quench their thirst at streams and wells before pressing onward to Leln, where the home of Defehl's family might serve as a temporary haven. And now that they've arrived at last, the thought of resting his throbbing legs—if even for only an hour—has made Echeret's weary mind almost delirious with anticipation. But the sound of Defehl collapsing with a gasp to the earth beside him pulls him sharply to his senses. She must've pushed herself too hard. He whirls around, arm outstretched impulsively toward her, when a pair of hands suddenly grips his legs behind the knees. Burning erupts in his already exhausted legs, and an overwhelming fatigue robs his feet from beneath him. He falls heavily to the grass beside his wife before he can think to react, entirely out of breath. Someone's found them.

No!

Echeret summons the last of his strength to scramble to his knees and reach for the weapon at his lower back—but now a slender hand appears at his chest, somehow pulling threateningly at all the power in his lungs, his heart—forcefully slowing the breath at his lips, the blood in his veins. When he manages to raise his head, the small gray figure that stands before him stares back with massive, golden-orange eyes. Eyes that throw back the soft light of the moons with almost stunning intensity. It's them. The people of the woods. Onei's people. They stand at all sides, watching soundlessly. Echeret's mind races at the sight of them. What were the words she gave him?

"Si . . . siel . . . ," he wheezes, struggling to speak with lungs of stone and a straining heart. The orange-eyed figure stirs at the sound, and after what seems like an agonizing eternity, the hand pulls away from Echeret's chest. His heart resumes its racing pace with a sharp leap and a shudder, and he gasps and chokes terribly as the night air returns in a cold wave to his breath.

"What did you say?" the gray figure growls, bearing an accent Echeret's come to recognize.

He looks into his captor's waiting gaze. "*Sielil dehvt hiri.*" He repeats the words as well as he can remember them.

The stranger's hands form little fists at his sides. "Where did you learn those words?" he rasps.

"From a friend. One who wants more than anything to end the deaths in these lands," Echeret tells him.

The gray voránjevin grips Echeret's shoulder, threatening again to steal away the strength there. "If you caused her any pain—"

"She wasn't harmed!" Defehl cries out as she struggles to lift herself on weary arms. "Echeret kept her safe."

Echeret nods in agreement, still regaining his breath. "I tried to set her free, but she wouldn't leave. She wanted to help our people establish peace with her clan. But our king's refused her proposal. She was alive yesterday morning, when I was made an outcast. If you go after her now, she may still be," he explains.

"We hear your king fled to the north." The slender stranger eyes the two of them carefully as he speaks. He carries no weapon, but his frame bears the solid stance of a soldier. A fighter.

"He's likely taken her with him to our northern garrison," Echeret pants, and he straightens his back. "So long as you'll promise to end the killing, I'll take you there myself, help you make an agreement with our king. Please, take back Onei and spare our people.

These lands have seen enough death. There's hope yet for a treaty if you'll honor Onei's wishes."

"You would betray your king? Walk his enemy to his door?"

For a moment Echeret hesitates to reply. The sight of Talek's hardened, remorseless expression returns like a chill to his mind. The face of a man who insists on leading his men to battle with an enemy they're unable to fight. A man who was once a friend and a brother—who now didn't hesitate to demand Echeret's death. "He's lost himself to madness. He's no longer my king. I only wish for our people to live on in peace."

The gray stranger stares back in silence, with a stonelike expression that Echeret can't hope to interpret. "If you don't wish to die, you'll take your people and leave these lands," he says. His words are flat, impassive. "I know the way. I don't need a guide." Then he turns away without waiting for a reply, vanishing into the night. The others follow soundlessly after him.

And the former first officer and his wife are left kneeling alone in the grass. Echeret lets his breath ease out. "They worked. The words Onei gave me worked," he marvels softly, turning to Defehl. "But I fear I've condemned an old friend to death."

13

Two days were all he needed. Two days of sprinting through the woods with a blaze in his heart and the wind at his heels. He pressed on without sleep, not caring for food, not caring to slow his pace for anyone. Only Hylveh and eight heln have managed to follow like sleepless shadows in his wake. But the rest aren't far behind. The Iftav have come like a rolling tide over the land, gathering to the northernmost settlement of the eastern arai. A place the foul men of Rand call Tol. Now, as morning begins to send its shallow fingers over the walls of the garrison, they'll descend like a dark cloud over anyone unfortunate enough to be found within it.

"Go. Search every structure. Every corner. We'll find her." Faleth sends his hunters into the settlement before turning to the false arai woman beside him. "Come. Show me the face of the son of Rand."

The night still fights to keep its thin shadows veiled over the ground as they stalk into the empty village paths. It's a small garrison, with only a handful of little barns and cottages huddled in a seemingly random arrangement. The Iftav search each of them, breaking through shuttered windows, overturning every crate and table, leaving every door open. But smoke rises from only two cabins in Tol this morning. Faleth finds the first unlocked, occupied by a single sleeping guardsman.

"Not him," Hylveh confirms with a single glance. "Just one of his men."

Faleth turns to continue onward. Hylveh follows close behind, towering strangely over her comrades in her pale *virsevin* form. The sight of her walking among several voránjevin hunters seems to confuse the guard who keeps watch outside the door of the second cottage. His bewildered stare has little time to dart between the faces that approach him before Hylveh pulls the life from his chest, and he slumps to the ground with little more than a gasp. Faleth steps around the soldier's limp body to push open the cabin door.

Only three arai fill the room beyond. One stoking the fire, another slouching on the bench in the corner, and a third seated at a humble table with his head resting in broad hands.

"Him." Hylveh steps past the threshold with her arm raised, pointing to the man at the table.

The soldier beside the fire straightens at the sound of the door, then reaches for his dagger. But he scarcely manages two strides toward the door before meeting Faleth's outstretched hand and collapsing to the floor. The arai from the bench isn't far behind. He rushes forward only to be sent gasping to his knees by Hylveh's swift touch. Faleth hardly notices.

"Talek, the son of Rand," he speaks calmly to the only remaining man in the softly lit room, using the language of the arai.

"Beast of hell," the man curses as he rises to his feet. "What do you want?" He backs subtly away as Faleth nears.

A king? Faleth muses to himself as he watches the anxious twitch in the man's vein-laced fists. Are the eastern arai not proud of their bold leaders? But who's this trembling creature?

"I want my Onei. I want to end the one who took her from me," he replies.

The arai draws a short blade and lets out a sudden violent growl as he swipes at his enemy. Faleth moves aside and lays a palm to the man's leg as Hylveh dodges to drain the power from his arms. And in an instant, Talek the king falls helplessly to his knees with a gray voránjevin hand hovering threateningly over his heart.

"My soldiers will carry on without me," he breathes, "keep fighting . . . until these lands are rid . . . rid of your curse. Our people . . . will be avenged." His voice strains as Faleth's hand pulls mildly at the strength in his chest.

"Where's my Onei?"

A scoff escapes the king's tight jaw. "The captive? Slain . . . no more use to m—"

Faleth tears the life from the heart beneath his palm before the word can be finished, then shoves the man's heavy body away. It hits the floor with a sickening thud. And for a time, the fire's soft crackling is the only sound to fill the dim cabin. Until the hunters can be heard shouting from the south.

"*Neseo setat!* We found her! She's alive! Come quickly!"

Their voices come calling from beyond the cottage walls, echoing crisply through the morning air.

Words like sweet dew, like new breath. Words that send lightning through Faleth's cold and drowning heart.

Onei!

All reality seems to meld and blur away as he bolts out into the morning air, every thought swallowed up in the sound of the distant voices. He flies down the worn dirt paths between the cabins with his feet scarcely touching the ground, running with hope pressed and pounded into every footfall.

Alive!

He spots the others gathered in a clearing near the southern outskirts of the settlement. Several heln, kneeling low in the grass with their arms reaching down into the earth. An unfinished well. The sight pours terrible heaviness into Faleth's bones.

"*Where is she?*" he shouts as he closes in. The others are too focused to notice until he comes skidding to a stop at the well's edge, pushing them aside.

"ONEI!" He grips the coarse rope that hangs down into the blackness of the well. Far below, almost entirely veiled by the shadows, a dim shine appears. The glimmer of two weary eyes gazing up.

"Faleth?" Her voice skips breathlessly along the cold stone and earthy walls of her prison. Faint.

"I'm here! Tie yourself to the rope!"

Maybe she's attempting to speak, but strained and ragged gasps are her only reply.

"Don't speak, Onei. I'll get you out of here! Just secure the rope as well as you can—give it a jerk when you're ready."

He waits in agony at the well's edge, hands trembling and rigid over the rope's coils. Why has it come to this? She could have escaped them, could have come back to her people with no more than ruffled fur. How could it possibly come to this?

A mild tug travels up the rope from down below.

"Hold on!" Faleth cries down into the blackness as he heaves the rope over his shoulder. Someone snatches up the end behind him, making an anchor.

Pull!

She weighs almost nothing at all. In a moment Faleth reaches down to grasp Onei's quaking shoulders. He pulls her swiftly over the stony edge and into his arms, sending her all the strength he can muster. He sends it coursing like hot waters through his palms, his arms. But her breath is a feathery whisper at her lips, and all over he can feel her life flickering like cooling flames, fading. Threatening to extinguish entirely. And now the darkened shape in her torn tunic catches Faleth's eye—a shining wet stain that's soaked her right side. Blood.

"What have they done!" The tremor that clatters through his bones erupts into his voice as he stares into Onei's partly open eyes.

"Give her strength!" he shouts to the others.

They gather around with open hands, pressing their palms to the spine and heart of the filíl whose life seems to be slipping steadily away before their eyes. Hitérian energy shifting has always had a miraculous way of healing wounds. But it can't replace blood. They've come too late.

Faleth curses at the cold grass. "Onei, stay with me, you hear? Stay with me!" He wraps his sash around her bleeding side, moving desperately to stop the warmth from flowing out into the grass.

I heard a cry in my brother's heart.

It was something the sasarian woman said. Words she spoke some time ago, which meant nothing to him then. But now, they carry hope. Somehow, she's always been able to find him. Find *anyone*. He closes his eyes.

She's leaving me! Please, save my Onei!

The light comes subtly at first. Soft enough to be mistaken for the dawn peering through the bodies of the trees to the east. When Faleth looks up to see the sasarian's radiant countenance standing no more than an arm's length away, it seems unreal. Bathed in light, her glimmering robes pool like sparkling dew over the grass where she kneels.

"Give her to me," she says.

Onei's warmth has vanished almost entirely as Faleth lays her gently in the sasarian's waiting arms. All around, the scouts and hunters of the Iftav gather nearer, watching wordlessly.

Éliva looks to their leader with a startling light in her eyes. "I don't do this for you," she says, "or for any of you, who have robbed away the lives of many. I do this for Onei. She has yet to complete her purpose in this life. I can feel it." She holds Onei like a frail child in her arms. Then she closes her eyes, and the silence of the trees becomes suddenly apparent. As if all the birds and the wind itself have paused to watch the angel at work. Muted, waiting—until the stillness is broken by a coarse, desperate gasp that erupts at the heart of the scene. Onei takes the morning deep into her lungs. Her wide eyes stare suddenly up at the glowing being that holds her before falling peacefully closed again. Asleep.

"She may sleep for several days, but she'll survive," Éliva whispers.

Faleth leans nearer, peering at Onei's sleeping face. She's so thin, so pale.

"Your kind can wield Hitérian, can't they?" he murmurs.

"Hitérian was a gift from our kind, given to the voránjevin race long ago. Before that day, the power to share life energy was borne by sasarianë alone," Éliva tells him. "The energy's everlasting within us. Endless."

She returns Onei to Faleth's still-trembling arms. But she remains kneeling for a moment longer. Somehow, her silvery glare has risen to an almost blinding intensity. "Her wounds are mending. You've received mercy because of her. What mercy was there for the people of Votyón?"

Faleth stares back, attempting to scoff at the memory of the pitiful village he and his hunters decimated. But something catches in his throat. It's a crippling sensation. A deafening silence that manages to momentarily intercept any thoughts he may have had and send them sizzling down to ash.

What mercy was there?

The question simmers—boils away all else until only the sight of Onei remains. The one who always spoke of mercy, always questioned the order to kill, always tried to soften his coarse edges.

The sasarian's words pour terrible bitterness into the air, and for some incomprehensible reason, it burns like hot embers in Faleth's cold and lifeless heart. The words cut in a way he never could have anticipated. And he has no answer to them. He sits in suffocating speechlessness as the sasarian rises to her feet and turns away to the west. She vanishes midstep, trailing the dawn at her heels.

14

He's seen countless sunrises through the years. Seen the newborn face of the sky bloom in marvelous, dazzling blends of color and light more times than he could number. But today, the morning breaks with hues Echeret can't name. And as he watches, the warm spread of color at the horizon lays a blanket of silence over his heart. He's not sure how long he's sat on the step of the cabin, watching it all unfold, when Defehl comes slipping out the back door to sit beside him.

"Thought I might find you here," she whispers.

Echeret draws a long breath into his lungs, then lets it slide like a receding tide from his chest. "I was a fool to think they might spare him," he says.

Defehl loops her arm through his, gripping him just above the elbow the same way she always did in the early days, when their love was young. "You tried to do what you could. No one can ask for more."

It's strange to think that seven days have already slipped by since the morning they found the king's lifeless body at Tol. They'd pressed onward to the garrison as quickly as they could, gathering aid and desperately hoping to reach Talek before the enemy. But they were too late. Far too late. The people of Rand have lost their king. And little remains to battle the panic that's begun to spread among the settlements.

"Word's just come from Sóvrun," Defehl tells him, reaching to gather her dark hair into a simple bun behind one ear. "They'll come to the council."

"That's all of them, then." Echeret nods in quiet approval, surprised. The leaders of the settlements haven't gathered for a council in many years—not since before Talek was named king. Echeret wasn't certain that any of them would react gladly to a plea to do so now—especially at the invitation of a recently outcast first officer. But he needed to try. And now that they've all agreed to gather at Leln in three days' time, the true severity of the people's troubles seems to tower like an impassible mountain on the horizon. The lack of a king, the looming threat of the Iftav . . .

"You need to eat something. Come back inside." Defehl gives his shoulder a mild squeeze as she rises and turns back to the door.

* * *

A thin fog still hangs like shallow gray waters at the roots of the trees as Echeret walks along the edge of the woods later that morning. It flattens and distributes the morning light into a cool, even glow over the grass. Not moving, yet not entirely still.

"Hidden lights are found at dusk."

A man's voice speaks a name Echeret hasn't heard since the day he and Defehl made their vows. His full name. The voice belongs to a young man who now stands between the trees to his right. A shining man, clothed in robes that glisten like still waters in the brightness of dawn.

"They call you 'Hidden,' don't they?" the glowing man asks, eyes full of stars.

"Yes." Echeret stops in his place, searching the stranger's bright face. "You . . . you appeared to our king not long ago, didn't you? Who . . . what . . . ?"

"I'm just someone who wants to aid your people."

"Have you come from the heavens?" Echeret questions.

"No more than you have. I was once a boy of Ethein. My common name is Tolaiyë," the man replies, stepping closer. The light of his presence moves like dusk from the trees as he leaves them. "I seek to aid the children of Claya any way that I can."

"I heard you make an offer to our king when you visited last. Our king no longer lives." The words glide out of Echeret's mouth, and their reality strikes again like a sudden gust of wind in his weary mind. Talek is dead.

"The offer I extended to the king still stands. If your people will accept it, we can provide an escape from those who haunt them," Tolaiyë tells him. He's stopped an arm's length away—near enough that Echeret can see the shards of ethereal light that glimmer at the edges of his eyes.

"Refuge from Onei's people? From the Iftav?"

"If you leave these lands, the Iftav will give us their word never to harm your people again. They'll honor our covenant."

"I see." Echeret stares back. "You would have us leave North Emér? Where would we go?"

Tolaiyë holds out his arm toward the trees where he stood moments ago. "To the south, to lands we'll dedicate to your people. South of Emér, the voránjevin clans dwell only along the western shore. We'll guide you to a place where even their scouts have never wandered," he says.

South? From the time Echeret was a boy, no one but wanderers and wayward soldiers have ever journeyed south of the settlements. And of those who returned, few claimed to have ventured beyond Rand's Mark. There's no knowing what wild lands lie south of it. But perhaps south is the only option. It was the oppressive rule of the lords of Old Sketza far to the north that drove Rand's people to settle North Emér. To the east, the forests and plains quickly melt into endless sands. And the people of the western settlements would sooner fight battles than allow their longtime enemy to flood their villages—refugees or not.

But will the people of Rand agree to leave their land? Again?

"More than anything, I wish I could help my people escape these times," he tells the glowing man. "But I've only just met you. And I'm not even sure what you are. Can I trust you?"

Tolaiyë smiles, and an unspeakable brilliance shimmers from his face. But despite the angelic rays, the smile's a human one. The smirk of a humble gardener's son. "You can, and I hope you will. But the choice is yours, Echeret. I can't force you," he says.

Echeret looks down to the dewy grass at his feet, bringing a hand to his hip in thought. Here he is, talking to some kind of angelic being—a being who offers to provide the people with an escape from their enemy. No one would believe him, should he tell of it. Even Defehl needed time to believe when Echeret returned late one night to tell her of the godlike man that was speaking with the king. It may be rash to trust this stranger too quickly. Even so, he must try. Would it be any better to remain in North Emér, awaiting the next massacre?

"How can I find you again?" he asks at last, feeling suddenly at ease for reasons he can't entirely explain to himself.

"If you need me, think of my name, and I'll come," the angel says. "If the people are willing, take them south until the last shores of the Emér can be seen in the west, until you reach the great plateau that overlooks the southern wasteland. We'll meet you there."

15

The slumber that shrouds her mind is thick. It blackens out any thoughts or memories that might arise and leaves her adrift in a soundless, dreamless sleep. And when it loosens its grip at last, a single fleeting image is all that comes to her mind's eye: the face of an arai goddess that shines like the sun.

The morning is a soft yellow-green glow in the leaves overhead when she opens her eyes. She shifts her shoulders, feeling stiff and heavy all over. A familiar dark sash hangs drying in the branches to her left, embroidered with the simple emblem of the Iftav. And an old scent floats mildly in the air. The smell of wind-tossed fabrics and sun-dried meats. The smell of home. It floats like perfume from the heln who's fallen asleep on the blanket beside her with his head propped on one fist. Onei resists the urge to touch him. It's been too long since she was able to stare at his sleeping face. And so much has happened . . .

Faleth's chest rises in a waking sigh before he opens his eyes a moment later. Such bright, golden eyes.

A calm smile paints his gray face. "Welcome home," he tells her.

He leans to leave a kiss on her forehead, and Onei nearly forgets the storm of questions that clutter her mind. It'd be wonderful to fall into his arms, to let the fears and pains of all that's happened melt away into the embrace she knows so well. But things have changed. *Everything's* changed.

"How did you find me?" She almost coughs as her voice comes to life. It seems like only moments ago when death was knocking kindly at her door. When the world had been shut away beyond cold, earthen walls. And darkness reigned . . . such darkness. The memory of the well sends a subtle shudder through her lungs.

"An arai man told me. He said he tried to let you go. Why didn't you come back to us?" Faleth asks. There's something different in his tone that's difficult to label. Something less coarse . . .

Onei sits up. "Echeret. So he's still alive. I was trying to help them make peace," she murmurs, then looks back to Faleth's waiting gaze. There's no sense waiting. She must ask. "Love, why has so much death come to the arai? After all these years, all our talks of forgiveness, of peace—what could they have done to deserve this? He told me . . . he said . . ." Her voice quavers with the memory of all Echeret told her.

An entire village.

Faleth looks momentarily past her, his face like stone. "I thought they'd killed you," he says.

Onei brings his eyes back to her with a gentle hand at his cheek. "Even if they had, no amount of death among them would return me to life," she says. "We can't undo what's been done. But we can end this now, Faleth. We *must.*"

Faleth rises to his feet. "I can't tolerate the arai of Rand here any longer. None of us can. They'll leave these lands if they wish to live."

"They're no threat to us. Why must we become their demons? You've gained me back, and in the process destroyed many families of the arai and broken countless others. The sorrow you've brought them is enough! How far must you go, son of Drinehn?"

The silence that follows her words is almost unbearable. Silence like simmering coals, like rising steam. Faleth's yellow gaze is unwavering. "You've made friends with them too, then?" he whispers. "The creatures who stabbed a knife into your side and threw you to the bottom of a well?"

Onei opens her mouth to reply, but a call through the trees interrupts her words before they can begin.

"Messengers, returning from the east!" someone shouts through the leaves, and Faleth turns toward the sound, ears twitching forward. He looks back to Onei, waiting only a moment.

"Faleth, wait—"

Then the gray heln slips away through the leaves before she can speak, and is gone.

16

He's never forgotten that summer, over twenty years ago, when he managed to hunt and capture his first stag. He was thirteen, barely tall enough to leap onto the wild animal's lurching back from the forest floor. He returned to the camp with his kill borne between the shoulders of his comrades—with a grin on his face that would have lasted for days.

Mother and Father weren't in the camp when Faleth arrived that day. But he knew where to find them. He sprinted off toward the arai village, replaying every detail of the triumphant hunt in his mind as he went. It began with the perfect hiding place, then a sleek and soundless dart into motion as the helpless creature fled through the leaves—and an intercepting leap at the perfect moment. He leaped the way Father always taught him. With careful precision, not holding back. And it worked.

Ever since the arai had appeared from the north several months before, it wasn't uncommon for Mother and Father to spend countless afternoons at the newcomers' nearest village. Some days they passed hours with the tall, narrow-faced arai—learning their language, exchanging herbs and fresh kills. Many in the clans of the Shardehn and Iftav were fascinated by the seemingly new race. But Faleth had yet to share their sentiment. He'd seen the way some of the arai looked at his people with such anxious, darting eyes. The way they clutched their gardening tools more firmly in the company of the clans. Faleth had decided long before that it was best to keep his distance from the strangers. After all, as hunters of the Shardehn often said, the larger the beast you encounter, the more carefully you must tread.

It was a windless day. Mother was kneeling in the still grasses near the incomplete framework of an arai shelter when he spotted her.

"Mother, I caught a stag! You should *see* it! Where's Father?" he called out to her as he came running from the trees. But his sprint melted into a slow shuffle when she turned to see him. Her forehead was furrowed together, eyes wide and gleaming with wetness. Something was terribly wrong.

"Faleth, my sweet boy," she said to him, scarcely audible above the slow rustling of his feet through the grass. Her eyes were violet ponds of crystal waters—pools that suddenly sprang into fountains and began to pour down her dark face as Faleth came nearer. It was the first time he'd ever seen his mother weep.

A young arai boy sat watching from the shadow of the half-built shelter, pale and silent. He stared back at Faleth with reddish hair falling in swirls around his furless face. He was a boy Faleth had seen many times. The son of a man Mother and Father had most likely come to visit that morning.

"Mother, what's happened?" Faleth whispered as he stepped nearer. She was hunched over, cradling something dark in her arms. Some*one*. Father's green sash lay crumpled in the grass beside her. And Faleth's heart began to shudder and seize up at the sight of it.

"Your son," Mother whispered between gentle sobs. "Your son is here, my love."

Faleth stopped in his place. Paused at the wall of cold air that seemed to meet him where he stood, wishing he could turn back.

But Mother bade him closer. "Don't be afraid, Faleth. There's been an accident. . . . Your father needs to see you."

Father?

Each step closer seemed sharp. Like stumbling downhill, like fumbling over rocks in the dark. Jarring. The reverberations jolted through his spine as he came to Mother's trembling shoulder. Beside her, Father lay with his head cradled in her arm—his body pinned beneath the weight of a massive log. His strained expression softened at the sight of his son. But he didn't speak.

"It would have crushed a man and his child. Your father saved them both," Mother breathed. She said something more, about someone running for help, about time running short.

But Faleth scarcely heard—hardly felt anything but the slow turn of his own head from side to side and the numbness that swelled in cold vibrations along his fingertips.

A wet glint of red appeared at the edge of Father's mouth, threatening to trickle out and stain his dark chin. "Faleth, be strong."

The words slipped like unswallowed water from his teeth. Breathless. Then something changed in the hues of his half-open eyes—a soft flutter of light . . . then shadow. And he grew still. Mother brought her face low to the ground beside him. Silent.

That's when the men came. They came yelling in their strange language, throwing stones and gripping torches in their massive hands. The pale boy was dragged away into the crowd, hidden away behind a stampede of broad feet and waving shovels. Mother did all she could to pull Father's lifeless body free. Faleth fought desperately to keep the men at bay, stealing strength from as many of their thick legs as his young body could manage. But there were too many of them. They came like a herd of thrashing, wild boars. A tumbling avalanche. They set flames to the half-built structure where Father's dark figure lay pinned, and the starving fire leaped and scampered along the timbers.

When Mother turned away at last, the flames licking frantically after her, she took Faleth by the wrist and led him swiftly away to the safety of the woods, saying nothing at all.

They ran nearly halfway back to the camp before she collapsed to the earth, weeping bitter rain into the emerald-green sash clutched in her arms.

He was thirteen years old the day his father was killed. The day the arai lost any hope of friendship among the Iftav.

17

"Farther south? Deeper into the nest of the beasts? Need I remind you, we never knew of their terror until we came down from the northern shores." The chief guardsman of Kehnin raises his noticeably thick eyebrows as he speaks, an uneasy melody chiming in his otherwise deep voice.

"Our enemy dwells in clans all along the northern and western sides of Emér," Echeret answers him. "But we'll be following the eastern shore straight south. To a land where they haven't ventured."

"How have you learned all this?" Someone speaks up from a back corner of the room. A collective murmur spreads through the council.

The leaders of the settlements have gathered for only a short time here, in the village hall of Leln. But the sweat's already begun to gather in the creases of Echeret's broad palms. "The king kept one of their people hostage for several months. We learned many things from her," he tells them.

"Can we trust the word of a parafa?"

"It could have told you anything!"

Many voices erupt at once, colliding like crashing waves in the air until the eldest woman raises her hand to silence them. "None have gone south to Rand's Mark so much as Kelef of Leln. And in his many ventures there, he's never mentioned the beasts. The lands beyond may very well be free of them," she suggests.

"Even so—say we go south, but the beasts follow us, disguised as men?" a younger man questions. "They could come along—creep into our camp! Slay us in our sleep!"

Echeret rises from his seat to look over the crowd. "My people, these are trying times, and our options are few. To the east the plains turn quickly to desert. The people of the western settlements have long made clear their desire to remain independent of our kingdom. We can flee back to the north, to the land of our kinsmen—can return to the servitude of the lords of those lands and forget the reasons why our families ever left it all behind. Or we can muster the courage to come together and search for a new home. We can find a haven for our people. A land unclaimed, untouched." He takes a slow breath. "It's true that we have no way to be entirely certain of the plan I propose. There will be risk. But our risk is greater if we remain here. I've come to love this woodland as you have, and it pains my heart to leave it behind. But we must. To remain in North Emér is to sentence ourselves to death. As you know for yourselves, the enemy has little interest in mercy."

The hall falls silent in the wake of his words, and from wall to wall the people sit with stern eyes and mild frowns on their faces. Some shake their heads in soundless dismay. Others simply stare at Echeret, as if they expect him to somehow reach into his pocket and draw out the answers and certainties they so desperately need.

Then a man with his age painted as silvery streaks in his hair rises to his feet. The chief guardsman of Urást. "Can we trust a man who was made an outcast? Our king made the order himself, in the final days of his life."

It's a question Echeret had been expecting. But it was asked more calmly than he would've anticipated. "Talek, son of Rand, was a dear friend of mine from the time I was a boy. More so than a brother," Echeret answers. "But the hardships our people have suffered in the past year changed him into a man I couldn't understand. He was obsessed with the idea of remaining here with all our people to defeat the enemy in battle. An idea that I couldn't accept. But as his people you're free to trust his final judgment. I'm no king. But I dearly hope that our families will have a chance to live on."

The man stares serenely back with a slow nod at his chin, as if he'd expected every word. But the gleam in his eyes is difficult to read. "How far is it to this land in the south?" he asks.

"I suspect no less than five weeks of travel by foot to the southern shore. Perhaps more, with all our people moving together."

"Very well. The families of Urást will join you on this journey. Hauten long served as a wise and strengthening voice among us. I'll trust his son before any others of the second generation," the man announces with a fist held ceremoniously before his lips. Then he turns to the council. "We'll find a new land for ourselves, however difficult it may seem. We've done it before. Who will join us?"

The council members stare thoughtfully at one another—some looking to the guardsman of Urást with careful approval, others muttering heatedly amongst themselves. Now their voices rise. Their words float up and flood the room like warm, shifting steam, full of doubts and opinions. A stifling rain of sound at Echeret's ears. Until the keeper of Sóvrun raises her slender hand. "The families of Sóvrun will join you. How soon must we be prepared?" she asks.

"As soon as possible. How soon can the people be readied?" Echeret struggles to hide the raw urgency in his voice.

"We of Kotán need no more than five days. Where's the meeting point?" a man near the back of the hall calls out.

"At the fork of the river just south of here. We can head out together from there, no?" someone answers over the crowd, and Echeret turns to send Defehl a silent, raised-brow glance. Could it be? Will the settlements agree to leave North Emér?

He raises his hand to quiet the council. "Four days, then, and we'll meet at the fork of the Held river with all who'll join us. We'll begin our journey with the dawn of the fifth day—the eleventh day of this month."

"Yes, four days!"

"Agreed!"

"Fine then!"

Shouts ring out through the council, some readily approving, some sharp and strictly obligatory, others scornful. Not all will agree to go. But those who will are far more numerous than Echeret had anticipated. He dismisses the council with his heart at his throat, hoping desperately that the messenger called Tolaiyë wasn't just some wild creation of his own mind.

"So much to be done in a few days' time," Defehl murmurs at his side. "Where to begin?"

Echeret lets out a desperate laugh and shakes his head, as if nothing could ease the tremors in his gut. "With a prayer for miracles."

18

The afternoon sun sets a warm stain on the cliffs as the people of Ethein move slowly up from the desert sands. Their shadows lie like black ghosts over the dry stone, growing steadily taller as the daylight yawns and reddens in the west. The steps they follow are low and wide—carved like flat teeth into the stony wall. An earthen ramp runs alongside them, which the wagons of the Ethein have followed upward for the greater part of the afternoon, one broad switchback at a time.

The children are first to the top. They've run ahead, and now their voices can be heard echoing back down the wide stairs and out over the Sand Sea. Thrilled, breathless shouts.

"Is this the place?"

"We've made it at last!"

"It's a palace! A castle!"

Pressing forward with her back bent into the slope, Kadeis glimpses white shapes along the edge of the cliff tops as she nears the final switchback. Tower rooftops, sleek marble walls and columns. They peer over the rocky edges above like welcome ensigns, rising in pale, defiant contrast above the cliffs. And when the caravan comes at last to the cliff top, songs of praise and wonder erupt from the travelers' parched throats. Kadeis drops to her weary knees. The sight atop the cliffs is far beyond anything she had dared to anticipate.

A white sanctuary sits like a mansion of the gods atop the cliffs. A structure grander than the palaces of the lords in Old Sketza, more massive than any construction the people of Ethein have ever known— full of columns and archways; wide, curving stairs; and sweeping balconies. All chiseled of sparkling granite and marble, formed in places with blocks more immense than any human hands could move. Flowering trees and long grasses spring up in open courtyards between the marble halls, mirroring the green land that extends from the sanctuary's walls to the distant horizon. The heat of the sands far below has given way to cool wind that carries the scent of fresh water. And the people of Ethein leave their wagons and wander like orphaned children into the gaping halls of an emperor's castle, stepping slowly along the paved paths, the open colonnades. Marveling, forgetting to breathe.

Kadeis is helping the others gather water from a fountain in the central courtyard when white light falls softly over her shoulders.

"Families of Ethein."

Her son's voice bears the same calm tones as his father's. He stands in a pool of light only a few paces away when she turns to see him, and the brilliant light of his presence is no less dazzling to her eyes.

"The angel!"

The word is whispered and gasped among the people. Some drop their buckets and ladles; others bend to kneel on the cool earth.

"He's come again!"

Tolaiyë shakes his head, urging them to return to their feet. "My people, you've journeyed far through wood and plain, over hills and rolling sands. You've journeyed long to reach this haven. Now it's yours—a sanctuary from the world."

Shouts of praise and thanks ring out from the families who have gathered. Mothers and fathers, graying elders, young husbands and wives. The children cheer and squeal in high-pitched melodies as they race along the marble stairs and arched halls.

"A palace! We're gonna live in a palace!"

Kadeis steps into Tolaiyë's radiance. "So this is the place you spoke of. The sanctuary beyond the Sand Sea. We've come at last," she says to him. "It's like a dream!"

"Mother, this is my realm. A place dark spirits can't enter. You and the people will be safe here."

"There could be no better place in all the world. Many of us spotted a pale shape above the cliff wall from the sands below. But we thought it was an illusion, a mirage. I never would have imagined . . ." She takes his hand. "Your father would have loved to see it."

"He *will* see it—before the next dawn rises. I'll go to free him now, Mother. Wait for us here," Tolaiyë assures her.

Kadeis stares back, watching the way the sun rises endlessly in her son's determined eyes. Eyes that could never lie.

Kehljen . . .

"May the winds make you swift," she whispers.

* * *

The sasarianë stand in silence for a time, at a place where black mountains collide like sharp earthen waves over the land. The darkness of night crawls along the valleys below—gray and voiceless as it paints over stone and grass and tree. Here, they listen carefully to all the earth. Their guides float idly at their sides, throwing shards of the setting sun from their single eyes. Tolaiyë watches the horizon. "Palarian, the people of Ethein have entered my realm, concealed from the shadows. We're ready to find the dark spirit who hides between the realms."

"Will you tell us his name?" Éliva's request comes calmly, but Tolaiyë can feel the urgency floating like undissolved salt in her words.

"This servant will tell you the name," the Palarian answers in a whisper, "directly into your hearts. Speak it aloud, and the one you seek will certainly hear."

"He'll turn his thoughts toward us at the sound of his name. It should be easy to sense his presence," Éliva affirms, and the Palarian drifts nearer.

"He will not look long. He knows that you seek him. You must move quickly once the name is spoken."

Éliva and Tolaiyë exchange a careful glance. The name is cold and ancient when the Palarian sets it in their minds. Like etchings in a tomb, like words on a scroll long ago disintegrated. And the chill it brings when they speak it aloud is undeniably tangible.

"Kyvóike Sekýnteo."

The Palarian was right. The attention of a single entity turns their way as the name is pronounced, somewhere far away in Claya's forgotten shadows. For only a fleeting moment. But that's all they need.

"Now!" Éliva shouts, and the two sasarianë leap into the wind. They follow the entity through the heart of the earth—plains, forests, and seas melding together in colorful collages on all sides—until they stand at the edge of the place between realms, only several paces away from a figure who stands shrouded in darkness. A figure Tolaiyë could never mistake.

Father!

He rushes forward, grasping the wrist of the man in the shadows before he's dragged away.

"Kyvóike Sekýnteo, I command you to leave him! Be gone from this man!" he shouts into the blackness. A sharp cry cracks the air, and a terrible twisting, writhing motion erupts in the shadows. Then the darkness pulls sharply away from the man it once cloaked, tearing like a thick blanket from his shoulders. He stumbles and falls soundlessly forward, vanishing out of the shadows altogether and tumbling into the realm of the living. Tolaiyë follows.

The sun's morning rays have begun to paint diamonds in the waves of the Atayu Sea when Kehljen appears on the sand—as if he's washed ashore at last, rejected by the shadows that once so mercilessly tossed and imprisoned him.

"Father!" Tolaiyë manages to catch the man's arm before he collapses to the ground, laying him slowly down.

Father lies for what seems like ages on the cool sands, eyes closed, heart fluttering like a candle's flame in his chest. The waves of the Atayu surge loudly beside him, fighting to rise from their depths, reaching fruitlessly after him. Their voice swells and sighs in endless rhythms. For a time, it's the only sound.

Tolaiyë brings his palm to his father's chest and wills his strength to gather there. The energy pools in a warm eddy over the shuddering lungs and seeps down into the exhausted corners of the heart. And the man lying in the sand draws a sudden, heavy breath. His eyes are as blue as ever when he opens them. A pale, dusted blue, like the morning sky after the gusting of a harmless windstorm.

"Tolaiyë . . . ," he whispers, and he smiles wearily—a smile Tolaiyë's sorely missed. He takes another ragged breath. "I knew you'd find me if I held on long enough." He makes an attempt to laugh, though it crumbles into a cough. "You look like a god, son."

"Some say I take after my father," Tolaiyë tells him.

Éliva appears beside them now, her bare feet scarcely touching the sand. "He's fled. We'll have to find him again once Kehljen is safe," she says.

Tolaiyë nods. No longer carrying a captive, the dark spirit may move even more rapidly through the realms. But he'll still be easier to pin than before. Now they have his name.

Tolaiyë looks back to his father. "Come, I'll take you to Mother."

19

The buckets are an awkward strain on their arms as they carry them back from a spring, and Echeret wonders again how he forgot to bring a water cart along for the journey.

"It's good—keeping us from becoming lazy," Defehl pants at him when he gives her a weary look over his shoulder. She hugs a single broad bucket to her stomach, smiling over the water that sloshes inside and threatens to spatter in her face. Where does she find all that positive energy?

Five days have passed since the people gathered from the seven settlements and set off on their journey to the south. Only a handful of households remained behind, choosing instead to seek out land among their brothers and sisters to the west. There are times when Echeret's thoughts drift back to them, wondering if they've found a refuge for themselves. Wondering if they survived the trip. Defehl only shrugged her shoulders when he wondered aloud the second morning.

"There's no use fretting over them," she told him. "We've got more than enough to be concerned about right here."

She was right. The fate of those settlers isn't something he's likely to find out soon—if ever. And the road ahead is long. They've moved in a parade of feet and wheels, flowing in massive formation over the hills. Nearly every family spent the first four nights lying awake with blades clutched in their anxious fists. Now, as the fifth night edges in, most groups are planning to keep watch in shifts. Walking for days with their homes tugged in wagons and packed tightly into bags on their backs is already exhausting, and a lack of sleep only adds to the burden. Some say they've spotted the eyes of the parafa in the trees at night, creeping among the shadows. If the stalkers are truly nearby, they have yet to attack. But no one wants to be caught relaxing too soon.

Echeret pauses to set down the buckets and work a knot out of his shoulder when he notices the lack of sloshing water at his back. He glances over his shoulder.

Defehl's stopped in her place, staring off into the trees. He follows her gaze. A little figure stands at the edge of the trees, watching motionlessly, just outside the view of the travelers in the camp. A fur-covered being dressed in a simple tunic—with massive, tannish eyes that Echeret's come to know well. He leaves the buckets and steps carefully to the trees, Defehl following at his heels.

"You escaped!" he exclaims in a whisper that comes out more hoarsely than he had intended. "Did they rescue you? Your people?"

Onei nods. "Yes—at the expense of your king and his men," she answers, glancing to them both. Her stare glosses over with wet shine. "My friends, I'm so sorry, for everything," she says, voice wavering. "I can't seem to stop them. The sooner you can leave these lands, the better. I've come to aid you."

"It isn't your fault," Defehl tells her. "Aiding us won't endanger you among your own people?"

Onei shakes her head. "I'll leave my tribe if I must. The other clans are peaceful toward your kind— I'll seek out their scouts along your path and ask for their help. They can protect you."

Echeret kneels in the grass. "The words you gave me saved our lives. Now this—how can we repay you?" He fails to hide the surprise in his voice. How could this little creature possibly care for the people of Rand? The people who took her captive?

"I only ask that you deny the Iftav a chance to take any more lives. They have yet to send their hunters after you. But I wouldn't suggest staying long at any campsite," Onei tells him, and she glances to the surrounding trees, ears twitching. "I'm going on ahead. But I'll be back."

She turns and slinks away into the leaves before either Echeret or Defehl can respond. And the two of them are left kneeling beside nothing more than quivering foliage, staring silently into each other's faces.

20

He should've known. The arai were thieves from the start. They stole away the hearts of his mother and father, fooling all the Shardehn—lulling them carefully into false friendship and drawing them in like practiced trappers. Deceivers. It was the arai who took the life of Drinehn of the Iftav. Mother was too enamored with them to see it, and now she's abandoned her son because of them. They even dared to take away Onei, the only one who truly remained to him. And it was a miracle that freed her from their hands, away from the edge of death. But now . . . now it seems as though her rescue came too late. The arai have taken her heart too.

She was gone when he returned from meeting with the scouts that morning. Gone without any explanation, without any goodbyes. But the morning hunters spotted her heading south. Alone. Faleth left after her with only the supplies he had tucked in his sash.

Cursed arai! Spawns of hell!

Why would she turn to them? The brutes who stole her away, who left her at death's door?

Now the day fades along the treetops, softly surrendering to the darker hues of the night. But Faleth doesn't slow his steps. He leaps like a wild animal through the leaves, his steel gaze locked toward the south. Running, running.

How dare they take her! How dare they steal her away!

Running . . . running . . . running till the woods become no more than a darkened blur in his path, until the outrage stains deep swaths of blackness into his heart.

I'll kill them all if I must. Kill any and all in my path.

The darkness is consuming. It comes gliding along the night air and clings to the hot rage in his breath. It cloaks his soul and drowns away any reasoning that remains in his cold and weary thoughts—overpowers him until he can no longer hope to control it. And in time his steps are no longer directed by his own mind, but the mind of another.

An entity that crawled from the gap between the realms—a presence more blackened than a moonless night sky.

21

Mother's waiting near the polished handrail of the grandest balcony when they return. It's a wide, curving stone patio that sweeps out along the westward edge of the cliffs, overlooking the Sand Sea far below. And despite her plain clothes, Mother looks like nothing less than a queen peering anxiously out from her royal porch. Tolaiyë and Father come arm in arm to meet her, appearing like a sudden mirage in the air and stepping softly down onto the marble tiles of the sanctuary.

"Kehljen!"

Mother throws herself into Father's trembling arms the moment he arrives, and the two of them stand almost motionless together, eyes closed, breaths in rhythm. Silent. They remain in each other's arms as Tolaiyë slips carefully away, and the sight of them leaves a familiar sensation in his bones. A grounded, rooted sensation, like the strength of the ancient trees near Ethein. And it brings a smile to his face.

* * *

The two of them are by the fountain in the central courtyard when Tolaiÿë returns the following morning, watching the sunlight stretch playful fingers among the archways. The light slides in a clean gloss over Father's freshly washed hair—a vibrancy that matches the brightness of the woven blue tunic and dark trousers he now wears.

Tolaiÿë smiles. "You're looking much more like yourself today, Father."

There's a calm grin on Father's face when he turns from the bowls he's rinsing. "Your mother's cooking has a way of doing that, you know," he says.

Beside him, Mother shakes her head. "It's the fruit that grows here," she corrects him. "Sweeter than any found in North Emér."

Father stacks the clean bowls at the edge of the fountain and moves to the nearest bench, setting himself slowly down with a sigh that makes him seem suddenly much older than he truly is. "I'm glad to *look* myself, at least. I'll never be the same again, after all that's happened," he tells them.

"Tell us, how did the darkness take you? When did this all begin?" Mother joins him on the bench.

Tolaiÿë steps nearer and sits contently on the grass at their feet. The shining of his countenance lights a warm glow on their faces, as if they sit watching a massive, blazing bonfire.

"He attacked me the night the other men of the peace treaty were killed. Some kind of powerful spirit. It took all my strength to fight him," Father explains, staring down in thought. "But with that being constantly striving to push me out of my own body, I began to inherit strange abilities."

"Abilities?" Tolaiyë questions.

"*His* abilities," Father clarifies. "In time, I began to sense you and your mother. I could feel that you were alive, and that you, my son, had become something much more powerful than an ordinary man. You had the same power as my captor, but stronger, full of light. I could feel you moving all over the earth. I began trying to reach you. And it worked—but when you came for me, the darkness would drag me away, out of your sight."

Tolaiyë's mind drifts momentarily back to the gap between the realms, to the dark presence they found writhing in the shadows there. "Seems like your captor accidentally passed that skill to you when he brought you across the realms, beyond the veil that hangs between the living and the spirits," he explains. "He was once a sasarian, as I am now. Long ago. But he used his gift for darkness and now roams the earth as an exiled spirit. He longs to return with a body to the physical realm."

"This being . . . it sought to steal your father's body. Did it hope to regain its former strength?" Mother places a firm hand to her husband's arm, almost possessively.

"I don't think he could ever truly return to his full strength. But there's no telling what he might attempt with the abilities that remain in him," Tolaiyë tells her. "We're searching for him constantly now, throughout the realms. But don't worry, Mother. He can't come here. He can't enter my realm."

"Good," Father says. He sighs again as he raises his head, looking toward the northwest at nothing in particular. "The abilities I gained from that demon seem to have stayed with me. Even now, I can feel a stirring somewhere deep in the earth. A stirring that resonates in my heart."

"The earth lives and is always speaking. We sasarianë can hear it. Now you've begun to hear it too."

"Yes, but it's quiet—no more than a half-spoken whisper," Father says, and Mother takes his hand.

"Teach me this skill! If we can hear the voice of the earth itself, then nothing in all the world can truly separate us. We could always find each other. And we could know always that our Tolaiyë is safe," she reasons.

"It could be a useful skill to master," Father tells her, nodding slowly. "But it may take years for us to learn in full. We can't cross the realms as our son now does."

"We can learn together," Mother assures him, her voice free of doubts. "Along with any of our people who may care to study it."

Tolaiyë smiles. It's a whimsical thought. The families of Ethein have traversed the Sand Sea to reach their sanctuary atop the cliffs. Now they'll learn to hear the voice of the earth. What marvelous tales their children will tell!

"May these cliffs be a haven until the end of days. A land where families will live together in peace, communing with the heart of Claya," he whispers.

And the words sink deep into the warm center of the earth. Remembered.

22

Three weeks south of Rand's Mark, the land becomes an open canvas painted in pale and sun-faded colors. It lies like a crumpled blanket in all directions, almost treeless, broken occasionally by the edges of mild plateaus. Dry, dust laden. Not far to the west, the southernmost shoreline of Emér can be seen as a shimmering sliver of gray against pastel sands.

The people of Rand make their camp at the edge of the greatest plateau in sight—a balcony of earth that overlooks a vast rolling plain to the south. The barren hills ripple out from its feet, continuing on until they collide with dark mountains along the southern horizon.

"Quite a view for our camp tonight." Echeret stares out over the plateau's edge from where he kneels and nearly misses the tent stake with his mallet.

"So vast," Defehl whispers, looking out to the hills. "Such a lonely land."

She hands Echeret another stake, and he doesn't bother to suppress the sigh in his chest. Could the new home of Rand's people possibly lie anywhere nearby? In the heart of a wasteland?

* * *

Onei finds them after the evening fires have been lit. She comes crawling along a narrow shelf just below the jagged edge of the great plateau, a subtle shadow below the rocks. When she peers up at them from her perch, Defehl nearly spills the simple soup in her hands.

"Your steps are silent as the twin moons!"

Onei shows them a little smile, and her ivory teeth peek slyly into view. "Silence is the way of my people," she says, and she glances around, confirming that no other eyes are watching. "How far away is this land you hope to claim? I've never come so far along the shore of Emér."

Echeret resists a wince. "The others don't know this . . . but to be honest, I'm not entirely certain," he answers as he settles down beside the fire to stir the coals. "I was told to bring the people south until the southern shores of Emér come into view in the west. He said we'd find a plateau that stands above the hills."

Onei brings her slender arms over the edge of the little cliff and folds them under her chin. "Who said this?" she asks.

Echeret gives the fire another jab, then tosses a fresh wedge of wood into the mix. Searching for the right words. "Someone who can help us. Someone your clan is willing to make promises with," he tells her.

"Could it be . . . the sasarianë? One of them saved my life, not long ago."

"The what?"

"The immortals. Our clans have watched for them through many generations," Onei explains.

"You know of them? Where do they come from?" Defehl asks, but Onei shakes her head.

"The two who exist now began as ordinary arai children. My people kept watch over them both from the beginning. But how they changed and why—it's something I don't yet understand."

"Well, at the very least it's comforting to know that they *do* exist. I haven't lost my mind after all," Echeret murmurs.

"And now that you've come here? How long will you wait?" Onei asks.

"The one who led us here will come again, as he said he would. I trust his word that a way will be provided," Echeret assures her. Assures *himself.* It's possible that the mysterious messenger who proposed this journey won't provide any further direction. And what could be done then? Must the people abandon their homes and come this far only to wander aimlessly in the wastes? The thought brings more cascading worries into Echeret's mind than he cares to manage, so he waves it away. The people of Rand will find a way to prevail. And everything will work out. It *has* to. Somehow, he can feel it—a subtle whirring in his blood like the static before lighting, or the chill before dawn. It's the kind of sensation that can only come as a prelude, a premonition. Something awaits the people of Rand in the path ahead. Echeret only wishes he could guess what it is.

Sleep comes to him in uneven episodes that night. The wasteland's restless breath stirs in constant little whirlwinds throughout the camp, tugging playfully at loose tent walls and untied ropes. Rustling, whistling faintly. It wakes him again and again, as if searching for someone to accompany it through the night. Until sleep leaves him entirely.

"Echeret."

The voice sounds at the center of his mind. A remnant of the flitting dreams that so recently reigned there.

"Echeret."

Now the voice is clearer. He sits wearily up, blinks in the dim light that's begun to seep in through the tent seams. He shakes the sleep from his head, and Defehl stirs in the blankets beside him.

"Did you hear that?" Echeret whispers to her.

She opens her eyes. "Hear what?"

"Echeret."

The voice comes again. Not the echo of a dream, but a voice that rings in his awakened ears. He looks back to his wife.

"Someone's calling me," he tells her. "Can you hear it?"

The drowsiness in Defehl's face gives way to raised-brow curiosity as she sits up, shaking her head. "Someone in the camp?" she asks.

"I don't think so," Echeret answers as he unhooks the tent door and peers out into the crisp morning air. The sun has yet to rise, but its glow already lights the plateau in simple shades. No one stands waiting. But he can't be certain. And now that he's awake, there's a new thrumming in his heart that he can't ignore. A breathless, urgent sensation—tugging, pulling him out the tent door. "I need to go see."

"Let me find my shawl."

They walk in silence to the edge of the plateau—all the camp still asleep at their backs—to where the previous night's campfires lie, still smoking in little gray piles.

"Echeret."

Now the voice echoes up from over the edge of the rocks. Defehl gives her husband a silent glance. She hears it too.

The morning's just beginning to send sharp ribbons of light over the eastern horizon as they find their way down the mild cliff. It forces them to squint at the rocks at their fingertips. The descent is simple, full of wide steps and jagged edges for hands to grasp. And their worn shoes meet the dust of the dry prairie hills below after only a moment's effort.

"You've come at last to the land of your inheritance."

Echeret's still dusting the grit from his hands when the voice sounds at his back. The one who bears it stands several paces away, near the shadow of the plateau. And the white light that beams from her presence chases out all shadows from among the rocks. Her radiance rivals the brightness of the rising day.

Another immortal. The light pools and shimmers at her feet as she motions toward the barren land that surrounds them.

"New life is brought to the wastes of the south. Now we'll call upon the earth to sustain it," she murmurs, and she turns away before Echeret or Defehl can manage any response, raising a single hand high overhead, palm to the northwest.

A sudden quake in the earth nearly topples Echeret off his feet. He reaches for Defehl, and the two of them huddle together as a terrible roaring erupts over the hills—a deafening rumble that tears like vicious seizures through the stones. Now the earth groans deep in its heart.

"Hold on!" Echeret can scarcely hear his own shout over the raging stones. The shaking jolts them to their knees when a massive crevice opens its mouth in the distant prairie, running like a fracture in pottery. The land opens in a dark, jagged line from north to south, slithering away toward the mountains. Now wetness joins the barrage of sand and dirt that flies overhead, and a sudden white spray of water can be seen leaping over the westward edge of the plateau. It pours excitedly into the newly formed crevice that scars the land, tossing and spurting high into the air as it flows. A faint mist rains over Echeret and Defehl where they kneel together, speechless. And then the earth falls still, it's grumbling replaced by the thundering waters that race to fill its new scar.

Water! But where . . . ?

Echeret rises to his feet and scrambles back to the little cliff he descended only moments ago. Defehl follows closely behind. The sight that awaits beyond steals all words from their lips.

The sea of Emér is broken. Its southernmost shore—once a low, sandy slope—is now carved and divided by a massive trench that cuts through its borders. Its waters flee in a violent torrent along the raw earth, escaping to the south.

"A new river is born. A gift to the people of Rand."

Echeret turns to find the angelic woman standing beside him, smiling with a brilliance that nearly blinds him.

Then the voices of the people can be heard. Shouting, exclaiming.

"An earthquake! There's been an earthquake!"

"Anyone injured?"

"Look there! What's happened at the shore?"

The families crawl from their tents with amazement on their faces, with breath held at their teeth.

"A river!"

Echeret stands watching as they come wandering from the camp, then looks back to the angel—

But she's gone. And without knowing why, he laughs.

23

"Thank you, love." Defehl smiles as she pulls back her hair with the little leather tie Echeret's brought her. She weaves a loose braid at the back of her head before turning back to the sopping laundry in a tub before her, little runaway strands of hair still dancing at her cheeks. The rushing river waters make rinsing clothes a much more efficient chore these days. In the course of their hurried journey south, many families have had little chance to wash *anything* thoroughly. But now the bold scents of soaps and oils rise and perfume the air all throughout the camp.

Echeret bends to snatch another wet undershirt from the bucket at his feet to hang on his makeshift drying line. The people wanted to camp at the river's edge to rest from their travels, and Echeret didn't object. Several weeks have passed since anyone's claimed to have spotted any followers in the night. And the river's cool mist is simply too wonderful to pass by. *Everyone's* at the water. Those who aren't bent over soapy tubs are soaking dried beans and grains upstream or swimming in the shallows near the plateau's edge, where the young river cascades loudly down to flow into the prairie hills beyond.

Such smiles! Such laughter in the air!

Echeret watches the faces of his people, marveling. It's an odd feeling to suddenly stand at the banks of a wild river. Yesterday, there was no river at all. It's a miracle. One that no one can explain—not even the two individuals who witnessed its creation. Echeret and Defehl alone saw the angelic visitor who woke the earth. She was a being not unlike the one who suggested leaving North Emér. But she gave no explanation of herself. She called the river a gift. *A gift to the people of Rand.* Is this truly the land intended for the refugees from the north?

The Sketzan people have always lived near water. Far to the north, Old Sketza lies entangled in a labyrinth of rivers that weave and collide throughout its borders. Rivers are its roads—carrying the people and their goods, their messages. Running their mills and irrigating their fields. In the forests of North Emér, each of the seven settlements was built near the flow of the river Held, or alongside one of its branches. It was the pure waters of the Held that once inspired Mighty Rand to declare the end of his search for a new home. All the families that followed him grew to know the sweet scent of its waters.

Though the refugees have travelled within sight of the Emér Sea for nearly their entire journey southward, the presence of a river is different. Unlike the stirring waves of the inland sea, river waters have no home. They hurry constantly onward, taking only souvenirs from the lands they visit. Rivers flee from their birthplace—a trait that's resonated in the hearts of

Rand's people since the day they left the old kingdom behind. Now, it resonates with new depth.

A gift indeed. It's good to have a river again.

Echeret's thoughts drift in slow circles over all that's happened, his fingers moving almost mechanically to smooth out the wet creases in the shawl he's just hung to dry. Until the sight of a man standing at the edge of the camp catches his eye. A stranger who stares back with jovial eyes and a subtle smile on his amber-bearded face. A newcomer? Echeret finds himself ducking under the clothesline and walking toward the stranger before any other ideas can come to his mind. Until recently, he'd never dream of confronting an intruder in the camp without his sénsin rod. Or at least a dagger. But today seems different. And for no provable reason, he feels entirely at ease.

"Are you new to our company, my friend? I don't believe I recognize you," he questions as he comes into the sparse shade of the single tree the stranger stands beneath.

"You know the faces of all your people?" The man seems older than Echeret, though no less lively.

Echeret gives a fond laugh. "Well, I just about do, after these long weeks walking together," he admits. "Though I may not always remember their names."

"That's far more than most men can say of the people they lead." The bearded man bends to snap a dry reed from the prairie grass at his feet, poking it casually between his teeth.

"I'm no leader. I was only the first to speak up with an idea."

The stranger smirks. "You're a humble man, Echeret."

Echeret pauses to gaze more carefully at the man before him. "Have we met before?"

The man shakes his head. "But now we have," he says. "I come from the far east, beyond the Sand Sea. I was once a man of Votyón. My name is Afai."

"Beyond the Sand Sea? Is there such a place?" Echeret wonders. Only Rand's appointed explorers and cartographers ever ventured near the Sand Sea in days past. And none of them dared enter it—let alone cross it.

"The way's far but not endless. Beyond the sands the people of Ethein have found themselves a refuge atop the cliffs."

Ethein. The westward settlement that many say was cursed. Its inhabitants must have abandoned it after all.

"Sounds like you've had a long journey, to say the very least," Echeret marvels. "What brings you to the southern edge of Emér, to the humble remains of the people of Rand?"

"Someone's coming your way. I've come to stop . . ."

Afai's words fall to broken silence as he glances abruptly in all directions. His calm smile melts away. "I know this spot. You need to get awa—"

Echeret has little time to react before he feels a sudden weight clap onto his shoulders. A slender gray arm appears at his chest, and all at once the breath seizes up in his throat. The earth comes up to meet him as his heart comes to a wrenching halt, held in place for an agonizing instant before Afai's strong hand tears the attacker away.

Breathe!

Echeret grips the dry soil at his face, gasping desperately, willing his heart to continue its rhythm. It's a sensation he's experienced once before. But this time it's far more powerful. Overwhelmingly so.

Breathe! Fight!

Fatigue boils like fire through his heart—a heart that hiccups and shudders terribly as the life ripples over it in irregular spasms. It takes all the power in his bones to keep it from falling silent. When it calms at last, leaving a horrible ache beneath his breath, the sounds of a struggle nearby become suddenly audible.

The Iftav. They've come. And Echeret's thoughts erupt at his temples.

The people! Families, children—all washing and playing unsuspectingly at the river's edge, entirely unaware, unprotected—

No!

Echeret summons the remaining strength in his breath to lift his head from the grass, rising on trembling elbows. Ready to fight in any way that he can. But there's no crowd of invaders when he looks up at last. No organized attack. Only one Iftav hunter stands in view. A gray-furred figure with a dark sash over his shoulder. He stands rigidly over Afai with a wild rage in his orange gaze and clenched teeth. The red-haired man has collapsed onto his back, chest heaving beneath the voránjevin's palm. But he looks his attacker in the eye.

"Leave him . . . demon . . . of an age long gone. . . . I command you . . . leave the body of this heln!" His words are faint, rasping like smoke at his lips.

But the gray hunter shudders fiercely at the sound. He writhes and stumbles backward, shaking horribly until he shrinks down into a squat, head in his hands. Silent.

Demon? Echeret takes a few breaths, swallowing the throb in his throat. The gray hunter's attacked him before. But this time, he came like a wild animal.

Still lying on his back only several paces away, Afai coughs. "You can't take the life of that man," he says, gesturing limply toward Echeret. "His family . . . will someday give rise to one . . . one who'll bring new life to all of Claya. Trust me. I've seen it." Now he strains to sit up, bracing against the earth to look at the voránjevin who sits curled up an arm's length away. "Faleth, we never took them from you. Your father . . . Onei . . . they're yours. Always have been."

The one who leads the Iftav. Few know him as well as I do.

Onei's words return faintly to the corners of Echeret's mind as he looks on. Maybe this is the one she spoke of. Somehow, Afai knows him too.

But there's little time to wonder. The two men are still struggling to lift themselves from the ground when the gray hunter's trembling shoulders fall still. He rises slowly, lifting his head to stare with terrible sharpness at the red-bearded man sitting in his path— the fire in his eyes now changed from madness to something darker. Sharper. Free of whatever power had possessed him a moment ago. And the scene that plays out next is almost too quick for Echeret to follow.

The hunter darts into motion, knocking Afai backward and leveling a hand to his broad chest—

"No, Faleth!"

A little figure comes leaping over Echeret and bolts to the hunter's side. A voránjevin figure. A *familiar* figure. She snatches his outstretched arm and pulls it desperately away from Afai. But the hunter's fast. Focused. He pivots unconsciously to remove the obstruction in his path and brings his second palm to her heart without taking his sight from the man before him, without blinking. And the smaller voránjevin collapses with a gasp to the dirt at his feet.

"*No—!*" Echeret curses.

Then the gray hunter freezes in his place, as if the flow of time has somehow seized up—as if the moons and all the stars have ceased their dance. And without uttering any sound at all, he falls to his knees. The fires that raged in his eyes only a moment ago fade and flicker out as he turns to the lifeless body beside him, leaving only a cold, stony stare in their place. Afai pulls himself shakily up again, leaning forward onto his hands, but the hunter doesn't seem to notice. He doesn't notice Echeret calling wearily to men in the camp either, or the way the sun's come out from behind thin clouds to beam hot rays onto his face.

"Onei . . ."

Now several men who remain from the king's army come rushing from the tents, leaping over stacks of supplies, ducking laundry lines. But the gray voránjevin's already gone when they arrive at Echeret's side. Gone through the trees and away over the hills to the north. Cradling a lifeless body in his arms.

24

South of the plateau the hills become steeper. Like shrunken mountains that lie together in sweeping ranges, sometimes clustering together as if hoping to hide some secret in the labyrinth-like valleys between them.

The people of Rand have come at last to their new home. They spread in little caravans over all the land, with the pride of Sketza still visible in their sun-darkened brows, following the path of the new river as it weaves and coils through the hills. Some pitch their tents within distant view of the plateau, tilling little gardens amid the shaded valleys. Others continue onward to the south—both east and west. They march with new trails at their heels and songs at their lips— songs of the Nakuë, the river that was born in a single morning before their eyes. The gift of the gods.

Nearly two weeks have slid by since the river appeared, and already its banks have begun to blossom with new life. Tiny clovers, miniature ferns, and infant blades of grass that poke in sparse clusters through the dirt. A delicate blanket of green. Watching from a hilltop, Echeret can spot the river's rushing waters winding far into the open hills, branching like veins in the earth's wide face. He lets out his breath in a slow sigh. After two weeks, his strength has returned in full at last. If it weren't for the newcomer, he wouldn't have had a chance. Afai saved his life. When anyone questioned why he came, how he knew where to find the camp, he simply showed them an honest smile.

"I could feel it. The man who led Rand's people was about to be in trouble, and I couldn't allow it," he always told them.

Now, the settlers have all gone their ways. The river beckons the people onward. Many families who once settled Táutha have gone westward along the first branch of the Nakuë. When morning comes again, Echeret and Defehl will join them.

The day grows old. Echeret sends one last glance over the hills as he turns back to camp, more than ready to roast the fish he caught when the afternoon was still simmering at its hottest. But a shadow on a nearby hilltop catches his eye midturn. The shape of a small-shouldered individual sitting low in the grass, motionless beneath the shade of a single young tree. A gray blemish in a sea of pale prairie grasses.

Could it be . . . ?

The sun's begun its descent in the west by the time Echeret's crossed over several hilltops and climbed near enough to recognize the being whose eyes match the hues of the fading daylight. Then he stops in his place, sénsin rod drawn and gripped warily at his side. The voránjevin figure sitting several paces away doesn't look up. Doesn't stir at all.

"She would be honored to know that her grave lies in the new land of your people." He speaks almost too softly for Echeret to hear, as if whispering any louder might disturb the one who sleeps silently in the grave before him—a grave marked with a single stone.

"She once told me that few knew you as well as she did," Echeret answers, unsure of the tone in his own voice.

"She was all I had left." The hunter closes his eyes.

Afai knew his name. The name Onei called out in the moment of her death. *Faleth.*

Echeret steps closer. "It was you, wasn't it? The one who led the attacks against our people. The massacre at Votyón." He fights to suppress the shudder that grips his bones with the memory of it all. So many lives . . .

Faleth opens his massive eyes and stares back. Emotionless. "We killed more than you'll ever know," he says flatly.

Echeret's fist tightens involuntarily on his weapon's leathery grip. For so long the enemy was too unknown to name, too hidden to visualize. Now the devil sits in open daylight, and it seems like all the lives he took away are watching at Echeret's back. Waiting to see what vengeance will come down on the beast who so heartlessly robbed them.

But for some reason the rage that urges Echeret to lift his sénsin rod doesn't remain. It boils and rises up like steam in his lungs, only to seep out on his breath and away on the breeze. And instead of charging forward in a vengeful blaze, Echeret finds himself simply staring calmly at his enemy, out of words. Out of thoughts. Waiting.

"So many years," Faleth murmurs to the stone on Onei's grave. "So many years I spent at secret war with the race who killed my father. Thought I could take back everything the arai stole from me. I wanted to dig my enemy's grave and throw him in it with my own hands, because it would somehow set me free. But now I see I dug the grave for *myself*. I've destroyed everything I sought to protect."

Standing nearby, Echeret wonders what to believe. Is it real? Somehow, the merciless leader of the Iftav melts into something else before his eyes. Something powerless. Broken.

"The Iftav will honor the request of the sasarianë. These lands belong to your people alone."

Echeret holds his breath. This voránjevin can't be trusted. Afai was the only other witness to his ruthless attack two weeks ago. But if the people spotted him at all in these lands, they'd lose hope of ever finding a home where the creeping fingers of their tormentors couldn't reach.

The Iftav will give us their word never to harm your people again. They'll honor our covenant.

The words of the godlike messenger have rung like a recurring dream through Echeret's mind since the day he first heard them. A statement he risked everything to trust in, despite endless uncertainties— one he's often considered himself half-mad for believing. But the immortals kept their promise. They created the Nakuë, and the people of Rand have found their new haven alongside it. If the Iftav ever break their promise and come haunting again, the creators of the river will know it.

"I have every reason to end your life," he tells the gray hunter.

"I have every reason to let you," Faleth answers without taking his gaze from the grave, and Echeret finds himself staring with him at the stone that rests there. It's plain, without any sudden edges or intricate layers of sparkling minerals. Simple. Like Onei's desire for the Sketzans and the voránjevin clans to live together in peace.

Then Echeret slides his sénsin rod back into the metal sheath at his hip. "You'd best be far from these lands by morning," he warns as he turns back to the southeast, where smoke from the little campfire Defehl's tending to draws thin, weaving stripes of gray over the fading face of the sky.

"Afraid to take the life of your enemy?" Faleth's voice mutters gruffly from behind.

Echeret pauses to look back, shaking his head. And he smiles.

"Let mercy run."

25

It must have been a simple trick to steal the body of Faleth of the Iftav. Like a thief who creeps in on a stormy night, concealed beneath the quaking thunder and the clamor of rain through the treetops. The voránjevin hunter wore rage and hatred like an open door on his chest. A door that let the dark presence of Kyvóike Sekýnteo enter easily in.

But the victory didn't last. The fallen spirit had yet to entirely expel the rightful owner of the body he stole, and Afai's command sent him reeling out into the open air. There, Tolaiyë and Éliva were waiting. The chase that ensued was rapid, wild. Almost unreal. The sasarianë pursued the enemy like flashes of lightning, darting and bolting through the realms. Never tiring, never pausing in any spot for long. They pursued him through the heart of the earth, through seas and valleys, forests and desolate mountain peaks.

Until the demon fell at last into their grasp.

He was leaping into the blackened gap between the realms when Tolaiyë caught hold of his disembodied, immaterial wrist.

"You have no power! I have no end!" The spirit-man thrashed and flickered in Tolaiyë's grip—sometimes clearly visible as an image of a man in long robes, sometimes nothing more than a quivering dark shadow that fluttered like an infant bird against the sasarian's palm.

"Only the goddess can bring about your ultimate destruction." Éliva raised her hand as she spoke, stepping closer. "But we have all the power we need for now."

The captive spirit let out a terrible, straining cry—quaking the realms and nearly rending the barrier between them. The blackness of the gap seemed to twist and contort at his back as he writhed and coiled fruitlessly in his place. Tolaiyë held him down as Éliva touched a single fingertip to the ghost's dark forehead.

"Kyvóike Sekýnteo," she declared, "you have haunted and tormented the living bodies of the children of Claya for too long, seeking to take back a privilege you lost. We now revoke it further. You no longer have power to touch or possess the bodies of the living. Human, voránjevin, or beast—all are beyond your reach."

Her words sent a violent quake through the shaded being before her, as though the merciless force of all the earth's tides had come down in one massive torrent onto his shoulders. And when Tolaiyë released him, Kyvóike—the dark king of old, the fallen sasarian, the demon, the ghost—wavered and drifted like smoke in the windless gap between the realms. Weakened. Changed. But no less sinister.

Tolaiyë brought a hand to Éliva's shoulder. "Come, we shouldn't stay long between the realms."

Éliva nodded, raising her hand to tear an exit in the darkness. The two of them were already gone when Kyvóike's rasping voice echoed after them.

"I never die," he sneered as he let himself drift backward into the shadows, until all but the soundless glare of his reddened eyes was hidden in the blackness that pooled there.

26

"Did you hear it?" she asks as she comes stepping out of the wind to appear beside him, the subtle scent of evergreens trailing after her.

Tolaiyë nods. The voice of the goddess was unmistakable when it came to him only moments before. Like the calls of songbirds in the wake of dawn. A voice that called him to a place in the heavens, among the gods. Away from Claya indefinitely.

"Why would we be asked to leave?" He stands watching as the fishermen of a seaside village bring their boats in for the evening. Sails rolling, seabirds gathering as baskets of fresh catch are heaved onto the docks.

"I'm not sure either. The heavens have their purposes," Éliva tells him.

Away over the western sea the sun begins to settle down and melt into the waves. Nearly a year has slipped away since the creation of a new river south of the Emér Sea. In the past months, Tolaiyë's visited nearly every nation, every village on Claya's face.

Watching. Appearing in dreams to kings and chieftains, queens and magistrates. Urging peace, coordinating negotiations, warning of unseen dangers. He's tried everything.

"The world's a stubborn place, isn't it?" he says to her. "Even after all our efforts, too often the people choose to live in turmoil. You hoped to bring the Sketzans and the voránjevin clans together, but the gift you gave them was used for murder. I hoped we could establish peace between the western settlements and the people of Rand. But peace only came to North Emér when more than half of them left their land altogether. We hoped to put an end to the fallen sasarian who's haunted and threatened the world. But when we caught him at last, we could merely lessen his power." He turns to look into Éliva's radiant eyes. "We've hoped to mend a broken world. To make it perfect—or something closer to perfection. But the pieces are missing. You're right. We've only ever toyed at the edge of our potential. Our true purpose as sasarianë has yet to be completed. We need more time. How can we leave now?"

Out over the far edge of the sea, the clouds have begun to gather in thick, graying layers. The beginning of a mild summer storm.

"Don't despair, my brother. We've done all we know to do. Remember Afai's vision—what he told us of those who'll rise in generations to come," Éliva assures him. "Our aid to the people of Rand has made that future possible."

The dream came to Afai more than a year ago—a vision more spectacular than anything he'd ever seen. *Glorious*, he said. *Magnificent*. The man swore he glimpsed the reality of heaven itself, saying the vision showed him the face of a sasarian yet to be born, descended from the line of Echeret and Defehl. A figure who stood over a world turned to glimmering crystal. It was this vision alone that drove Afai to return westward over the Sand Sea and prevent the death of a stranger. Now the people of Rand are building a new home for themselves along the banks of their river. And if Afai's vision must be fulfilled, Tolaiyë can only imagine what kind of nation they'll build in the years ahead.

"The Shardehn clan found me on a sandy shore like this when I was a little child," Éliva says, and she smiles at nothing in particular. "Broken as this world truly is, it pains my heart to leave it."

Tolaiyë gazes out at the pale sands, wondering how many generations have left their footprints across them since time began, and how many are yet to come. Wondering if there are seas and sandy shores in the heavens. And he smiles too.

"We won't be far."

NORTH EMÉR (EAST)

EAST

SETTLEMENTS

Tol

Sóvrun

Kotán

Kéhnin

Léln

Ethrin

Taintha
(CAPITAL)

Urnot

Votton

Hud River

Hud River Branch

LAKE
Hud

Hud River (main)

Arai's
Hideout

EMÉR
(THE INLAND SEA)

About the Author

A short introduction: I grew up in the upper Midwest, where the forested hills and cloud-dimpled skies always flooded my heart with the inspiration to write. My husband, Daren, was raised in northern Alberta. He and I live with our children in rural Minnesota.

Now, why do I write?

Since I was about eight years old, I've had dreams of another earth called Claya. These dreams sometimes come at night. But most often, they come to me like sudden, vivid memories as I sit pondering in the middle of the day. Claya is a world full of diversity—from the Black Shores of the west to the vibrant, emerald forests of North Emér, to the blowing sands of Ketsa in the far east. The people who wander between these lands are no less diverse. Claya is home to many tribes and nations—each of which has more history and heritage than I could ever hope to record entirely.

While I've written about the things I see in dreams for many years, *Anamnesis* was my first attempt to share my writings with a public audience. I owe my wonderful husband for all his tremendous support in this effort!

I've created my website as a resource for readers who are interested in knowing more. You can visit the site at memoriesofclaya.com. There, you can take a deeper look into the geography, languages, and cultures of Claya. I plan to expand this site as my other books are completed.

Thank you for your interest in my work!

Whitney H. Murphy (Lorëu)

See where the story continues…
Read Ages of Claya Book 3!

When life's winds threaten to choke the hope from our hearts, we can let them destroy us ...or learn to rise above it all.

AHEBBAN

AGES OF CLAYA

BOOK 3

Find your copy on Amazon.com today!

Have you enjoyed this book?

To discover more information about the Ages of Claya series, please visit www.memoriesofclaya.com.

Thank you for reading!